DEADVILLE

ROBERT F. JONES

DEADVILLE

A NOVEL

Skyhorse Publishing

Skyhorse Publishing books may be purchased in bulk at special discounts for
sales promotion, corporate gifts, fund-raising, or educational purposes. Special
editions can also be created to specifications. For details, contact the Special Sales
Department, Skyhorse Publishing, 307 West 36th Street, 11th Floor, New York,
NY 10018 or info@skyhorsepublishing.com.

Skyhorse® and Skyhorse Publishing® are registered trademarks of Skyhorse
Publishing, Inc.®, a Delaware corporation.

Visit our website at www.skyhorsepublishing.com.

10 9 8 7 6 5 4 3 2 1

Library of Congress Cataloging-in-Publication Data is available on file.
ISBN: 978-1-62636-008-2

Printed in the United States of America

Once again, for Louise

Still, it is not so much the anthropophagi and men whose heads do grow beneath their shoulders that one listens for in this firelight as Othello's other themes, antres vast and desarts idle, moving accidents by flood and field, hairbreadth 'scapes i' the imminent deadly breach, and being taken by the insolent foe. . . . Murder, starvation, massacre, endurance, the will not to die.

—BERNARD DE VOTO
Across the Wide Missouri (1947)

EDITOR'S NOTE

THE THICK PACKET of manuscript known as the Griffith Papers was discovered in the storage rooms of the public library at Hidalgito, New Mexico, during an inventory of donated materials preparatory to that institution's centennial in 1995. Ms. Wanda Chatsworth, who found the papers, recognized immediately that they held more than ordinary historical interest and called them to the attention of this editor, a professor of American studies at Rocky Mountain College.

Written late in life by Capt. Dillon Griffith (1815–1907), the papers are of historical interest in that they deal, among other things, with the middle and later years of the author's longtime friend and business partner, James Pierson Beckwourth, a controversial figure in the early Rocky Mountain fur trade. Beckwourth (1798–1866), one of the rare "mountain men" of African-American descent, is often mentioned in early chronicles of the fur trade, usually—given the prejudices of the period—in less than kindly terms.

In *The Oregon Trail* (1849), Francis Parkman wrote: "Six years ago a fellow named Jim Beckwourth, a mongrel of French, American, and Negro blood, was trading for the Fur Company, in a large village of the Crows. Jim Beckwourth . . . is a ruffian of the worst stamp; bloody and treacherous, without honor or honesty; such at least is the character he bears upon the prairie. Yet in his case the standard rules of character fail, for though he will stab a man in his sleep, he will also perform the most desperate acts of daring . . ." Beckwourth's own autobiography, *The Life & Adventures of James P. Beckwourth: Mountaineer, Scout, and Pioneer: And Chief of the Crow Nation of Indians* (Boston, 1856), ghostwritten by one Thomas D. Bonner, was roundly condemned by two generations of American historians as bombastic, self-serving, and totally inaccurate. Beckwourth entered the literature as a "gaudy liar."

He appears quite otherwise in these papers. Perhaps it is time for a reappraisal of Beckwourth's career. This memoir provides a good starting place. I am presently at work on such a scholarly study.

THE PAPERS, HANDWRITTEN in India ink on high-grade vellum, had lain unread for more than sixty years in a calfskin trunk at the Hidalgito Public Library. They had been carefully wrapped in oilskin, tied with a red ribbon, now faded, and overlaid with a jumble of daguerreotypes and photographs; a brace of cap-and-ball Colt Walker pistols; an assortment of tomahawks, arrowheads, lance points; and half a dozen crisp, woolly items that proved to be Native American scalps. (An attempt is under way to return these latter items to the tribes from which they were wrongfully taken.) Existing records do not indicate who donated the trunk to the library. A label attached to its handle bears the date "May 26, 1934" and appears to be written in the hand of the late James Quiller Parkes, who served as Hidalgito's public librarian from 1923 to 1946.

Ms. Chatsworth, knowing my keen interest in the history of the Rocky Mountain West, especially the fur trade, and having read my earlier studies of such figures as Josiah Pilcher, Samuel Tulloch, Zenas Leonard, Peter Skene Ogden, and the Patties, father and son, asked me to appraise the manuscript for authenticity. Such internal evidence as dates, handwriting comparisons, and analysis of both paper and ink was found to be consistent with the story's purported provenance. At Ms. Chatsworth's request, I have edited the papers for publication, all proceeds save my personal expenses and a modest fee to go to a fund that might save the library from impending extinction.

Beyond correcting some minor spelling errors and anachronistic punctuation, there has been little editing to do. The narrative falls logically into three parts, two written by the hand of Capt. Dillon Griffith, another by the hand of his older brother, Owen. These parts I have broken into chapters where it seemed the author's intention. As to the story, I found it compelling, though the squeamish might be forewarned that the narrative is fraught with violence, not to mention attitudes and expressions regarding women and minorities offensive to enlightened contemporary sensibilities. That, though, might be said of all Western history "in the raw" and, indeed, of human history from the beginning of time.

—Dr. L. J. Kenton
Audie Murphy Professor of American Studies
Rocky Mountain College
Sixgun, Colorado

PART I

BUENAVENTURA

ONE

EIGHTY-FIVE YEARS have sped beneath my boot heels, and suddenly I find myself old. I can no longer walk, thanks to a bullet which nicked my spine half a century ago but only last winter crippled me for good. Yet I still remain capable of driving a carriage, and even of riding a horse, if someone will be so kind as to hoist me into the saddle. Each morning I go my rounds of the rancho, one way or the other. Herds of blood horses range the grasslands, intermixed with clusters of portly shorthorn beef cattle. The cattle feed on grama, that most nutritious of grasses; the horses snort, flirt their tails, stare at me with fiery eyes, then gallop away. Great golden eagles turn high in the cobalt skies; coyotes sing at night to the rising of the moon. Everywhere is the perfume of dust and flowers. Groves of oranges and lemons surround the house, watered from a crystalline stream that descends from the surrounding hills. All told, it is not a bad life.

Still, I had never thought to see the year 1900 turn up on the calendar, and it's coming soon. What an odd and alien number it seems. As this century ends—my century—I cannot help but think back on the changes it has wrought. Changes in me, of course, and not only the ones inherent in aging, but changes to the people I've loved as well; changes to the very land that's sustained us so long and so well.

3

Sitting here of a hot, lazy summer afternoon, at the cusp of this new age, on the veranda of my modest estancia, La Casa Pequeña, up in the dry *cerillos* just south of Santa Fe, I find myself looking out at the baldheaded mountains and the sere, yellow plains beyond. The images come ghosting back to me. So concrete are they, so urgent, almost palpable, that I feel I must record their histories before they pass from human remembrance. No one will ever read this memoir, so I can tell the truth about what happened.

The ghosts beg for truth.

I see the great buffalo herds, long gone now, careering over the plains from horizon to horizon beneath a boiling tan cloud of their own generation, and the great grizzly bears that descended like avalanches upon our *caballadas* to carry whole horses off between their jaws, while bullets bounced from their dirty white hides like so many puny snowballs. I see the heavy-jawed lobos lurching ungainly over the prairie, their yellow eyes set on destruction; the bighorn sheep bouncing from crag to crag in the high country; and antelope flashing their heliographs through a shimmering haze of prairie heat.

I see the tribes, Crow and Blackfoot and Apache, Cheyenne, Comanche, Kiowa, Ute, in all their painted fury, proud and fierce, fearsome in war yet deeply spiritual, and capable of tortures beyond even the imagination of old Torquemada. I hear their drums, their war cries.

I see my brother, tall and pale, his eyes deep-sunk in madness.

I see his haunted lover, doomed, maimed, murderous, lance in hand, death in her strong dark face.

I see my wife, as she was so long ago, a warm, cheerful, devil-may-care Indian maiden out for a jolly good time; then later as mate and mother, serious, loving, resourceful.

I see Spybuck, the embittered Shawnee who was my friend from the start, and I see red-whiskered, wild-eyed Lafcadio Dade, who became our mortal enemy.

I see my children, living and dead, and must look away for a moment.

IT'S A SAD thing outliving all that you loved.

*   *   *

BUT MOST CLEARLY I see Jim.

He it was who taught me the West.

Ah, Jim, how you'd laugh at all of this today. Steel rails, which had scarce reached the Mississippi when I first crossed that noble stream, now gird the continent; humming wires carry messages from coast to coast at the speed of light, where once only smoke signals blossomed. My granddaughter has had installed in the hallway of our home a device called a telephone, which allows her to speak with her friends in Santa Fe as if they were in the next room.

There are streetlights now in the dark *calles* not only of Santa Fe, but of San Francisco de Taos and Nuestra Señora de Socorro.

And just today I had a visitor arrive in a horseless carriage, the first I'd ever seen. A Duryea it was, I learned later, red as hellfire, puttering and backfiring its way up the mountain. To my amazement, it wheeled through the gate, belching smoke and clattering like a tinsmith's shop in an earthquake, and exploded its way to a halt at my door.

"Captain Griffith, I presume?" said the driver, dismounting and lifting a pair of rubber-rimmed goggles. He wore a white duster over his city clothes, and a little checkered cap atop his blond, oiled hair. He had a little waxed mustache, too, which he smoothed back with a delicate finger. He had one of those unctuous southern voices, educated, elegant, smooth as Kentucky bourbon.

"Could be," I told him. "Depends on who you are and just what you presume to do."

"Wentworth Champion of the Santa Fe *Republican*," he announced with a slight bow. "At your service, sir. I have driven all this way from the capital in my brand-new Duryea motorcar just to interview you for our Sunday edition."

"What do you feed that thing to make it fart so loud?" I asked.

He was taken aback at first, then laughed a weak little waxy laugh. "It eats gazarene, Captain Griffith, a whole gallon to get it this far. But I fear the poor beast is suffering from indigestion at the moment. Perhaps some water in the feed line?"

"Give it a dose of castor oil," I said. "That'll do the trick."

He removed his duster and the checkered cap, mopped his brow with a monogrammed handkerchief. It was hot in the sun, cool in the shade of the veranda. "May I join you?" he asked.

"Suit yourself."

No sooner had he seated himself in a cane chair opposite me than my granddaughter Esperanza emerged from the shady kitchen with a platter. On it was balanced a pitcher of lemonade tinkling with ice, some glasses, and a plate of her crisp sugar cookies. 'Speranza is a pretty girl—I'd say a beautiful one—with lustrous black hair and a golden brown complexion. She has confided to me that she feels her nose is a bit too long, her eyes too black, too wide-set, too large and catlike—too much like those of an *indio*—but she looks just like her grandmother. I have assured her that her beauty is that of the angels of this land, but still she glances doubtfully at her image in the hallway mirror each time she passes.

She poured our lemonade and withdrew.

"Very well mannered," said Champion. "And prompt, too. It's so hard to get good servants these days. Most of these Indians and mestizos, I must say, they're as bad as niggers . . . but then after all it is the Land of Poco Tiempo, is it not?"

"I guess so. Now what did you wish to ask me?"

"I'd like to know what it was like in the old days," he said.

I pulled a jug of aguardiente—the old Taos Lightning—from beneath the Navajo blanket that covered my thin shanks and sweetened my glass of lemonade, two quick glugs' worth. I offered the bottle to Champion. He pursed his lips, frowned, and said, "No, thank you," then withdrew a notebook from the inside jacket pocket of his seersucker suit. He unscrewed a fountain pen, poised it over the page, and asked, "Is it true you were a mountain man?"

I laughed.

"I'm a man, sure enough, and if you misdoubt me I shall whip back this blanket, unbutton my fly and display the proper credentials, wrinkled though they be. And you know I live on a mountain, having driven your spiffy *Door-yay* up here to my door just this very afternoon. Not to put too fine a point on it, Mister Champion: yes, in that sense I was a mountain man, and indeed remain one to this very day."

"No, no, sir. You miss my meaning. I have reference to the fur trade of the 1820s, *et sequelae*. The beaver trade, as it then was. I have heard talk from certain usually trustworthy sources in the capital that you played a part in that era of glory. The Opening of the West. The Taming of the Tribes. The Blazing of the Emigrant Trails. Forerunners to the pioneers. Et cetera. Were you that kind of a mountain man, Captain Griffith?"

"The term wasn't used much in those days," I said. "Easterners made it up. We were just trappers. Or fur traders if you want to play it elegant. As to the opening of the West, why, it was pretty much open when we got here. Those very tribes you say we tamed had trails all through the durned place. And we didn't tame them so much as they *wilded* us."

"But you did participate, I take it. When did you first come west?"

" 'Thirty-three."

He made his first note, then said, "So you must have known some of the great ones. James Bridger, Thomas Fitzpatrick, Jedediah Strong Smith, William Sublette, the Bents?"

"Never met Smith. The Comanch' rubbed him out in '31, I believe. Down on the Cimarron crossing. The others? Ayuh."

" '*Ayuh?*'? Is that an Apache word?"

"No, it's Vermontish. Where I grew up before I came west. Means 'yep.' Your Indians mostly say, 'Ugh.' " Well, they don't, but I was sick of this fellow already.

"I'm told you once knew the notorious nigger scalp hunter, horse thief, and braggart Jim Beckwourth. I recently read his preposterous autobiography and wonder if you could corroborate a few points for me, or refute them preferably. Clear some things up?"

"No."

"I'm sorry; what do you mean?"

"I mean I won't corroborate or refute anything for you, nor clear up any matter save this: that you're not welcome here. Esperanza Quemado, the young woman who served us our lemonade, is my grand-daughter. She is one-quarter white, one-quarter Crow Indian, and half Mexican. Her father, Sergeant Victorio Quemado, served with me against Sibley's Texans at Valverde and Apache Canyon, during the late unpleasantness known as the Civil War, and later married one of my 'half-breed' daughters. Captain James P. Beckwourth was not only a business partner of mine for many years, but my closest friend. He was no 'nigger.' I know your type, Mister Champion. If I'm not mistaken, there's a touch of Dixie in your manner of speech. You're contemptuous of Indians, Mexicans, Jews, 'breeds, and especially blacks. You also despise 'squaw men,' and of course I am one of them. No man with your attitude could begin to understand the West I knew and grew up in, and anything I might tell you of the truth of it you will doubtless warp to your own prejudices. Now if you've finished with your lemonade, I'll thank you to remount your clattering steed and depart my *estancia,* pronto."

"I . . . I . . . Well, sir, I *nevah* . . ." He stood and I swear it looked to me as if he were groping for a gauntlet with which to slap my face and call me out for a duel at dawn under the moss-draped live oaks. Or perhaps he was reaching for a derringer to assuage his honor right there.

"*Never* is the right word," I said. "Not in a million years."

From beneath the Navajo blanket I withdrew a revolver, my old .44-caliber Colt Walker. It is an awesome weapon, and had its desired effect.

Wentworth Champion skedaddled.

What would you make of all this?

Ah, Jim.. . . .

IN HIS DAY he was the Bloody Arm of the Sparrowhawk People, who inflicted traumatic baldness on a thousand thousand enemies. He was the Big Bowl, the Bull's Robe, the Antelope. He was the White-Handled Knife. He was the Morning Star, the Medicine Calf. He was Is-ko-chu-e-chu-re, the Enemy of Horses, the greatest thief of riding stock ever known among a tribe of excellent horse thieves. Best in the West, he always said.

To hear him tell it, he stood seven feet tall in his moccasins with shoulders a yard wide. He had more Indian names than wives, for a fact, and he had a full dozen of the latter—ten with the Crows alone and anyway two among the Blackfoot.

His smile was bright as the Ghost Trail that splits the sky of a cold clear prairie midnight. His scowl could set the Rocky Mountains themselves to trembling from the Río Bravo del Norte clear up to the Milk. His scalp yell diverted whole rivers. Oh, yes, it did.

He had by his own testimony—and who so brave as to doubt him aloud?—run ninety-five miles in a single day, dawn to dark, pursued by half the howling Blackfoot nation. It took him three whole days just to rest up from that escapade.

He was my friend James Pierson Beckwourth, trapper, trader, explorer, poet, war chief, and no man dared call him nigger.

OLD JIM HE was a wonder, sure. Lived among the savages all those years; I only really got to know him later, and he could spin a yarn some, but most of it sounded like the truth. Some newspaperman in California named Bonner wrote a whole book about him, most of which was bosh, but as Jim said, he wrote an elegant prose. Still, it was too damned slick for me. I read it some years ago. To hell with it. Read this account instead if you want Jim straight.

That winter in Absaroka we lived in a buffalo skin lodge all black near the top from wood smoke and the smoke from dry buffalo dung up in the foothills on a south-facing slope. Lots of snow to the height of five feet on the ground but plenty of sun. Plenty buffalo down in the flats.

The first name the red men gave him was the White-Handled Knife. The white-handled knife Jim always had with him. He used it on beaver and buff' and the heads of the slain, though he never cut any wood with it. It was your customary butcher's blade with the haft wrapped in a long strip of white silk Jim had taken from a Blackfoot war chief he had killed on Hams Fork some years earlier. He always washed the silk clean when it got too dark from the blood of his enemies. I saw him wash it three times that winter while I was with him on the Absaroka. He boiled water over a special medicine fire he built of white osier. He got that name from the Sho-sho-nees he came up with when he was with Gen. William Ashley in 1823 or '24. They call them the Snakes by sign. Good people, but they, too, will kill you if they take a mind to it.

"I next met up with the Blackfoot," he told me. "And I married one. You can just bet it was nice to be with a woman after all that time with mountaineers. They called her Plume in Blackfoot. She was very pretty but had a sassy mouth."

One time the Blackfeet brought three scalps into camp. They were white scalps, and Jim said he got mighty sore. Would not dance the scalp dance that night and told Plume she could not dance either. That was the hair of his friends and partners, he said. But she went out and danced anyway. A white trapper named Dick Gant was living in Jim's lodge at the time and looked out and says, "Your lady is a mighty fine dancer, Jim; look at her go." Jim looks out the lodge and sees her whooping it up out there and waxes wroth. He grabs his battle-ax and goes out and walks right through the dancers and whacks his wife alongside the head.

She drops like a brainshot elk.

Well, the Blackfoot grabbed him, angry as you might imagine, and wanted to take his hair right then. But Plume's father, Old Lodgepole, stopped them. He said, "She was too sassy; her ears were blocked. You kill your wives if they do not obey you. Why shouldn't he?"

So they saw the wisdom in that.

And Lodgepole said, "Here, Knife, I give you my second daughter for a bride to replace the sassy one. She's prettier anyway and very obedient." Jim took the younger sister, whose name was Painted Turtle, and went back to his tepee. He was under the robes with her that night and just dozing off when he heard something whimpering outside the tent. "That damn dog," he said, and pulled open the flap. In crawled Plume, her hair all stiff with blood. He hadn't killed her after all. "Now my ears are unblocked," she said, "and I will not be sassy anymore." So Jim had two Blackfoot wives now to keep him warm on a winter's night, one to each side of him under the buffalo robes.

* * *

THE WAY I met old Jim, I had come up the Platte River from Cabanné's trading post near where the city of Omaha now stands in the spring of 1833 with my brother, Owen Griffith, and a small party of fur traders bound for the Rocky Mountains. We headed up the North Fork of the Platte River, past Scott's Bluff, crossed the Chugwater and Laramie rivers in early May, and then in the Black Hills of the Medicine Bow range while running buffalo were jumped by a band of Arikara Indians. The very sky rained arrows. None of those boys could shoot with any accuracy. They were green and scared. Not that I was any braver. The Rees rubbed out most of the party, took their scalps, cut off their private parts, tied some of the boys upside down to a tall wagon wheel, and burnt them on a slow fire. They screamed some, all but Captain Wofford, the leader of our expedition. He did not have time to yell. The first arrow to fall took him right through the brainpan.

The wagon had lost one of its wheels in the chase and lay lopsided. When the Rees saw that they could spin the opposite wheel freely over the fire, they took turns at it with a man tied to the rim, so that he cooked even slower than he would hanging head-down over the flames.

They laughed at that one you can bet.

When the whooping stopped only my brother Owen and I were left alive, along with a Shawnee scout named Golightly Spybuck. The three of us were trussed up like hogs for the killing.

"Oh, these bastards!" said Owney.

Then a couple of Rees grabbed me, slapped me around some, and cut at my face with their quirts. They began to tie me to the wheel.

Well, I am ashamed to say I wet my pants about then.

"Be brave, Dill!" yelled Owney. "Don't yell; don't give them the satisfaction!"

I heard the Shawnee Spybuck chuckle at that.

The Rees were saving him for last.

* * *

THEN A BIG war party of Sparrowhawks came swooping in to save us, and a big Negro was their leader.

Well, the lead and arrows flew thick as the good red devils drove the bad ones off. Fusees banged, bows twanging. The ugly wet sound of hatchets slicing meat. I saw a flint-tipped lance shatter on the skull of an old Ree, and his battle-ax come around to chop the Crow who'd speared him, blood everywhere. The toughest of the Crows—we could tell they were of that tribe from the length of their hair, some with coiffures nearly as long as the warriors themselves were tall—was a dark stocky fellow riding a speckle-rumped Nez Percé pony; he swung his ax fast as a dragonfly's wings, took down at least five of the Rees by himself in that quick, loud little fight. Then he reined in and trotted his pony over to where I lay tied to the wheel. And he cut me down.

Seeing that he was a Negro, or at least part a one, I immediately thought of a man I had heard about, Edward Rose, part African, part white, part Cherokee Indian, who was said to be a good friend of the Crows, some say a chief among them.

"Mister Rose," I said, "oh, bless you for saving us!"

It was like I'd shot him. His face, black enough to begin with, now went even darker. He said something in Crow to his warriors. Two of them jumped down from their ponies and grabbed me upside down and tied me that way again to the wagon wheel. There was tinder and pieces of dry, fast-burning sagebrush piled up in the fire heap, with broken floorboards from the wagon bed on top of it, and these boys grabbed out their fire steels and pieces of flint and started to strike sparks. They were grinning all the while like it was only a Sunday school picnic.

"Wait a minute," I said. "What are you doing? Are you going to burn me anyway?"

The black chief had turned his back on me, but now he spun round again.

"I am *not* Mister Edward Rose," said he. "Mister Rose was a *Negro* and a very bad man, a thief, a damned liar, and a disgrace to everything America stands for. And anyway, he was rubbed out last winter up on the Yellowstone, along with old Hugh Glass, by these same damn river pirates, the Arikara. I am a *white* man, born in the Old Dominion, though I live amongst these ignorant but innocent Sparrowhawk Indians and am honored to be one of their war chiefs. My name is Captain James P. Beckwourth, and I am surprised you do not know of me."

I tried to swallow there, upside down on the wheel, and had a hard time. You try it once. Then I said, "Well, Captain Beckwourth, I am sorry I mistook you for Mister Rose. Please forgive the error. It must be that the sun has darkened your skin so, living out here on the prairie as you do, but now I can see you are white all right, whiter even than I."

He smiled then, and yes, his smile was bright all right, and very welcome to me at that moment, I can assure you. He jumped down off his pony and strode over to cut me down from the wheel. He pulled me to my feet and slapped me on the shoulder.

"I knew you would see reason," said he.

Just about that time one of the sparks the Crow warriors had struck took fire in the tinder and the sage began popping. Flames as tall as a man started climbing the wheel.

And I looked over at the black, blistered faces of the others in our party, dead now with their teeth shining through snarling crisp lips. The Rees had burnt them on the wheel all right, and I can tell you I was mighty relieved to be free of it.

WELL, CAPTAIN BECKWOURTH was no seven feet tall. He was about my size, a handspan or two more than five and a half. Average height. But he was plenty strong and thick-muscled, and for all his denying it he was indeed a Negro or, anyway, half a one. From a distance you might have mistaken him for a Spaniard, I guess, but the wide nose, full lips, and curly hair, his skin the color of a black walnut gunstock, those traits gave him away.

"Now," says he, "who are you and these others with you, my friend?"

"We are the Griffith brothers of Vermont and Pennsylvania," I says, "headed west for beaver. I am Dillon Griffith and that's my brother Owen there with the cut on his forehead, and the other fellow is a Shawnee hunter name of Golightly Spybuck who scouts for us."

Jim frowns. "Looks like your Indian did not scout so good, did he? My Sparrowhawks don't like the Shawnees much," he says. "They are a sneaky lot, being woodland Indians from east of the Mississippi originally, not noble buffalo Indians like these of the prairies, and I am not sure I can vouch for my men's good behavior in regard to this Indian."

Golightly now comes stepping up to us, picking his way through the dead bodies, and looks Beckwourth in the eye. He is a tough coot all right: a tall Indian, with a long, thin scarred-up face and his hair all knotted in a bun atop his head, usually contained in a green-and-yellow bandanna which resembles a pirate's turban, but now it has come loose a bit, hair straggling out, and his eyes are flaming.

"I can take care of myself, Captain Beckwourth," says he. His hand is on the haft of a pipe tomahawk he picked up off a dead Ree. "Give me back my fusil and my powder and ball and I will leave here now afoot and not raise any temptations amongst your people."

I cannot help saying, "Hurrah for you, Mister Spybuck!"

"No need of that," Beckwourth tells Spybuck, smiling now. "I admire your spunk and will now guarantee their good behavior. But keep that ax handy anyway."

I saw right then, and never forgot it, that old Jim valued courage and forthrightness in a man; whether red or white or black, it mattered not. So long as he said what he believed, Jim would treat him fair and square. Though I later grew to distrust him for his sly deviations from that credo.

Two

---·◆·---

Jim Beckwourth now walks over to my brother Owen sitting dazed there in the dirt, blood streaking his face from where a battle-ax had clipped him atop the head. Owney is twenty-three years old, five years older than I. A powerful built man, my brother, wide shoulders, long arms, big blocky fists, a clever boxer either bareknuckle or with the gloves. Years of hard work in the coalfields of Pennsylvania had given him the muscles of a lion.

Our Da, bless his memory, had taught us both to box.

Owney mumbles some words: "Cactus and schist, I care not." His eyes are glassy, his head swaying weak on his neck.

For all the years of his grown-up life he had risen in the dark, gone down to the dark, emerged again in the dark, his world black and white. Imagine how he marvels now at color! Stunned by it. Wildflowers blue and red and yellow as butter, songbirds so bright, coinage fresh from the mint; the electric blue of darning needles and skeeterhawks, red buttes aglow in the distance beyond the acid green rivers, blue-black peaks topped in sprawls and skids of spring snow off to the north and west—the Rocky Mountain Front.

"Prickly pear," says Owney.

Prickly pair indeed. I know where his mind is wandering; he's dreaming of Mam and Da.

"Vicious bitch," Owney says, mumbling still as Beckwourth stares down at him, "but Da no winner neither, look'ye Dill. A rum lot the two of 'em, should never been hitched to begin with."

She was a little wee woman, scarce five foot tall, Mam, maybe five-two or -three, hair cut long and brushed over sideways to hide her baldness. Pursed little mouth like a arsehole, flinty eyes, a tongue like the tail of a hornet.

Owney spots a black cactus, gone dead, dark and shiny with spilt blood drying on it, and it throws him into a dream of old Da coming home with the "pillows."

Those big, fat old pillows and Da telling us about how you had to hit left and right, right and left, high and low, mix 'em up, and throw your punches so they could not be seen. And then hit him hard, take him down, kill the bastard . . .

And I remember. Da kneeling on the floor to lessen his height, thus his advantage. His old face blue-gray still with the Welsh coal dust that would never wash out, the random blue scars on his balding head, tattoos of coal dust where the dark had cut him underground, back in the old country, in Wales.

Old Da's elbows close to his sides, patting at Owney with the fat black shiny pillows, patting himself.

His old eyes twinkling, *colcarreg* black in the light of a lamp.

The fat black pillows weaving the air.

Old Da, suddenly younger, patting Owney in the belly and on the chin, saying, "Hit me now, Owney; c'mon, ya can hit me sure enough; look'ye now rather; now hit me, left hook!"

And he hit old Da in the gut and old Da coughed. He coughed and he coughed, and finally he coughed up a great thick wad of coughup, a great sloppy black wad of smelly black tar that ran down his chin like the hot macadam they laid on the hunchback road from Ffaldau to Blaengarw, and Owney must have felt like the worst little shit in the world, and he crept back to his corner and rolled himself into the sour sheets next to me, his little wee brother there in the dark, and listened to Mam and Da wrangle high and low, screechy growly, to the end of the night and the break of another day.

Later, much later, we went with the folks and our two sisters on across the sea and lodged next in a place called Dorset in the frown of the wet green hills of Vermont. Da said it was a land of riches, with iron and copper, lead and silver and gold lying in wait beneath the earth to enrich the first man to reach them with pick and shovel. And marble? Enough to erect the Heavenly City itself. But when we arrived Vermont looked much like Wales, all up and down, all cold and hard and very poor. The state was still all abuzz with talk of the Newfane Lump, a nugget of pure gold that weighed more than half a pound, found up in the Green Mountains. But try as he might, plying his pick on the hillsides, Da could find neither gold nor silver, nor yet enough copper to shape a farthing, and finally had to settle for a job as a quarryman. He plied a chisel-tipped drill half the length of a man, hammering it home full twelve hours a day, six days a week, carving channels in cold, hard marble, and earning at best $1.40 a day for his labors. The company where Da cut marble till his breath got too short let us rent a rickety wood-sided house, and Mam was almost happy for once then with a yard all her own and a garden plot wherein to grow her Swedes and cabbages and leeks as long and thick as a strong boy's leg. We had chickens as well, a tall red-and-black rooster and his *hareem*, Mam called them, of dumpy, fat hens. Fresh eggs of a morning for breakfast.

Ah yes, Owney and his brother Dillon were happy, too. We had a little wee dog now, a wicked quick ratter called Thump. After school we would grab a spade from the garden shed and whistle Thump up and run with her down to the dump, there to hunt rats until supper-time. Thump-in-the-Dump, we called it. Weekends we prowled the marble-studded green hills back of town and down along the loud brown Mettowee River after rabbits and groundhogs and muskrats— Thump was a great leaper, too, who on at least three occasions man-aged to grab a partridge from the air when it flushed beneath her nose—and, now and then when we were especially lucky, a fox. Thump dug like a little wee coal miner when the prey went to ground.

Fought it out in the dens and runs below, growls and yips and horrendous yowls funneling up from the bowels of the earth, Thump emerging always a-grin, dirty and splattered with blood, some of it her own, but she did not care, did not feel it even, so hard she was, and we dug down to extract the meat. Mam would cook up the rabbits and groundhogs that weren't too badly chewed, Da skinned the muskrats and the rare foxes, stretched their pelts on stiff, circular wire frames, fleshed them, showed us how to rub them down with salt and tanbark and sheep's brains, and we sold them cured to the hideman over in Rupert—two shillings apiece for the rats if not too sorely torn by Thump's long fangs, a whole solid Yankee dollar for a prime fox plew, whether red or gray.

Then one day while we were hunting Norway rats over near the marble quarry, Thump lost her balance and fell down an abandoned lead-mine shaft. That whole countryside was riddled with shafts, like a worm-eaten apple. She survived the tumble, though, and we could hear her frantic barking, echoing up to us from far below. The shoring in the adit was rotten, and even Owney, who usually had no fear of the terrors beneath the earth, was afraid to try a descent. All our efforts to coax her out failed, and we returned home that night despondent.

For the next two days we returned to the shaft, dropping food to her and hoping she might find her way back up. But we could not drop water, of course, and her yipping grew weaker and weaker. After much soul-searching we decided that to prevent a slow, agonizing death by thirst we had best blow her up. At the general store in Factory Point, Owney purchased a one-pound cannister of gunpowder for seven cents along with a foot of slow fuse for a penny more—all the money we could muster. With tears in our eyes we returned to the mine shaft. Thump was whining from the depths. Without a word, Owney lit the fuse and dropped the can down the hole. We could hear it clattering downward, down, down, down . . . then a blast, and the earth shook beneath our feet.

Her cries were heard no more.

Soon after we got home, though—sadder than we ever had been in our short sorry lives—imagine our surprise when we heard a familiar scratching at the back door. We raced to open it and, yes, there was

Thump! Thinner and dirtier than ever, to be sure, but at least alive. The explosion must have blown loose an escape route, and she was able to dig through what rubble was left. Though she emerged in a totally different area from the one where she had fallen in, she nonetheless found her way home in no time. That little terrier had an uncanny bump of direction, and all the heart in the world.

And then when Da lost his quarryman's job—he had inhaled marble dust enough for a emperor's tombstone and could no longer wield a chisel well enough to channel the stone—we moved to Swartsburg in the Allegheny Mountains of Pennsylvania, where Da found work in the *colcarreg* again. *Colcarreg* is Welsh for coal, the infernal stuff. By now Owney was big enough to join him in the pits. I was good with ciphering and wrote a fair hand, so took a job as an apprentice clerk in the coal company office. As a beginning miner, Owney worked the graveyard shift alongside Da. That was the end of the sunlight for both of them. Our sisters married, moved away, and Mam kept house till the day the mine collapsed on Da's night shift. Owney was home with the pleurisy that night. The whole town shuddered, screaming ponies and a hundred and thirty men dead—I would rather not remember it—and Owney and I could not bear our mother any longer, and knowing that coal would only kill a man sooner rather than later, as it had Da and so many others, and having pooled our meager earnings, we struck off west, even farther toward the sunset than Da had tried to reach, to seek the riches of the Great West.

So far, though, all we had met with was Rees, and now Captain Beckwourth.

JIM RUBBED SOME balm on Owney's cut scalp, bound the wound with a dirty strip of cloth ripped from a dead trapper's shirt, and we built a little wickiup to keep Owney out of the sun. The Crows had found a bag of coffee beans in the wreck of the wagon, so Spybuck and I built up the fire and ground some down fine and boiled a big pot of it to share out among the Sparrowhawk warriors. By God that coffee smelled good.

"Indians love coffee only a little less than they love whiskey," Jim said. He picked up the pot and drank it straight and steaming right from the spout. Then he passed it to his warriors. When it came around to me I poured me a dose into the pewter cup I'd pulled from my possibles sack, blew on it to cool it, and drank some. "I will not trade my Indians' whiskey for their peltry," said Jim. "Not like some others I could name. It ruins the red man for trapping. They would rather sit around the lodge getting drunk than go out wading the beaver streams."

Spybuck is standing off to one side in earshot; he chuckled. He, too, loves the bottle.

"So you trade with them?" I says right smart.

"Oh, yes, for Mister McKenzie of the American Fur Company down to Fort Cass, where the Bighorn enters the Yellowstone. But latterly I have been so preocupied with this chieftainship business that I have no time to trade. These incessant wars are very prejudicial to the company's interests I admit. All the time Blackfeet and Shi-ans and Rees attacking the Crows, stealing horses and women, killing Crow soldiers from ambuscade, so of course the Sparrowhawks must strike back in reprisal. I cannot keep them from it. These very Rees we rubbed out here"—he kicks a dead one with his moccasin—"had just stolen about forty head of horses from us, and we must get them back, along with some scalps, if our honor is to be assuaged. You saw how well my men fought. I reckoned that if I could make the Crows the best warriors on the plains, a terror to their neighbors, perhaps I could, as they say, conquer a peace. Blackfoot and Shi-an would have to sue for mercy, beat their tomahawks into beaver traps, their lances into plowshares." He shakes his head. "But making good troops out of red men, well, it takes time, and Mister McKenzie he no like."

Right about then some of the Crows who had gone haring off after the defeated Rees come trotting back into view. They have a string of ponies with them, pintos and chestnuts and even some plowhorses, the mounts the enemy had stolen. At the head of this war party is a woman. A handsome one, too. Strong neck, square shoulders, flashing eyes. Her long, shiny black hair spills down her back to below her rump; her firm little breasts are heaving.

"Bar-che-am-pe! The Pine Leaf returns triumphant!" yells Jim with a welcoming smile. He shouts something in Crow to her, and she nods her head haughtily, lifts her bloody lance, and shows him two fresh reeking scalps.

"Best soldier I've got," he tells me. "Braver than any two men, runs fast as a prongbuck, shoot the eyes out of a gnat at a hundred paces, arrow or rifleball, either, 'fraid of nothin'. When she was just a girl, maybe twelve years old, the Blackfeet killed her brother and she vowed then to avenge him with the scalps of one hundred enemies. I reckon she is up to about eighty by now. I plan to marry her when she makes her limit."

"All the more reason to stay on the warpath," says I.

"You have the right of it there, bub," says Jim with a laugh.

By now it was getting on toward dark and the Crows prepared to make camp for the night. Some of them busied themselves butchering out a mule killed in the fight while others busted up more of the wagon for to fuel a cookfire. There was no wild wood in that country, not a stick of it. I went over to where Owney lay in his wickiup. "How are you feeling now?" I ask him.

"Some better," he says. "What is happening? Are we prisoners still?"

"No, praise God, we are rescued!" I say. "By a kindly trader to the Crow Indian nation name of Captain Jim Beckwourth."

Owney props himself up on an elbow, looks around. Jim is over by the fire giving orders to the night guard.

"What?" Owney says. "The Negro?"

"Do not say that word," I say. "He claims to be white and he like to burned me on the wheel for mistaking him for another gentleman of the black persuasion. Just play along with him for now."

Then the girl named Pine Leaf came over to us and stood there looking down at Owney. She said something in Crow. We looked at her blank-like. She leaned over with those breasts in her shirt and felt of Owney's head where the ax bit him. She started cooing some Indian words to Owney, caressing his sore head. She took some herbs from a leather pouch she carried and offered a handful of the stuff to Owney, making like he should eat it; it will make him better.

I see Beckwourth looking at the scene, and his face is like stone.

The Pine Leaf glances back at him and gives a sassy little grin. Then she pats Owney on the head and stands up and goes away to where her ponies are hobbled.

Owney eats the herbs.

"Who is she?" he asks. "She is awful nice, I must say."

"She is a warrior like the others, name of Bar-che-am-pe, or the Pine Leaf, but Captain Beckwourth is sweet on her," I tell him. "Looks like she wants to make him jealous; I would be careful with her, Brother."

"Well, whatever it is she gave me to eat, my headache is going away now," says he. "She is a mighty fine nurse no matter what her game might be."

Supper that night was half-cooked slabs of mule meat and a potful of mashed-up roots of some kind that the Indians carried in their possible sacks and boiled on the fire in a brass kettle. I had gone over the battleground earlier and collected my and Owney's gear where it had been scattered when the wagon crashed. Blankets, a couple of heavy wool capotes, Owney's .53-caliber Hawken rifle that he paid forty dollars for back in Saint Louis, and my own .69 H. E. Leman smoothbore fusee, along with powder and ball and small shot enough. I also retrieved our heavy leather bag with half a dozen two-spring Mackinaw beaver traps in it, folded up flat with their chains wrapped around them, and of course spare moccasins for both of us. I stacked all this in a pile over by Owney's wickiup.

"We will be on our way back to the Absorkee come first light," Captain B. says, picking stringy bits of mule meat from between his big, square teeth. "Where do you fellows plan on going?"

"Back to Cabanné's, I guess," says Owney. "I have had enough of the jolly trapper's life."

Beckwourth laughs.

"Not I," says Golightly Spybuck. "I came here for beaver, and beaver I shall get. Even if I have to go it alone."

"A man alone would not last long in this country," says Beckwourth. "What about you, Dillon Griffith?"

"I would have liked to make a try at trapping," I said finally, "but blood being thicker than creek water, I reckon I must stay with my brother if he wants to go back . . . *to the coal mines of Pennsylvania.*"

Owney flushed some in the firelight. The Captain laughed again.

"One for to go, one for to stay, and one tore plumb down the middle," he says. "Might be I have a solution to your impasse. Come along with us to Fort Cass up on the Yellowstone; we will protect you that far. You can buy passage there on a keelboat, or maybe even a steamboat, that will bring you back safe and sound to the States. And, say, if grubbing in the earth is your desire, you need not travel all the way back to the coalfields of the Alleghenies; you can do as I once did and dig for galena up on Fever River in the Illinois country. Indians there are Sacs and Foxes, not near so murderous as the Shi-ans or the Sioux, nor even the shave-headed Pawnees for that matter."

"I am for the fort," Spybuck says.

"Sounds good to me," says I. "What say you, Brother?"

Owney frowns into the fire, silent. Then the Pine Leaf gets up from the flickery shadows and pours a cup of coffee and brings it over to my brother. She hands it to him, then feels again of his head; smiles brightly in his eyes as he looks up.

"Well, I guess I am outvoted then," Owney says. "Fort Cass it is."

IN THE MORNING when I went over the frosty ground to where the remuda was grazing, I found a big ugly Crow in charge of our horses. Owney had a little buckskin he bought off the suttler at Cabanné's with the U.S. brand on its flank, and I had a sprightly chestnut mare, ditto. I made to unhobble the horses.

"No," says the Indian. "My ponies, you no take."

The horses stood there, smoke blowing blue from their nose holes.

"Give me them horses," I said.

"I give you this," the Indian said. He whipped out a toadstabber long as my forearm.

I had left my fusee back by the bed, elst I would have shot him sure, but was about to tackle the red devil barehanded when Captain Beckwourth came up.

"What's this?" he says.

"This here thief has stolen our horses!" says I.

"They are not your horses," he says. "They are Crow horses now, by right of war. They ceased being your horses yesterday when the Rees took 'em from you and we took 'em from the Rees."

"Well, damn me for a sucker," I says. "So that is how the law works out here on the prairie. Then how do we get to Fort Cass, pray tell—afoot?"

"Rest easy; I will sell them back to you," Beckwourth says. "You can owe me for them until you have trapped, say, two packs of beaver."

"How many beaver to a pack?" I asked.

"One hundred pounds," says he. "Say sixty-five or seventy plews."

"How much a plew?"

"Three dollars at the fort," says he.

"Why, that is four hundred dollars apiece for these ponies, and we only paid eighty in toto for them on the Missouri!"

"Prices are high in the mountains," Beckwourth says. "You have got to figure in the cost of transportation." He pulls a piece of paper from his shirtfront and hands it to me with a sharpened stub of pencil. It is a contract. "Just make your mark here by the X."

"But we transported the ponies ourselves!"

"All right," says Jim, grabbing back the paper and pencil and walking back toward the breakfast fire. "Then go it shank's mare to Fort Cass, if it suits you. I don't give a damn."

Well, he had us by the short and curlies all right.

I signed.

THREE

LATER I LEARNED that Golightly Spybuck had got his horse back with no trouble at all, just walked into the remuda and roped it easy as pie. I didn't tell my brother about the price we would have to pay for the ponies; he was still feeling poorly that morning as we rode north toward the Absaroka. His face all ashy white; took him three hops to get up on his horse even after I had saddled it for him. The Pine Leaf rode beside him, steadying him when he reeled now and then over the rockier ground.

It was a nice spring morning, though, with bands of antelope flashing their white rumps at us like so many mirrors in the slow-rising sun, off in the distance a few black clumps of buffalo grazing their way north with the season. Of the Rees there was no sign, God be praised.

Still many worries ran through my mind as we trotted north, chief among them, *How do you trap a beaver?*

Owney had had it in mind to search the mountains of the Great West for precious metals; he was a whiz at sniffing out anything hidden underground. Back in Vermont he had demonstrated his prowess time and again. Once we were driving a borrowed rig over the Green Mountains to Brattleboro, where Da had heard he might find work in a new mill there, and Owney suddenly raised his head, sniffing the breeze like a hound dog. "There's iron up there," he said, pointing to a peak that loomed overhead.

"Bosh," said I. "I cannot see any rust streaks even."

"I can smell it," Owney replied.

I laughed aloud.

"No, do not laugh," Da said, pulling the mules to a halt. "My own daddy could sniff out iron deep in the ground. Also coal, lead, copper, antimony, and silver. He could smell a gold watch through a rich man's vest pocket."

We hiked up the mountain until Owney said, "Stop." Then he dug through the rocky rubble with pick and shovel until he came up with a big black chunk of smooth stone. "This is it," he said, "but it does not come from underground; it comes from the sky."

Later Da took it to the professor at Sheldon's Mineralogical Academy in Brattleboro who pronounced it a "meteorite." He even paid Da a sum of money, a dollar I believe, for to keep it in a glass case at the academy.

After that Owney began studying on every book he could locate about the search for precious metals. He even took a course on natural philosophy at the academy, bringing home books on that subject and many more. Gold had been found in 1799 down in North Carolina, he told me, and later elsewhere in the Appalachian Mountains of the East, but only in small amounts. Worse still, all the land was owned by someone or other, which left us poor boys out. Gravel bars in certain creeks had been "salted" with small amounts of gold by unscrupulous land agents to drive the price of mineral rights even higher.

But land in the Great West was free for the taking; the Rocky Mountains were high and vast, cut through with rivers and creeks in which free gold might be found, washed down from the crumbling mountains themselves.

So I knew Owney could find gold in the Great West, if indeed the metal was there to be found.

But we also knew we would need more money than we had to get the necessary tools for our mining effort. I suggested spending the summer trapping beaver at the then-going price of five dollars a plew in Saint Louis, and had reckoned on learning the craft from one of the seasoned trappers in our party, but all of them had gone under yesterday. Worse still, we had seen little beaver sign on the Chugwater or the other rivers and creeks we crossed on our way to the Black Hills, and I had heard grim talk that all the easy streams were pretty well trapped out by now. Yet I knew that even if there was beaver in plenitude in the streams of Absaroka, I sure would not know how to take them.

Finally I swallowed my pride, chucked up my horse, and rode ahead to where Golightly Spybuck was riding near the head of the column.

"Golightly, old friend," says I with a smile, "have you ever trapped beaver before?"

He gives me a stare. "Could be I have," he replies.

"Is it hard?"

"Not if you know what you're looking for," he says.

"What do you look for?"

"Depends," says he.

"On what?"

He laughs. "On whether you're talking prairie beaver or mountain beaver, pond beaver or river beaver. Say, have you ever even *seen* a beaver?"

"Not in Vermont where I lived," I must admit. "Nothing but musk-rats left there, and some foxes and squirrels. And damn few of them anyway."

Says he, "Well then, when we get to good beaver country I will show you what to look for by way of sign, and how to make a foolproof set, and the skinning and stretching of the plews. But you must pay me for the lessons, like you would pay a teacher in a private school back east. How many traps do you have?"

"Six," I tell him. "Good Mackinaw traps, weighing five pounds each, say eight with the chains attached. We purchased them for eigh-teen dollars apiece at Cabanné's post."

"Good traps, then. When I have taught you, you will be taking six beaver a day in your sets, so long as the animals last. The price of your lessons shall be one beaver a day for the season."

"And how long is that?"

He purses his lips and says, "It is now early May. We can trap until freeze-up, probably the end of October or early November in the mountains, later on the plains."

I do some quick reckoning. "So that comes to, say, 180 plews or thereabouts, at three dollars apiece—540 dollars in sum? Why, that is *steep*, I must say for even a teacher of natural philosophy, back where I come from."

"Yes, perhaps," he rejoins, "but everything costs more in the mountains. A man of my acquaintance, Mister Osborne Russell, figured it out once and estimates a 2,000 percent advance in the price of goods and services out here over what they bring in Saint Louis. Why, at the rendezvous on the Popo-asia three years ago I had to pay five dollars a pint for diluted rotgut whiskey that cost only fifteen cents a gallon back east. It is the added expense of the transportation, don't you know? Or so say the goddamn traders."

It was then that I explained to Golightly our indebtedness to Captain Beckwourth in regard to the horses, and he laughed and told me how he had just taken his pony free of charge and ridden off on it.

"Listen here," he said. "This Beckwourth fellow is a notorious sharp trader. I know him of old. And he works for McKenzie, the sharpest trader of them all. Beckwourth is loved by the Crows for his leadership in their petty wars and the gifts of horses he brings them from his raids, but he will screw them gladly for their furs. He is a gaudy liar, too; he would lie to his mother on her deathbed if he could make a dollar from it. You should have walked back to the Missouri rather than sign that paper. He has you now in his power, and will keep you there."

I was saddened to hear this, and said, "Maybe when Owney is stronger we can just sneak off at night, taking our horses with us, and flee for the East."

"Never attempt it," Golightly says. "White men do not steal horses from the Crows; they steal horses from you. He and his Wolves would track you down before you knew it, and they would hang your scalps to dry on their lodgepoles. Best stay here until you know the mountains better." He looks at me kind of sorry-like and says, "Tell you what. I will not charge you a plew a day for my teaching lessons after all. I will only charge you a plew a *week*."

Taken aback, I know not what to say.

Then finally I say it: "Bless you, Mister Spybuck," and ride on back to Owney at the rear of the column.

No, you never can figure an Indian.

Had I known what I learned later that summer at Fort Cass, I should have realized that both Beckwourth and Spybuck were screwing us over financially, and quite royally at that. But that is the way of the mountains.

TOWARD SUNDOWN CAPTAIN Beckwourth called a halt. We were on a hogback ridge overlooking a wide expanse of prairie, the Wind River mountains looming blue and ghostly to the west, and I rode up to where he sat his horse just under the backside lip of the ridge. Two of his minions were with him, his Wolves, as Spybuck calls them, toying with their long black hair and studying the grownd below.

Beckwourth says, "Ah, young Griffith, we are planning to make some meat. Do you see them?"

I follow his eyes and spot maybe a dozen buffalo feeding slowly along through the sagebrush down below. The bushy plants resemble a field of gray boulders from our vantage point.

"I do."

"Then let us see how well you can shoot that fuke," he says, nodding toward the Leman gun where it lay athwart my saddle bow.

Now those buff' were anyway two hundred yards distant from us; no way in hell my ball could reach them at that range. The most I could count on it for was sixty yards, and that with a following wind.

I says, "I cannot hit them from here, not with a smoothbore gun."

Says Jim, "Why, my Indians can kill them, and they, too, have fusils!"

I says, "Not without riding among them."

"Then *ride* amongst them, young sir, and kill me some meat!"

And thus it was I ran my first buffalo.

THE CROWS WERE stripping for the chase; off comes their blankets and shirts, off comes their foofaraw sacks, they open the cocks on their light Northwest trade guns, check the flints for sharpness, and tap in fresh priming powder. Their eyes are glittering black and bright as chunks of Lehigh anthracite.

Oh, yes, their blood is up!

I load my piece: a fresh charge of fine-ground musket powder from the horn, then a patch tamped down on top, and a nicely rounded ball along with a handful of buckshot, another patch atop all that, and stick a new percussion cap on the tit. Lastly I pull off my hat and hand it to Captain Beckwourth.

I says, "Keep this for me if you will, kind sir, and in a minute I will trade you a buffalo liver for it."

He laughs. "Brave talk for a greenhorn!"

With the Crows leading we wound our way slow and easy down the scarp, at an angle away from the buff' so as not to spook them. Once in the flat we were pretty much hidden from them by the height of the sagebrush, also downwind from them so as not to alert them with our scent. Then we circled out so as to pin them against the scarp and ride toward them abreast of one another about twenty yards apart, riding slow and quiet, the Crows leaning low on their ponies' necks to reduce the scary man profile, gradually picking up the pace; then when within a hundred yards of the buff' the Crows suddenly kicked their ponies into a hell-for-leather gallop, and the buffalo wheeled on their tiny quick feet and ran for it. . . .

Well, wasn't it something? Quick as knife we are among them. *Bang!* goes the lead Crow's gun, and a fat cow goes skidding headfirst into the dirt in a great cloud of dust, and *Bang!* goes the other Crow's gun, and with a heart-wrenching bellow down goes another buff', and I am bucketing along now beside a yearling, its buggy eyes rolling back in its black curly head, its shiny black horns hooking toward me like doom itself, and I drop the reins, guiding the chestnut with my knees alone, raise the fuke, and let the yearling have it right back of the skull. . . .

Next thing I know I'm flying through the air smack into a jungle of sage, all tangled up with my horse's legs, dust and the stink of sage in my nose holes. *Whump!* I hit the ground, no breath left in me, dazed, you can bet, from the spill. Then through the dust cloud I see that yearling charge, straight at me, coming fast as a freight train, near half a ton of angry muscle, blood streaming down its face, and those deathly damn black spikes leading the way.

Oh, Christ, you're for it now, Dillon!

But no. From afar the providential shot rings out. The yearling drops in its tracks.

Up on the hogback I see Beckwourth laughing, laughing so hard the tears streak down his face. He points an arm to the side, and I see Owney standing there, 200 yards off at least, with the Hawken still smoking in his hands.

"Oh, yes, that is brotherly love at its finest!" yells Beckwourth. "Well shot indeed, Owen Griffith!"

Then another great peal of mirth, and now all the Indians are laughing too, Bar-che-am-pe as well, hanging there on my brother's arm. A jolly band indeed. There is naught for me to do but laugh along with them. Oh, I am banged up some from the spill, ribs sore, shoulder wrenched, patches of skin scraped off by the rough sage bark; my pony is limping a bit, but a quick check shows nothing broken. Ah, but my fusee is another story: barrel full of dirt, the stock split right at the wrist, even the hammer wobbly on its pinscrew.

But I put a good face on it, walked over to the spikehorn yearling who had near done for me, and with my butcher's knife removed its liver as promised. Then, blood to the elbows, I carried it up to Jim Beckwourth—a heavy load, let me tell you. He accepted it with good grace, sliced off a chunk, raw, and popped it in his mouth.

"Bring me the gallbladder," he says when he has swallowed. "You have not ate liver lest you dip it first in the gall."

One of his minions fetches the desired organ; Jim cuts me a slice of liver, slathers it in the yellowy goo, and proffers it to me. I ate it down, and mighty good it was, too: spicy and pungent as mustard.

"Don't I deserve a bite?" says Owney, walking up to us with the Pine Leaf at his side.

"More than a bite," Captain Beckwourth says. "The whole damn animal, with that pretty shot you made."

"I want to thank you for that, Brother," says I. "Forever in your debt. I guess you are recovered from your hatchet wound sure enough. Steady as a rock."

"You don't know the half of it," Owney replies. He pats the Pine Leaf on her shoulder and gives me a big wink.

Beckwourth turns on his heel and strides off toward the main party, barking orders in Crow like a damn major general.

THE INDIANS BUTCHERED out the three buffalo lickety-split, and soon we were all broiling fat hump rib over a fire of buffalo chips and sage. The sky to the west over the Winds was salmon pink by now, a mackerel sky that promised weather by the morrow.

The Pine Leaf had Beckwourth's goat by the horns all right, and womanly she knew it; kept flirting with Owney all through the time we were eating, feeding him choice bits of hump from her knife tip, but the captain said not a word, just stared grim at the fire. Except at the very end, when he gave her some sharp orders in Crow. She sassed back at him some, though it was weak I could tell, even not knowing the language; but then he threw her such a stern look that finally she gave in, grabbed her blanket, picked up her gun and her lance and her bow and quiver, and went off as he had told her, to stand watch over the horses.

THAT NIGHT GOLIGHTLY Spybuck showed me how to repair my injured gun. He cut a hunk of rawhide to size, soaked it limp in a kettle of water, and sewed it tight with a moccasin awl over the split in the stock. When the buckskin dried it would shrink even tighter, he said, rock hard and unbreakable. He had a kit of gunsmithing tools in his war bag and found a new screw to replace the loose one holding the lock.

"How much are you going to charge me for the repairs?" I asked him.

"This one is on me," said he. "If we're going to be trapping together I want to be sure your gun is in working order. It could save my life someday."

FOUR

———◆◆◆———

S URE ENOUGH, NEXT morning it came on rain; then sleet; then
a heavy wet snow commenced to fall, and it fell all day. It made for
slow going. The Indians did not seem to mind the bad weather, just
wrapped themselves tighter in their buffalo robes and rode through it,
heads down, letting their ponies pick the way over the slippery trails.
Owney and I and the captain pulled on our capotes, thick-hooded
jackets sewn from the wool of four-point Mackinaw blankets; Spybuck
carried a dark blue *grego*, or pea coat, in his blanket roll, which he now
donned; but soon the snow had soaked us through and through, and
each was as wet as the other. It eased up some by nightfall, when we
reached the Wind River country, then Wind River itself, where we
made a wet camp. It took awhile to get the fire started, but using
pinecones and dried punk from the heart of dead birch stumps we
finally had a good blaze going. I ground up some more of those coffee
beans, and soon we had a big speckled pot of it boiling, buffalo meat
sizzling on the ends of our ramrods, and buffalo tongues baking in the
red-hot coals at the edge of the fire; the river roared into the night.

Owney said, "How came you to live amongst the Crows, Captain?"

"Funny you should ask," says Beckwourth, "for it all started right
about here. A bunch of us Ashley men were camped on Wind River

back in '28, alongside a big band of Crows. We'd had a desperate fight
with the Blackfoot during rendezvous earlier that summer, and the
Crows wanted to hear all about it, chapter and verse. They hate the
Blackfoot, mortal enemies, those two tribes, and anyway, Indians love
a good war story above all others. The only man among us at the time
who could speak Crow was a trapper name of Caleb Greenwood, who
had a Crow wife. Well, he got so damn sick and tired of telling the
story, over and over again every night, that finally he latched onto me.
I had taken five scalps in the Blackfoot fight.

"Anyway, Greenwood told the Crows that years ago, back in the
Way Back When, the Shi-ans had stole a Crow baby from the People:
the infant son of a great Crow chief. Indian fashion they raised the boy
as a Shi-an warrior; he become a great hero amongst them. But for all
the honors heaped upon him, for all the horses he won in battle, for
all the beautiful girls who begged to marry him, he nonetheless always
felt as if he was not a true Shi-an, and one day went off to live among
the white men, or the Spiders, as the Shi-ans call us. There, too, he
distinguished himself for valor in the Spider wars. But then this boy,
now a great man among two great peoples, grew lonesome for the
prairies, and he came back west.

"By now the Crows are all agog, their mouths hanging open, ears
pricked. . . . 'What next? What next?'

" 'And that great man,' Greenwood tells them, 'is none other than
the Five-Scalp Hero, the White-Handled Knife, who sits beside you
now at this very fire: Jim Beckwourth!' "

Captain Beckwourth smiles his bright smile, takes a pull at the
coffeepot, and continues: "Of course the Crows will have it no other
way but that the great White-Handled Knife come back to his true
people. They even appointed an examining committee to make sure I
was of their tribe. An old squaw whose son had been stolen by the
Shi-ans said, 'If he is my son, he will have a birthmark on his left
eyelid.' They pull down my lid thusly"—he winked at us there in the
firelight—"and lo and behold!"

By God, he *did* have a birthmark on that eye!

After we had finished laughing at the story—and Captain Beckwourth could spin the yarn far prettier than I recount it here—he told

us that a short while later he had been trapping the country adjacent to Powder River, which is a fork of the Yellowstone, with the far-famed James Bridger. One day the two got separated and Captain Beckwourth suddenly found himself surrounded: "By an innumerable drove of horses, and I could plainly see they were not wild ones. Their Indian owners of course had discovered me long before I saw them—a gang of long-haired warriors, all bristling with lances and arrows. At first I reckoned I was finished for sure, surrounded on all sides, escape impossible. I resigned myself to my fate: if they were enemies they could kill me but once. I took the chance between death and mercy; I surrendered my gun and my traps. But never was I really frightened, for I had already recognized them as Sparrowhawk soldiers, and the Crows claim they have never killed a white man. I went to their encampment with them, where were some of the people who had talked to Greenwood a few weeks before. They welcomed me as a brother. During my stay among them I traded a pocketful of foofaraw for some of the best cured beaver plews I had ever seen. From that moment on, with the concurrence of my superiors in the American Fur Company, I have lived amongst them, trading and serving as one of their war chiefs. And that, sir"—he nods to Owney—"is the answer to your question. Now shall we turn in for the night? We've a long way to travel tomorrow."

WE FOUND THE main Crow village in the foothills of the Little Horn Mountains, where the Wind River becomes the Bighorn and spills its waters onto the plain. Great herds of horses grazed on the greening slopes, more horses than I had ever seen together in one place before. Bands of antelope flirted and fed in the highlands; hawks swung against the empyrian. It was a warm, sunny day, gentle spring in all her fairest ascendancy, with flags in flower blue and white and yellow along the watercourses; as we splashed across a bubbling brook on our way into camp I saw many specklebacked trout, some as long as my leg, swirling away in panic from the ponies' hooves. In Vermont the largest trout I ever caught was scarce a foot long. "Oh, yes, this Absaroka must surely prove a sportsmans paradise!" I exclaimed aloud.

"There's no country like Crow country," Captain Beckwourth agreed. "Old Rotten Belly, one of their chiefs, says that the Great Spirit put it in just the right place. To the south of it is nothing but prickly pear and sagebrush prairie and the water is warm and bitter; to the north is the land of eternal winter, not enough grass to feed a horse herd, and the Indians there must pack their goods on the backs of dogs. To the west is Digger country, where the people are poor and go naked, and must eat fish and bitter roots to live. East of Crow country is the Big Muddy, what we call the Missouri, where the water is not fit to drink unless you let it die overnight to settle the dirt out of it. No, young Griffith, Crow country is best: if you leave it, you live poorly; if you stay all your life in it, you fare well."

CAPTAIN BECKWOURTH SENT his warriors charging ahead into the encampment, whooping and discharging their guns in the air, and leading the herd of recaptured horses. Bar-che-am-pe led the way, her handsome face daubed black with fire ash and tallow as a symbol of victory, and brandishing on high her war lance, from which swung the scalps she had taken on this raid. A mob of old men, wrinkled squaws, the young warriors who had remained behind to guard the village in the war party's absence, toddling naked children, and last the young women who had tarried to don their finest outfits for this festive occasion—all came swarming from the tepees to greet their conquering heroes. Along with them come a great swarm of dogs, big ones and little ones, piebald and yellow and black and white and brown, all of them yapping and barking fit to be tied.

The outcry that went up was like unto a congress of crows, no pun intended. The captain's many Sparrowhawk wives were among the welcoming throng, ranging in age from the senior wife, a dumpy, sharp-tongued old wench of perhaps thirty years, misnamed Still Water, to the most recently acquired, a slim, shy little thing whom he called the Little Wife. She looked to be no more than twelve or thirteen years of age, but then the Indians marry young.

That night there was a festive Scalp Dance that went on loud and friendly until the moon was setting, and a big feast of buffalo meat. For the first time I cracked roasted marrow bones and ate the rich, buttery contents. My, was it good! We slept that night in Still Water's tepee, me and Owney and Spybuck, that is. Beckwourth went to the Little Wife's tent. A couple times during the night we could hear young girls lurking outside our tent flap, giggling and talking, and one of them even dared to peek in: a pretty little thing with fun in her eyes. But Still Water threw a billet of firewood at her and shrilled something in Crow.

"Goddamnit, she is a sourpuss all right," I said. "I am going to sneak out of here and have some fun with those girls."

"No, you dassen't," Owney said. "We are guests here and must not rush things; you don't want to end up with a tomahawk in your head, do you?"

"And anyway, you can spare no time for dalliance," Spybuck adds. "Tomorrow we start you as a beaver man."

GOLIGHTLY SAYS, "FIRST thing you look for when you want to trap beaver, the first thing is—"

"Sign," says I. "And I see it." I point to the sharp gnawed stubs of alder and popple in the thicket alongside the Bighorn, and to the stumps of the bigger aspens chewed down by the bigger beavers.

"Sign of what?" asks Golightly, grinning as always in his superior way.

"Well, *beaver* of course," says I.

He laughs. "No, you damn fool; first thing you look for is *Indian* sign. Lest you end up dead with a raw spot atop your noggin and an arrow or ball through your guts. In short, gone beaver."

We are standing beside the Bighorn in early light, me with the sack of traps in one hand, the Leman in the other. Golightly's fuke rested in the crook of his left arm in what they call the Indian carry. We had left our horses on good grass, picketed and unsaddled so they could roll to their hearts' content. The saddles we'd hung in the trees, well hidden from the eyes of man and out of the reach of hungry bears.

Owen had gone off to the mountains with Bar-che-am-pe to hunt for signs of gold or silver—"color," he called it. He'd brought a gold pan with him from the East.

"Why, we are only two, three miles from camp," I argue back at Golightly. "No hostiles around here, I am sure."

Golightly walks over to the riverbank and stares pointedly down at the grass. I follow. Sure enough, there is a moccasin track in there, and another, and another, leading on out.

"Whose tracks are they? Crow, I would bet," says I.

"No, Oglala," he says. "That is Sioux footwear. See the pucker at the end of the toe? Sparrowhawk squaws do not draw the buckskin so tight at the toe tip, but the Oglalas do. Hunk-papas also, but they usually sew their moccasins out of elk leather, a heavier shoe than this."

I look up quick and start scanning the cottonwoods. Again Golightly chuckles.

"You won't find him skulking in the bushes," he says. "No, he is long gone. That track was laid down some time last night, early morning at the latest. See how the grass has begun to spring up?"

But there was beaver sign aplenty in that grove, and the Shawnee now proceeded to show me the craft of trapping. First thing we set the traps, with Golightly compressing the springs between two thick, straight rods of ash wood, tied together at the near ends to make a press; then he carefully spread the wicked steel jaws while I set the dogs on the pans. One trap snapped shut because I hadn't been careful enough, narrowly missing my finger, and Golightly hissed at me, poison in his eyes, "Quiet, you damn fool!"

That done, we walked soft and slow upstream, well above the cuttings, until we came to a small feeder creek. There Golightly bade me enter the water with him. The water was cold and when it reached my waist I could feel my skin start to shrivel. A few hundred yards up the creek we saw the beaver dam, and another beyond it, and the round bulge of the lodge where these animals made their home. Between the dams were quiet, limpid ponds with trout dimpling the surface.

All Indians know the beaver to be among the wisest of animals, else why would he build such snug little tepees for himself and stock them before winter set in with so much of his favorite food: juicy popple bark? Even Spybuck the Shawnee, who had spent much time among white men, still had great respect for the beaver, and he taught me a little prayer he always said before setting his traps. I cannot remember all the words just now, it was so many years ago, but still recall the most important part: "Forgive me, Father, for the taking of your coat, but I will have need of it in the winter to come, while you stay snug in your house."

Just then a beaver popped his head above water in the middle of the first pond; he saw us, and with a loud smack from the flat of his tail dived back into the depths. I guess he had not heard the prayer.

We waded back downstream and near every place where the Shawnee saw a beaver slide coming down to the water we stooped over near the bank and with our butcher's knives, wet to our elbows, cut a level shelf. Then we lay a trap carefully on the shelf, about half a foot deep in the creek.

Last, with the flat of a hatchet we drove a float pole into the creek bottom, through the big eye at the end of the chain, and Golightly anointed the tip of a willow switch with what he called his "medicine." This was a pale yellowy-brown glue, some call it castoreum, extracted from beneath the pecker skin of a dead beaver. This noxious fluid Golightly carried in a length of hollow deer horn he wore dangling round his neck, on a leather thong, and stoppered with a plug of popple wood. Phew! Did it clear the sinuses! He planted the willow withe, butt-end down, inside the spread jaws of the trap, with the sticky end about a foot over the water.

Says Golightly, "Now when Father Beaver—we call him Amaghqua in Shawnee—when he comes down the bank in search of breakfast, he will smell the medicine and pause to investigate, see if he can recognize its owner by the smell; he does not like interlopers coming onto his property any more than we do, and thus when he stands up to sniff the castoreum his back foot will engage the pan of our trap. If you want to nab him by the front foot, you just have to cut a shorter switch. When the trap snaps, he'll panic and flee for deep water. The weight of the trap will hold him there until he drowns. If he manages to pull the trap with him, the float pole will show us where he is when he dies. So as to spot it easier amongst the flotsam of the creek, you'll notice I've cut three wide rings in the bark, top and bottom, to make it distinctive."

"Clever," I admit. "Now let's get out of the water; I am damn cold and already talking in a squeaky voice."

"Not yet," says he. "First we must wade back downstream to where we went in and splash water over our tracks, lest Father Beaver know we've been here. Then we go on to another brook and *I* set my traps while *you* stand guard."

SO THAT WAS our routine from then on. The following morning my traps held five drowned beaver. Big, heavy animals, about twenty-five pounds apiece, with long, sharp, chisellike buck teeth, slightly orange in color, and with thick coats of lustrous long fur. Golightly said that the mountain beaver of this Crow country, especially farther up the Wind River, had the finest quality fur he had ever taken. We skinned them out as you would a muskrat—a cut up the belly and lateral cuts up the insides of the legs. We cut out the medicine glands and finally lopped off the scaly flat tails to bring them back to camp. Good eating, Spybuck said. You can eat the whole animal—the meat is sweet and oily—and many a trapper has done so when working alone in hostile country, so as not to alert his enemy with a rifle shot while hunting other meat.

With our butcher knives we scraped the raw red insides of the plews clear of any flesh or integument that might have adhered, then stretched them over hoops of green willow, loosely basting the edges to the hoop with laces of rawhide *babiche* through the holes punched by our awls. Later, back in camp, we hung these disks in the sun, high over the reach of the always-hungry camp dogs, and they spun and twirled in the wind like so many small war shields, alternately red and shiny dark brown in the hard, clear daylight. When they were dry, after a couple of days, we worked them back and forth over a smooth log until they were supple, then folded them fur side inward and flattened them down tight into packs. Each plew weighed from a pound and a half to two pounds, so each pack came to about fifty or sixty plews, or 100 pounds a pack: $300 at the fort, cash or credit. Down in Saint

Louis a pack of peltry would fetch from $500 to $800, but that was the price of living in the mountains. You get what you pay for.

We had no trouble from hostiles. Captain Beckwourth's Crows had chased that party of Oglalas clear out of the country after we reported their presence, and I guess the Blackfeet had other concerns to occupy them.

Life was pretty good in the Crow camp. Always plenty of buffalo meat to eat, varied now and then with elk or moose or antelope. With my smoothbore Leman and a load of birdshot I liked to go out on the prairie of an afternoon and see if I could scare up some sharp-tail chickens or maybe a covey of sage cock. A few of the camp dogs always came with me; although they sometimes helped put the birds to flight, when I knocked one down it was always a footrace to get to it before the dogs. Nor did I always win, and let me tell you, it only takes about three seconds for an Indian camp dog to gulp down a sage cock.

One afternoon I found a pair of the Crow girls from camp following me out onto the prairie. One of them was the girl who had peeked in the tent that first night. They kept a discreet distance from me at first, hanging back and giggling whenever I looked over my shoulder at them; but when a flock of chickens flushed right out from underfoot and swung behind me and I managed to kill two of them with one shot, as pretty a shot as I've ever made, the girls ran out ahead of the dogs to grab up the birds. One of them brought the birds over to me. She was the one who'd peeked in the tent, a bold and pretty little thing: long thick black silken hair in braids down to her waist; big wide-set eyes like midnight beaver pools with long lashes; a flush on her cheekbones that glowed beneath her dark, smooth skin. She smiled with her big square white teeth when she handed the chickens to me. She had a fine wide mouth and a nice smile.

By now I knew some sign talk and asked her, "What is your name?"

She made the signs for "Pretty Singing Bird," and then some additional flourishes which meant "the Plover."

"Plover," I said in American. "You are the Plover."

She laughed and nodded her head.

"And your friend, her name?" signs I, pointing to the other girl.

"Yellow Calf," she comes back at me.

The Yellow Calf walks over now, and she is as pretty as the Plover, though maybe a little plumper of bosom.

"You hunt with me," I tell them. "Fetch my birds; I share them with you later."

They nodded their assent and thus I acquired the two prettiest little retrievers that ever a bird hunter could wish. Late in the afternoon, we lay resting beneath the shade of a cottonwood along a quick little rill, my game bag full; the Plover rolled over against me and gave me a long, warm kiss full on the mouth, her tongue hungry for mine. Then I felt the Yellow Calf's soft hands touch me . . . privily.

Well, the events that ensued might best be described in biblical terms, if you know the passages to which I refer. The Song of Solomon comes to mind . . . frankincense; sweet dripping myrrh; breasts like unto twin fawns of the roe deer. Black flowing tresses adorned their pretty heads; their lips were smooth as hot oil.

The only women I had "known" until then were cynical old whores in the river towns of the Ohio, Mississippi, and Missouri; soiled doves, as it were, harlots with rotten teeth, sagging teats, and great wiry thickets of rank bush between their ponderous thighs. These girls' breasts were small but firm, with tender pink nipples, their teeth white as fairweather clouds, breath sweet from the chewing of wild mint; the nap upon the portals of their sex was minimal, yet soft and sleek as that of a beaver kit I had found one day in the cruel jaws of my set. The beaver kit had dragged the trap up onto a small shoal in the river; she was in process of chewing her forepaw free when I discovered her. Then she must have heard or felt my footstep on the gravel of the riverbed. She looked up at me with gentle young eyes, stared at me unafraid, no fight, no fear, not a whimper. . . . How could I kill her? I depressed the springs of the trap; she swam away . . . down, down into the blue of the river.

Since Indians are said to be descended from the Lost Tribes of Israel, I knew these girls henceforth as "the Daughters of Jerusalem."

BROTHER OWEN HAD met with but little success thus far in his search for precious metals. He had panned scanty traces of color from a few westerly creeks but found no nuggets from the riverbanks, excavating with his knife above the places where the pan found gold. Yet he was not discouraged.

"There's no mother lode here," he told us one night as we all sat supping in Still Water's lodge. "I'm pretty damned sure, though, that we'll find gold aplenty just over the next range of mountains."

"Ah, the song of the Argonaut," Beckwourth said with a laugh. "How many times I've heard those sad yet hopeful strains! Still, you may be right. There's an area over the divide, up near the headwaters of the Río de Santa Buenaventura, that's said to be chock-full of the stuff. Some padres from Santa Fe were up there as early as 1776, Dominicans I think. Escalante and Dominguez were their names. Later some other black robes came in, Jesuits I'm told. In a place called the White Hart Hollow, just over the divide, the Indians tell me they've plucked nuggets big as goose eggs out of the creek." He dipped his hand in the stew pot and snagged another hunk of buffalo. "By God, this woman can cook!" says he, grinning up at Still Water. "As sweet as I find the Little Wife, she still has a lot to learn about keeping a man well fed." He belches politely.

Still Water smiles now, and for once she is pretty. Though Plover and the Calf seem not to mind sharing their favors with me, I begin to understand that marriage is a different business altogether. These Crow wives did not wish their husbands to divvy the largesse equally among them but to have the most of it each for herself, and Captain B. had not spent enough time with Still Water so far.

Yet with nine or ten wives to satisfy, he would have to spread himself mighty thin to be truly democratic about it!

"How do I get to the Buenaventura?" Owney asks. I swear he looked positively fevered. "How do I get to White Hart Hollow?"

"You don't want to go there," Captain B. answers him. "Not without the whole Crow village goes with you. It's way up in the Encantadas. Four great rivers head in those mountains: the Snake, the Wind, the Arkansas, and the Río Bravo del Norte. Just over the hill from White Hart, the Multnomah rises, a mighty river itself, which some now call the Columbia. All that height of land is Blackfoot country, and they would have your scalp in a jiffy."

"What if Dill and Spybuck come with me, and maybe a few of your warriors?"

"Frankly, I do not think my warriors would go," says the captain. "The Indians take a dim view of white men plundering the earth of precious metals. What we call mere mining is the blackest sort of sacrilege in their eyes. They hold those gold and silver to be the slow-moving blood of the gods beneath; such materials may only be removed with the most reverent of prayers and ceremonies."

Owen drops his head and stares into the fire. I can see that stubborn set come into his jaw, the same look he used to give Mam when she got all shrill about chores or schoolwork or churchgoing.

LATER THAT NIGHT, we are wrapped in our blankets outside the tepee—Captain B. has asked us to do so, since he must perforce spend the night with the Still Water. Unless old Jim spends more time with her, she has threatened to leave his lodge and go back to her father, taking along the many ponies Jim has given her over the years. So the captain must put up with her, for he loves his horse herd above all else in the world.

"How many packs of beaver have you taken so far?" Owney asks.

"I have near on two full packs; Spy has two and a half, if I'm not mistaken."

"So you have between you enough to pay Beckwourth for the horses, free and clear."

This was a statement, not a question; thus it took me aback for a moment.

"How did you know about it?"

"The captain told me. Do not fret yourself over the matter. Of course he has fleeced us good on the deal, but what do you say we clear out of this place, head over to the Buenaventura, find us some *real* wealth? We can take Spybuck in as a partner, using the money we get from his peltry at the fort to buy the necessary—picks, shovels, two more pans, some sledges, saws, hammers, and nails to build our sluice boxes."

He was all lit up by now, eyes sparking like the very stars, a vibrancy in his voice that I had not heard in weeks. And yet . . .

FIVE

———◆◆◆———

And yet I was torn. I loved the trapping life. For all the miseries it entailed, the cold and the wet and the always being on the alert for hostiles and grizzly bears, for all the early hours, for all the agues and stiff muscles and catarhhs it caused me, it was still the freeest life I had ever nown. Three dollars a plew paid for a lot of anguish. Clerking in the coal company office back in Swartsburg, I was hunched over a musty ledger all day long—growing the hump, we called it—scratching away at row upon row of meaningless figures from six in the A.M. to six at night. I had had my fill of ink blots and frayed nibs. And all of that for three dollars a week, mind you, while miners earned a dollar a day or more.

Not that I felt the least desire to ply a pick and shovel down there half a mile under the ground, breathing coal dust in the dim-lit dark until, like Da, I was coughing up black phlegm day and night. The black lung would have killed him sure, and not long down the line, had the earth itself not fallen upon him first and put a merciful dot to his sorry sentence.

Yet who knows? Gold mining might be less of a hell than grubbing for *colcarreg*. Especially panning for the stuff. "The Spanish called it placer mining," Owney told me, "which comes from the word for

45

'pleasure' in their lingo. You work on top of the earth, not tunneling through it like some blind mole. Me, I don't mind it down there; the earth talks to me. In creaks and groans and mumbles, like, which tell me if I am hurting her too much so she wants to drop the roof on my head or, in hot little whispers, when I am digging in the right spot."

I called it "bosh" again, as I had when he sniffed that meteorite way back when in Vermont, though I would never say so aloud to my only brother of course; Owney was always a wee bit queer about things underground. Still, from what he said, in panning or sluicing for ore you worked the mountain streams, out there in the sunlight and fresh air, just like trapping beaver; you shoveled the gravel into a pan or a rocker and ran more water over it and over it again, until the lighter dirt and gravel washed out and all that remained was the heavy gold itself.

"Then all you need do," Owney said, "is put it in bags and tote it out to the nearest bank, where the least they will pay you is twelve dollars per ounce, hard money. Just think of it, Dill; that is like four full-blanket beaver plews, without the slippery, smelly mess of skinning or fleshing or drying the damn things. Twelve dollars an *ounce*—and there are sixteen ounces to a pound. Why, a mere pound of gold is worth near two hundred dollars, more by far than you earned in a whole year a-clerking!"

"How long do you reckon it will take us to dig out a pound of the stuff?"

"From what Beckwourth says, we should pan out a pound a week. More with a sluice box. We need only stay in that country for the rest of the summer, eight weeks at the most, to clear more than two thousand dollars."

The most Da had ever got paid for a year of coal digging was four hundred. It was mighty tempting.

But then there was the question of the Daughters. It was nice to have the Plover and the Calf under the blankets with me every night; even in the quiet times, when they were not pestering me to demonstrate my affections yet again, we whiled away the evenings talking sign or Crow. I was learning new languages right smart, in many respects. And practical things as well. One day while hunting we came upon a family group of that hateful animal the black rattlesnake, which were all too numerous in that country. The Daughters walked right through them without a moment's hesitation. The snakes wouldn't bite them, they said, for they wore protective anklets of badger teeth. The rattlesnake, they told me, fears no animal but the badger. As soon as the badger sees a snake he dashes at it full tilt with a fearsome grunt. The snake flees, but too slow; when the badger catches up he pins the snake down with one foot; in a flash he bites off the rattle, which he spits out, then proceeds to devour the snake from the bitten end, not unlike an Indian with a length of buffalo gut. The snake writhes in agony, holding itself straight from the badger, not even knowing to turn upon its captor for revenge. When within about two or three inches of the snake's head, which contains its poison, the badger wisely stops gobbling.

So great is the fear of the rattlesnake for the badger that a mere token of its presence on a person, such as these flimsy bands of teeth, will cause the snake to flee. The Daughters gave me such an anklet, which I have worn since that distant day, and never once in my long life have I been bit by a rattler, black or any other color.

"If I throw in with you on this venture," I told Owen at last, "I will want to bring my girls along."

"I can understand that," he said. "I will have the Pine Leaf at my side as well. We have spoken of the matter already, and she is game. Perhaps I can dragoon her into bringing some warriors with us, for protection. Now what about Spybuck? We shall need his plews for to buy our outfit."

I SPOKE WITH THE Shawnee next morning as we ran our trap lines; a hot day it was, now into July, with the prairies drying out and the buff' well into their rut. We could hear the bulls roaring from sky to sky.

Spybuck looks up at me right thoughtful, then reaches down the trap chain into the water and draws up a drowned beaver, flops it up on the bank beside us.

"Look at that fur," says he, pointing with his knife. "The muffoon is thinning fast now as we get into high summer." He ruffled the long, glossy guard hairs to expose the finely grown lead-colored underfur, which trappers called the muffoon. Spy had told me that this undercoat is what made beaver so valuable. Each hair was minutely barbed, so that when the fur was chopped to make felt the barbs interlocked, and thus the resultant product held together much better than any other fur. "No," he continued, "the spring hunt is finished, I fear. Oh, we could shift our operations higher up into the mountains and still get some worthwhile plews, but now is the time for a change. I am familiar with that Blackfoot country; it still holds plenty of beaver, and since it is of greater elevation than here we might could get some pretty good peltry out of it yet this summer. Yes, I will go with you, though it will be dangerous up there. Blackfoot country. They hate Americans. They don't like other Indians much, either, as I've learned to my dismay. Yet I feel it's time to move on despite the hazards. In return for the plews I've trapped already I'll want a full third of what you boys take by way of gold from those White Hart streams; and *I will not swing a pick or a shovel.*"

That is what I liked about Golightly Spybuck: he could size up a situation and make up his mind quick as a finger snap. Forty years in the wild will do that for a fellow. A moment's hesitation at the crucial instant can result in a hungry belly for the hunter or a prematurely bald head for the victim of Indian attack.

"That's fine with us," I told him, and reached out my hand. He had a firm grip. Done and done.

THE CROW CAMP was abuzz when we returned that day. Visitors had just arrived from the Snake country west of the divide. They proved to be a brigade of free trappers and Delaware Indians led by Lafcadio Dade, a short, bossy, sour-looking man of about Captain Beckwourth's age, perhaps a bit younger, yet gnarled as a cedar snag, with a shock of carroty red hair and a beard to match. Dade was the booshway, or leader, of the trappers.

"You remember when we met I told you about the deaths of Rose and old Hugh Glass early last spring?" Beckwourth said to me while the new arrivals were unsaddling their mounts. "They were killed just outside of Fort Cass by those same Rees as almost done for you fellows. I had just arrived at the fort with my Crows and their peltry from the fall and winter hunt, and was told that Johnston Gardner and Lafe Dade had been there just a few days before, coming upriver with a big load of trade goods from the settlements. Their camp was just up the Yellowstone about half a day's ride. I wanted to trade with them, so three men from the fort headed upriver to fetch them back. Rose, Old Glass, and another fellow whose name I disremember. They did not get far. In the morning we saw their bodies lying on the ice. They had been cruelly butchered, and when we rode up their corpses were scarcely cold. But I will let Mister Dade tell you of the sequel."

He did so that night after supper. Dade had brought his new Indian wife with him to the fire, a tall, lovely thing of about Plover's age, whom he treated with great solicitude. "Oh, yes, them damn Rees," he said, unslinging the spyglass he always carried with him in a leather case slung over his shoulder. His wife lit his clay pipe for him with an ember from the cookfire. "They rode up to our camp sassy as jaybirds. We could not make out their tribe, in the dusk light, but they was led by a half-breed from Fort Clark, down there by the Mandans on the Missouri: shifty fella name of Antwine Garro. He dismounts and comes over to the fire, all smiles. 'What Indians are those with you?' Gardner asks him. Says the half-breed, 'Oh, they are good Indians; they will not hurt you.' But I noticed the red devils lookin' over our horses pretty fondly, and grew alarmed at what they might have in mind. 'Garro,' I said, 'tell us right quick, what Indians are those?' By now they are making off with our horses!

" 'They are Ree-ka-ras,' says Garro. 'But do not worry. They are only borrowing your horses; they will bring them back right quick.' "

Dade pauses to spit in the fire, shakes his head at the recollected gall, then puffs blue smoke from his clay.

" 'Rees!' Gardner yells. 'To arms, men; seize them!' But they all skedaddled too quick for us, even old Garro, and we only grabbed two of them. Garro stops just out of rifle range.

" 'Give me back my Indians!' he yells.

" 'Not until you give us back our horses,' Gardner tells him.

"'Then we will have the tops of your heads,' the renegade says.

"'Take them if you can,' Gardner says. And with that they rode off—and all our horses with them.

"Tell these boys what you did with the prisoners," Captain Beckwourth says.

"Well, we had seized them up good with trap chains," Dade says, "and we had a tremendous fire blazing there, so we opened up the top logs, swung them two Rees into the flames, and rolled back the burning logs to cover them."

"Did they scream much?" Owney asks, after a long pause.

"Not a peep," Dade says, looking over at him as if to say, "How could you ask such a dumb fool question?" He had close-set blue eyes, slightly crossed or anyway out of kilter, sharp as icicles. "Writhed around some in there, but them Rees, they are a rum lot."

Dade said Gardner was already across the divide, over on the Salmon River. Himself, he was heading in to Fort Cass to trade his peltry for a new outfit; then it was back to the mountains. "I found me some pretty good streams up near the Targhee, along with this prize, my new Shoshone wife," he said, slapping the girl on her rump. "Good beaver, both." We laughed. "The streams are just on the edge of the Blackfoot country, so no one has trapped them out as yet. And no one better try, neither. That is my country up there. I have a special relationship with the Grovan, and don't you boys forget it." He picked up his spyglass, wrapped an arm around his beauty wife, and decamped.

Lafe Dade was not a man to take lightly.

THE FOLLOWING NIGHT we told Captain Beckwourth of our plans. His face tightened some, and a look of calculation come into his eyes.

"You still owe me for those horses," he said.

"We have the plews for you, two full packs and then some," Owney said.

"Let me see them."

Spy and I dragged the packs down from the cache we had built in a dead cottonwood and hauled them over to the fire. Captain B. went to inspecting the furs.

"Some of these are a bit sparse of hair," he says, his face black and stony as that famous meteorite. "They will not bring full price at Saint Louis; I should have at least another pack, maybe more, to fulfill your end of the bargain."

"We need the rest of the furs to buy our outfit at Fort Cass," I says.

"If you are heading to the White Hart country you will require pack mules to haul your gear," the captain says. "Mules are pricey. And you cannot have enough peltry in hand just yet to afford them, not at Fort Cass prices." He smiles a cold, false smile. A smile of triumph. "Now why don't you just stay here through the summer with us and make a fine fall hunt up in the Winds? Lots of beaver up there. Then you can winter over with us. We will have plenty of buffalo to eat, and in the spring I will sell you some good mules, cheap, to begin your venture into the Blackfoot country."

"No, we are set to go *right now*," says I. "You cannot keep us here with all your black trickery and wiles."

"Easy," Owney says.

But suddenly I was getting hot. This squaw man, after all, had stolen our horses, then insisted we pay him back an outrageous price for them. Now he had the gall to up the ante!

"We will go where we will go," I snaps at Captain Beckwourth. "We are *free* men, not *niggers!*"

He hit me so hard and fast I never saw it coming. "Do not *ever* call me that," he says, standing over me now, his big, hard fists clenched and his eyes spitting fire. "I am a *white* man, from the Old Dominion, born free, and I shall die free!'

I try to get up, but he nails me again, with a wide swinging punch that slams me back into the dirt . . . stars in my eyes.

"Leave the boy alone," says Owney.

Beckwourth steps back and kicks me, hard, square on the chin. . . .

Then they are at it, hot and furious. Owney straightens Beckwourth up with a solid left jab, fakes a right cross, then hooks him hard with a left to the mouth. Beckwourth lowers his head and charges like a griz', but Owney dances to his right and plants a solid shot on the captain's ear hole. That staggers him, but the captain comes right back, boring in low and fast, planting short rapid punches into Owney's gut. Big loops of blood are swinging from the captain's split mouth; he is blowing bloody bubbles. Then he misses with a right uppercut and goes lurching into the fire. A great cloud of sparks.

By now the Indians are all gathered around, whooping and cheering, dogs barking, and I see Bar-che-am-pe looking on with a wide grin across her face. My girls are dancing up and down, clapping their hands and yipping along with the dogs.

Captain B. staggers out of the fire, his moccasins smoldering, his eyes blood red from smoke or fury, and stares around wild-like, looking in vain for Owney. But Owney is right behind him. He grabs Beckwourth's shoulder with his left, spins him around, socks him flat on the chin with a wind-up right. The captain goes down to stay.

Then I notice some of the warriors have grabbed out their scalp knives and tomahawks. They are not amused. The big ugly fellow who had held my horses back there at the Ree fight is in the forefront. But just as they start to move in on me and Owney, Spybuck speaks up, somewhere back in the shadows. He says something fast and mean in Crow, and they stop to look over at him.

Now he steps into the firelight, and he has two cocked fusees—mine and his—aimed square on the mob of warriors, the muzzles at belly level, his fingers steady on the triggers. For a long moment all is silence; time stands still.

Then into the firelight steps Long Hair, the principal old man chief of this band, roused out of his tent by the fracas. He is an elderly man, face wrinkled like a old glove, once a great warrior but now leading from wisdom, and he is aptly named. He has the longest hair of any man in a tribe noted for the length and beauty of its warriors' locks. Usually Long Hair wears his mane wrapped round with a wide strap of buffalo leather and folded up into a big square bundle which he carries under his arm; but now he has unfurled it, oiled it up nicely with bear grease, and it trails along behind him, longer by far than the chief is tall: like a great black gleaming bridal train.

"Put down them weapons!" he shouts, giving his hair a flirt. It writhes behind him, snakelike. "I will not have Crow blood spilled in my camp, nor any white man's either. This was a fair fight: The Enemy of Horses got his ass whupped by the Gold Seeker, whom the All-God has clearly blessed with great art in the use of his fists. Now the Shawnee has the drop on you Crows, and Shawnees do not hesitate to kill their enemies. Begone to your lodges and your wives and horse herds; begone this instant or I shall call my Dog Soldiers with their pony quirts to disperse you!"

The warriors obeyed. I walked over to where Captain Beckwourth sat rubbing his chin and shaking his head sideways as if he had water in his ear. "Do not feel bad, Captain," I said. "Owen Griffith was the best boxer in the Alleghenies. He has beat men twice your size."

"Small comfort, that," says the captain.

I offer my hand and pull him to his feet. He stands up slow and wobbly-kneed.

"Now he has made me look weak before my warriors; they are hard enough to control at the best of times, but presently I do not know if I can check them should they take it in mind to lift your hair. Well, I desired you to stay with us and, yes, to continue trapping for me and the American Fur Company. But now you'd better be on your way, and quick."

WE CLEARED OUT at moonrise, taking with us my girls and Pine Leaf on ponies of their own, but leaving behind two packs of prime beaver: a more than ample payment for the captain's Christian charity.

.

SIX

FORT CASS WAS at this time the principal trading post of the American Fur Company on the Yellowstone River, providing foofaraw and arms and tools to the entire Sparrowhawk nation in return for prime Indian peltry, mainly beaver but also including otter skins, fox pelts, lynx furs, and buffalo robes. Old Manuel Lisa, the pioneer of the Rocky Mountain fur trade, had had a fort on or near this location in the first decade of the century: Fort Manuel, he called it. Much bigger than this one. It lasted until the Second Revolution broke out in 1812 and the British started raising hell in this region.

The place was small and hardly prepossessing, consisting as it did of an ill-lit log-built warehouse and trading parlor, the entire facility surrounded by a sixteen-foot-high stockade of upright popple logs, peeled and sharpened by ax at the tops. The stockade measured about sixty paces square. Termites and carpenter ants had already left holes and sawdust piles at the bases of the pilings. Slowly but surely the fort was being eaten away by the wildlife of these prairies, though it had only opened for business the year previous.

Some of these pests had red hides and walked on two legs, for already a sizable village of beggarly Indians had attached itself to the fort, their tents clustered near a grove of cottonwoods along the bank of the Bighorn; a scruffy, scraggly pony herd grazed on the yellowing summer grass of the hills all around. These Indians, the Plover told me with a hint of scorn, were the River Crows, a lesser breed of Sparrowhawks who lived along the lower Yellowstone and who were by nature lazy and dirty. "We know them as the Dung-on-the-Riverbanks Band," she said. The Calf giggled and covered her mouth with her hand.

The tribe which the Daughters belonged to were Mountain Crows, a small band called the Erarapi'o, or Kicked-in-Their-Bellies, while the main body of Mountain Crows was known as the Araraho. "Why the name Kicked-in-Their-Bellies?" I asked. Plover didn't know, but the Calf said it came from an incident many many winters ago when a proud old chief of the Araraho got kicked in the belly by a horse he had stolen from the Sioux. The Araraho laughed and laughed, so that finally the proud chief got very angry and took his whole family away to live separate from the main body. Oh, the Crows love a joke, they do, but they can be mighty rough about it.

These River Crows around the fort were a sorry sight. Their tepees were ragged and worn like they hadn't killed any fresh buffalo robes for years, all smoke-stained at the top and halfway down, some of the Indians reeling around drunk even this early in the morning. One toothless old woman lay passed out in the road, her white old head resting on a pile of horse manure over a puddle of vomit. You could smell the booze reek a rifle-shot downwind of her.

"Fort Indians," Spybuck said, riding up alongside me. "They grow dependent on the trader's goods, iron tools at first—arrowheads, lance tips, awls, needles, kettles, guns—then of course gunpower and lead, coffee and sugar; end up swapping their wives and ponies for a drink of diluted whiskey. I have seen it happen too many times; my very own people, once the fiercest, proudest warrior nation east of the Big River, have been unmanned by this hunger for white man's goods. It's not a good thing, but how can we prevent it? I'm afraid that only a holy war, red against white, can stay our doom."

Fort Cass at least appeared ready for one. The whole shebang was defended by two sturdy blockhouses, which dominated the northeast and southwest corners of the stockade. The blockhouses stood two stories high and had pointed roofs. On each of them was mounted a brace of swivel guns or blunderbusses, plus a one-pounder cannon apiece which could fire (I was told) sixteen musket balls per shot. Together these guns covered all four walls, and of course the main gate. So long as Mr. Samuel Tulloch, the company agent, and his half-breed engagés stayed alert, no Indian war party was going to break in on them for thievery or mayhem.

We arrived at the fort on the morning of July 14, 1833, discharging our weapons as we approached, both to alert the crew to our presence and to display our peaceful intentions. The gates swung wide. After exchanging introductions and pleasantries with Mr. Tulloch, a spry, small but well-knit man of middle years, and enjoying a fine breakfast of buffalo steaks, *boudins*, small beer, and the first fried eggs we had eaten since leaving the Missouri, we commenced trading. When Tulloch learned that the Shawnee wished to sell his catch of beaver, he broke out a keg of whiskey and offered Spy a drink.

"Not just yet," Golightly said.

"So be it," Tulloch replied, leading the way to the parlor. One of his pork eaters hauled in the packs of peltry.

"Fine plews for the most part," Tulloch allowed as he leafed through Spybuck's packs. "Good, thick muffoon; no spoilage." He slung the packs one by one onto the scale. They came to 260 pounds. "How many skins all told?"

"One hundred and seventy-five," Spybuck said.

Tulloch looked at him over his spectacles. "You do not mind if I inspect them individully, I am sure." He was afraid we might have freighted the pelts with sand to increase their weight, or perhaps slipped a few heavy but less valuable badger pelts into the packs.

"Help yourself," Spy said.

It was as the Shawnee had told him. Tulloch did some ciphering on a slate. "Will you be wanting hard cash or credit?" he asked us.

"How much of each or either?" Spy asked.

"I can pay you 500 dollars in coin of the realm, or extend to you 600 dollars in credit. I must say you have a remarkable command of the American language, sir, especially for a red man."

"Oh, we have been dealing with you for a long while now, beginning in the days of my illustrious uncle," Golightly said, smiling. "You may perchance have heard of him. He was known as Tecumseh?"

Tulloch's eyebrows shot up behind his specs, and so, too, I am sure, did mine. Every schoolboy in America had read of the great Shawnee war chief, and many had nightmares about him to this day. Or anyway, *this* one did! Tecumseh was the Shooting Star, the blazing Comet of the Shawnees, back in the days when they and their allies the Wyandots and the Delawares terrorized the Old Northwest with battle ax, scalp knife, and firebrand. In league with the British, Tecumseh and his brother, the Prophet, led a great, bloody, all-scourging holy war against the settlers who came in ever greater numbers across the Alleghenies, through the Cumberland Gap, and down the Ohio from Fort Pitt. It was not until Tecumseh ran afoul of Gen. William Henry Harrison at Tippecanoe in 1811 and two years later on the Thames River near Detroit that the Shooting Star burnt out. He died in the last battle.

"As to your price," Spy continues, cool as spring water, "I was told by Mister Kenneth McKenzie himself, only last winter at Fort Union, that the American Fur Company would be paying three dollars and a quarter *a pound* for prime beaver this year. Your own scale puts my catch at 260 pounds, which by my humble reckoning would come to 845 dollars."

Well, this was news to me. That damn rascal Captain Beckwourth had led me to believe the paying price for beaver in the mountains was only three dollars *per plew*, each of which weighed a pound and a half. He had short changed us by 50 percent, plus a quarter of a dollar, on each and every pelt. My plews should have been worth $650, where he valued them at only 400. *Oh, damn him for a thief and a liar!*

Mr. Tulloch quick says, "I have had advice by courier from downriver, only recently, that the Saint Louis price for beaver has fallen below three dollars. Seems like the fashion in men's hats has changed over in London. They now prefer silk to beaver pelt. . . . Say, I am a mite bit thirsty, what with all this 'rithmetic talk; won't you gents join me in a glass a of Old Killdevil?"

"No," says Spy. "But I will buy a keg off you once we agree on a fair price for my peltry."

"Oh, I dassen't *sell* any whiskey, not to Indians or white men, either one. The goverment is quite strict about that nowadays. Each keelboat that comes up the Yellowstone is inspected thoroughly for contraband. What I have here is for my personal use only, though I should like to share it with you all on this festive occasion."

"How the hell much are you going to pay for the damn beaver?" Owney says. I look over, and by God, his blood is up! He wants to get moving toward that gold, and all this dawdling is driving him bats.

"I can go up to $715, hard cash," Tulloch says. "Not a penny more."

"Seven fifty," Owney counters. "That is, *seven-five-zero,* or we will take the furs down to Saint Louis ourselves."

"Or, by God, burn them!" Spy adds.

"Seven forty-five," says Tulloch. "Eight hundred in credit."

Owney looks over at Spybuck. The Shawnee nods.

"Done. But we shall take it in credit, if you please. We must buy ourselves an outfit for the White Hart Hollow, and cash, I take it, don't go far in that country."

"No, it don't," says Tulloch.

"Now I will have that whiskey," Spybuck says.

MORE HAGGLING ENSUED as Owney ordered picks, shovels, axes, adzes, saws, sledges, hammers, spikes, and nails; gunpowder, lead, a spare bullet mold; and so forth and so forth. Pine Leaf and the Daughters had been out and around the fort, drinking cup after cup of hot sweetened coffee with the pork eaters. Now they came skittering into the parlor and began demanding foofaraw. Yipping in high excited voices, even the Pine Leaf. Finally Owney had to buy a quantity of colored beads for them, along with some moccasin awls, a pound of vermillion (for ten dollars!), one of blue paint, and another of yellow ocher (not quite so dear), along with half a dozen looking glasses, just to shut them up.

"Now we will need us some staunch pack mules to lug this lot upcountry with," Owney said when they'd finished. Tulloch led us out to the corral. Spy brought along the whiskey keg; by the ease with which he lifted it I could tell he'd depleted it some already. Yet he did not stagger. His eyes, though, were turning an ominous red.

Most of the horses were Indian ponies, swirling wild-eyed away from our approach like a calico whirlwind; the mules stood tall and calm, off in one corner of the corral; only the occasional twitch of an ear or a writhe of rump hide to scare off the flies betrayed the fact that they were indeed alive.

"What do you think, Spy?" Owney asked.

The Shawnee studied the mules for a few minutes. Then he climbed through the rails and went over to them, lifting lips, checking for galls, punching bellies, and knocking his knuckles against cannon bones. Finally he led four of them over to us by their halters.

"These the best," Spy said. "Rest too old, too sick. No last long on trail."

He sounded strange, his voice thick, his grammar that of a stage hall Indian. It was how the booze took him, I was to learn. . . .

"How much?" Owen asked Tulloch.

"Eighty apiece."

"Too damn much," Spy said. "Sixty." He spit in the dirt.

Wait a minute, I thought yet again. Beckwourth charged us $200 *apiece* to buy back our horses, and mules are more costly than horses out here. Once again my blood neared the boiling point. . . .

"Seventy."

"Sixty-five," Owney said, "with the pack saddles included; take it or leave it."

"Done," said Tulloch, grinning now for the first time. "You are a hard man to deal with; it was a pleasure doing business with you."

DURING THE NIGHT, after a fine supper of chitterlings, roasted turkey, Yorkshire pudding, mince pie, and coffee, I woke up restless. We were sleeping in the warehouse and I saw right away that Spy was gone. He had eaten only a spot of supper, pouring himself cup after cup of whiskey instead. I went to the door and looked outside. A gang of fort Indians was staggering around in the moonlight, and there was Spy with them in the compound, dead drunk, reeling like a fort Indian himself. Spy had a powder keg with him and was laying down a train to the little log house that served as the fort's magazine. *By God, I thought, he is about to begin his holy war by blowing the whole damn establishment to kingdom come!*

The fort Indians slipped into the shadows soon as they saw me, like the rats old Thump used to hunt at the dump. But these rats were all wasted with booze and consumption. I could hear them hacking and wheezing there in the dark. Anyway, I figure that's what set Spy off, the plight of those poor devils.

He turns and sees me now. Mutters something in Shawnee. "Ne-kah-noh. . . ." Which I later learnt meant "My friend." Then he looks at me more closely, and his eyes go squirrelly. "Matchele ne tha-tha!" he yells. "You are my enemy!

"Tschi!" he says. "Kill!"

Well, I coldcocked him easy enough alongside the head with a billet of firewood I had carried with me for a club, and dragged him back to his blankets, where I wrapped him up good. Then I took the whiskey keg out to the compound and poured the sorry few ounces that remained of it onto the ground. From the shadows came the sudden mournful howls of the fort Indians; as I closed the warehouse door behind me I saw them dash out into the moonlight and lap up what they could of the dregs.

WHEN WE WERE packed and ready to leave the following morning, Tulloch told us he had spent a lot of time up in that Blackfoot country where we were headed, trapping the headwaters of the Snake and clear on over to Day's River in the Oregon Territory. "That was back in the twenties when I was working for Smith, Jackson, and Sublette," he said. "Bug's Boys—the Blackfeet—is some tough. The Blackfoot nation consists of four tribes: the Siksika or Blackfeet proper, the Bloods or Kahna, the Pikuni or Piegans, and sometimes the Grovan of the prairies, who also call themselves the Atsina. Bloods and Siksika are the meanest; the Piegans are usually willing to trade but will kill you just as dead if they take a mind to it. The Grovan is just plain sneaky and murderous. Early in '28 me and four other Americans, one of them

Pinckney Sublette, was holed up with a British fur brigade under Peter Skene Ogden, of the Hudson's Bay Company you know; snowed in we were, and we had no snowshoes. Damn Ogden, he had plenty, I am certain sure, but he would not sell us any. We made some, but they did not work right. Snow eight feet deep anyway. Finally, in March, when the snow begun to melt, we got away, heading for the Three Forks of the Missouri, up where you fellers are going to, and Bug's Boys jumped us good. Grovans, I think they was, though we had no time to ask them. They killed Pinckney, an Iroquois named Baptiste, and two others of my party. Young Pinckney was brother to Bill and Milton Sublette; a good man, hard to lose him. And it would not have happened if that accursed Briton Peter Ogden had just sold us those webs we so desperately needed. Hell, I wouldn't have minded if he'd charged us ten times what they were worth. If we'd had them we'd of been long gone before the Blackfeet were on the prod."

He pauses to let the moral sink in.

"Now, boys," he says, "I happen to have some very fine snowshoes in the warehouse, Nez Percé webs they are, and at a *bargain* price. What say ye?"

"My brother and I hail from Vermont," Owney says. "We grew up on snowshoes, and know how to build them—snowshoes that actually work."

"Suit yourselves," says Tulloch, but he looks dubious nonetheless.

Spybuck groaned, rubbed the knot on his head where I'd hit him, and we rode on out of there, west by southwest for the Three Forks.

SEVEN

WE TRAVELED UPSTREAM along the Yellowstone, through open prairie for the most part, with small herds of buffalo grazing as far as the eye could see. Some of the fort Indians followed along with us for a ways, hoping, I guess, that we had another keg of whiskey in our packs, but when none was forthcoming they lost heart, stole a small brass cook pot and a few forks and spoons from our messware, and counted it a worthwhile excursion. I was for chasing after them and getting our stuff back, but Spy said, "Let the poor devils go. They have little enough in life. Besides, they will only stick a butcher knife in your guts if you catch them."

The sole landmark of note along the way was Pompey's Pillar, a great block of sandstone that rises along the left bank of the river 150 or 200 feet high. Lewis and Clark found it . . . or actually Captain Clark found it on his way back to the Mandans in 1806, coming down the Yellowstone in dugout canoes after their winter in Oregon. He named it for Pomp, the baby son of the Indian squaw Sacajawea and her husband, the Frenchman Charbonneau, who was their guide and interpreter on the trip. Captain Clark is said to have carved his initials in the sandstone.

We got there late in the day and made camp by the river; and while Spybuck and Bar-che-am-pe went out to shoot us some supper, the Daughters and I climbed the rock to see if we could find Captain Clark's initials. We found them, and fooled around some up there. It was a fine view of the prairie with broken, nameless mountains to the south of us and far to the west the great green heave of the Absarokas just topping the red horizon. A big angry eagle circled us where we sat up there on top of the Pillar, swooping down on us from time to time; and the Daughters shrieked and made like they was scared, so nothing would do for it but that I calm their fears with a bit of hugging and kissing and more. Oh they were always in the mood for it, yes indeed.

"You make baby for me just like that Pompey boy, hey?" said the Calf.

"No, he make *two* babies!" Plover yelped. "One for each of us."

God forbid, I thought.

We forded Clark Fork of the Yellowstone with no problems, and then the smaller Stillwater River ditto; these were good steady mules Spy had picked for us. Then with the Absaroka Range to our left, a big brawling stream that Spy said was called the Boulder River came crashing out of the mountains, and then the Yellowstone hooked to the south, up into some really high country. The river had been muddy and slow for most of the distance we'd come from Fort Cass, but now it got narrower, clearer, colder, and we could see big trout holding along the bottom and snapping grasshoppers whenever the wind blew them on the water. We left the Yellowstone and pushed on west over a low pass, to drop down into the headwaters of the Missouri.

So far we had seen not a single Indian, nor sign of their smoke.

"That will change from now on," Spy said. "We've been passing all this way through Crow country. Beyond this point are Grovans, whom some call the Big Bellies. We must post a guard each and every evening, taking turns through the night to keep watch over our stock. Picket pins *and* hobbles is the rule in this country."

"Are the Grovans as fierce as Tulloch said?" Owney asked.

"Yes, they can be. Like all these Missouri River Indians, they will steal everything they can lay a hand to if you let them. They will come into your camp professing peace and friendship, hug you and sigh fondly, rolling their eyes with the joy of it, and meanwhile pick your pockets. If you let loose of your gun, even for a moment, they will grab it and shoot you with it, then lift your hair. Yet on another day, when maybe their medicine is bad, they will play the Good Samaritan, feast you on the best bits of buffalo, offer their wives and daughters for your bed; even give you some of their horses free of charge if you are afoot. You cannot predict their moods. But the one thing the Grovans really hate, and all the other Blackfoot bands for that matter, is white men or other Indians poaching in their country, killing their beaver or buffalo, which is like stealing money from their pockets. Oh, they will trade gladly enough, but if they catch you alone on a trap line they will kill you quick as they can. Or maybe not so quick. We red folk are overly fond of torture. I suggest that Dill and I hide our traps right now, bury them deep in the mule packs, and bring them out for use only when we are sure no Blackfeet are in the vicinity."

That night we reached the Gallatin, the easternmost of the three rivers that join to form the Missouri. Next came the Madison, then the Jefferson farthest to the west; and beyond the Jeff, across the divide, were the Encantadas—the headwaters of the Río de Santa Buenaventura. Spybuck and Bar-che-am-pe said that White Hart Hollow was on the Garnet Creek, a tributary of the Buenaventura, between that river and the Jefferson; in short, quite a way upstream from the Three Forks. They debated long and hot over whether it would be better to go *down* the Gallatin toward the Forks and then work our way up either the Madison or the Jeff, easier going in terms of terrain, or to head *up* the Gallatin and then bushwhack our way west to the Buenaventura.

Spybuck argued that going up the Gallatin and across the mountains would take us around the flank of the Blackfeet, who were thickest at the Three Forks. But it would be tough riding, over the Spanish Peaks and right through the heart of the Madison Range.

Pine Leaf was for going straight down the Gallatin to the Forks, smack into the heart of Blackfoot country, devil take the hindmost. "Let's be bold," she said. "Fight it out with them if war is what they want. We are Crow soldiers, and we fear no one."

My girls snuck worried looks at each other, their faces solemn.

"Bold talk from a coup-crazy lady," Spy said, in English so that she couldn't understand him. "But we wouldn't last ten minutes against a concerted attack by a Grovan war party. She may not care if she dies, but I certainly value my scalp more highly. I say let's proceed up the Gallatin, then cross over through the back door to Garnet Creek."

"Yes," Owney agreed, "and let's proceed slowly. I would like to pan some of the riffles along this river, see if I can find color. All of these mountains look young enough to be auriferous, that is to say, gold-bearing. If we can locate a rich ledge or vein of it here, why, then we will not have to brave the terrors of those fearsome Big Bellies. I cannot help but think of them as cannibals, what with that awful name you gave them."

Spybuck said, "No, they get the name in translation from the French. Gros Ventres. The first coureurs de bois who encountered the tribe must have seen them just after gorging on a fresh buffalo kill. They are not true Blackfeet either, merely their staunch allies; they even speak a different language. The Big Bellies are cousins to the Arapaho, whom they hate, but good friends of the Rees."

That sealed our decision. I still had nightmares of my friends roasting on the wagon wheel.

And thus we went our way slow and careful up the Gallatin River. It seemed we stopped every quarter of a mile so Owney could grub around in gravel bars. He worked pan after pan of grit and sand in his search for gold but found none. His face grew longer and longer.

While Owen panned, I spent the time fishing. We had a packet of small fishhooks along in our plunder, so I clubbed a fool hen one day and tied up some flies from its feathers. I used a length of red wool from a blanket for dubbing the body, tied on the wings and tail with bits of feather stripped from the fool hen, using silk thread from a spool which Calf had swiped from Fort Cass when Tulloch and his engagés weren't looking, dabbed on a spot of buffalo-hoof glue to secure the whole shaggy concoction, and there it was, as pretty a trout fly as you could buy in the fanciest sporting goods shops of Boston, Philadelphia, or even, by God, New York.

The trout agreed. With a twelve-foot ash whip for a fish pole and thirty feet of greased string for a line, I was soon out among them, wading hip-deep into the riffles and swimming the fly down through the runs, a trout on every cast. These trout were different from the speckled natives we caught back home; bigger for one thing, some of them two feet long at least; and they had bright green backs with a red slash under their chins, like their throats had been cut by some underwater assassin befor they came thrashing into the hand. The Daughters served as my ghillies, grabbing the trout when I worked them in close, then braining them with a rock and stringing them on a peeled stick. Pretty soon we had enough for a proper fish fry.

"Your pole and pretty feathers are a clever way to catch fish," Plover said when we had waded back ashore. "Now I'll show you how the Crows do it."

She crept up the shoreline on her hands and knees, peering cautiously through the shrubs every few seconds, until she spotted a big trout lying in the slack water hard against the bank. Then slowly, slowly, with infinite patience, she reached down through the water until her hand was beneath its throat. Then with a whoop she reared upright, the great gleaming fish twisting and flailing with her fingers hooked through its gills. It was near half again as long as the biggest one I had caught.

"How did you get it to stay so still while you were reaching for it?" I asked her.

"Easy," she said, grinning. "I tickle its belly—like this!"

And quick as a flash she tickled my own belly. I grabbed her and dragged her down into the weeds; soon the Calf was into the wrestling match, and sooner still the fray had turned into another double seduction. Oh, how those girls could gang up on me.

When we got back to the others, Owen was a changed man. His eyes were on fire, his face lit up, a grin stretching from ear to ear.

"Look at this!" he yelled as we came within earshot. He ran toward me like a kid who'd found a penny in the street. He opened the clenched palm of his hand and revealed . . . a nugget the size of a nail head.

"Tain't much of a treasure," I said.

"That's not the point, idiot," he said. "The point is that it's here, in this mountain range. Oh, we're way downstream of the mother lode.

It may not even be at the head of this river. But it *is* in these mountains."

He turned and looked up into them, the great crags brooding over our heads, the wind muttering up in the bald, gray peaks. Owen's eyes were shining.

"All we have to do," he said, "is go up there and find it."

THREE DAYS UP the Gallatin and Pine Leaf, who'd been scouting ahead, came riding back to the pack train with her eyes shining. "Enemies ahead," she signed as soon as she got near us. "Blackfeet . . . four soldiers." She raised her bow and shook it. "We kill them."

"Not yet," Spy signed back. "Come in. We talk. Which way they headed?"

"Upstream."

"Let them go; no need to fight right now. Maybe more soldiers with them."

The Pine Leaf looked at him for a long moment, cold as Gallatin water, then spit on the ground and wheeled her pony. Off she went to battle, all by herself.

"Goddamnit!" Spy yells. "Well, let's go, then."

"Stay here with the mules!" I yell back at the Daughters.

We gallop forward through the lodgepole pines and aspens, Owney beside me on the buckskin, thumbing a fresh cap onto the tit of his Hawken. My fusil is newly loaded with ball and buck; I loosen the tomahawk in my belt.

Pine Leaf is still a hundred yards ahead of us when we see the Blackfeet, riding upstream on Nez Percé horses, now wheeling around at the sound of her hoofbeats.

Immediately they scatter.

Pine Leaf's bow twangs and the one farthest toward the river slumps sideways in his saddle with an arrow through his neck, then falls heavily to the ground. The other three Blackfeet abandon their ponies and quick fort up behind a fallen ponderosa, a big yellow tree-trunk log thick as a man to the waist, but not before she puts in another arrow; you can hear the whack of it hitting, this one into a buck's shoulder. She charges full tilt at the pine tree fort.

Bang! a fusee roars. Pine Leaf's pony stumbles, blood all down its throat, and she half falls, half leaps clear, dropping her bow now and pulling her battle-ax. She sprints toward the tree, ducks aside as an arrow comes whizzing, runs ahead. . . . Then Owney is pelting past me a-horseback, yelling and shaking his rifle over his head; and he jumps the log, reins around, fires the Hawken from the hip. I lose him in the bloom of smoke. . . .

Pine Leaf is over the log, ax swinging. . . . A *chunk!* and an ugly gurgle; then her war whoop. . . .

Oh, it's awful, just awful. . . . *But by God ain't it fun when it goes your way?* Well, I guess so.

Then I see a figure on horseback riding back toward us through the popple. I raise my gun, but it's only Spybuck. He had circled out and around us to cut off any Blackfeet that escaped Pine Leaf's onslaught. With him he was leading two of the Indian ponies. His face was dark, angry.

"There was no need for that," he said as he rode up. "No need at all to kill these men."

"They are my enemies," the Pine Leaf says. "They kill my people; they killed my brother."

Then we see she's bleeding from two holes, one in her neck and the other in her chest. Owney is off his horse in a flash, grabs her and holds her up.

"Get their hair," Pine Leaf says.

Owney lays her down behind the log. Pulls up her shirt to see the chest wound. Her breasts are quite lovely except for the blood on them. The hole is above the right one, bubbling like a soda spring.

"Shit, she's lung-shot," Owney says.

"Get the *hair!*" Pine Leaf says.

Owen looks up at me. "Get it," he says.

"But I never took a scalp before," I say.

"You want Blackfoot scalps?" Plover pipes up. They had come up behind us with the mules. "The Calf, she has one already."

I see the Calf just rising from the body of the first Blackfoot Pine

Leaf had killed. Something long and limp and black dangles from her fist, and her knife is bloody. She carries it over to Pine Leaf and lays it on her belly.

"Here, Dill," says Plover. "You take the reins; I'll cut the other scalps."

She squats over the body of the dead Indian, whips out her knife, cuts a quick circle around the top of his skull. Seems to me the Indian winced at the cut. Then she works the point of the knife under the skin, kneels on his shoulders, and yanks upward, sharp-like. *Pop!* it comes free.

"Now give it to me," Pine Leaf says.

Plover passed the scalp to Owen, and he offered it to Pine Leaf.

"Good," she said. Then she spit upon it and handed it back. "Now throw it in the river. That makes one hundred. At last I am done with blood-for-blood. Now at last we can sleep together like man and wife."

"Goddamn, I have had enough of this." Spybuck explodes, sitting his horse with the Indian ponies in train. "Take these critters and tie them up good so they do not run. I must go after the others, lest they get to the Blackfoot camp and alert them. *Kee-rist!* She risks all our lives just to take a couple of scalps so's she can sleep with her boy-friend! I would call that damn silly." He wheels and rides off through the timber.

"SO YOU HAVEN'T actually, well, *conjugated* with her yet?" I asked Owney that night.

"Not quite," he admits, a blush staining his cheekbones.

"What does that mean, 'not quite'? Either you did or you didn't."

"We express our affection in other ways," he says.

"Does she flail your wail?"

"Something like that."

"Like, tootle your flute?"

"Umph."

"Well, my girls do that all the time when they can. It counts for conjugation in my book."

"Not with me," he says.

"Aw, where did you learn about love anyway?" I rides him. "From Mam?"

He whirls on me and knocks me on my ass. "Now you lay off of that, pipsqueak," he says.

I did.

But conjugation was on everyone's mind that evening around the tiny campfire Spybuck built. Seems like killing will do that to people. The Daughters were all over me even though I had taken no hand in the slaying of the Blackfeet. Pine Leaf was already perky, the blood no longer flowing from the two buckshot holes in her. There was no sign of infection around the wounds. As they say, meat don't spoil in the mountains.

As for Spybuck, though, he looked downright melancholy.

"What's the trouble?" I asked him when we were alone for a minute.

"Trouble?" he snorts. "I'll tell you what the trouble is. *She shouldn't have killed those goddamn Grovans.* These men were part of a raiding party returning to its home base, totally unaware of our presence, intent on escaping with their horses and their trophies. Oh yes, they had Flathead scalps on their belts, and the Nez Percé ponies they'd stolen, but now, when they don't catch up with the rest, their soldier friends will backtrack those ponies that got away, looking for vengeance, and they will find us eventually."

"We'll be ready for them," I said. "But what I think is really bothering you is all this lovey-dovey stuff going on. When was the last time you had a woman?"

He laughs kind of bitter and says, "Long ago."

"Take one of mine," I say. "They're too demanding anyway."

"Well . . ."

"Which one do you want?"

"Neither of them," he says, sighing and slumping some there by the fire. Then he looks me straight in the eye. "You see, I have a wife back in Kansas. Her name is Mary Ann. I love her dearly. She didn't want me going to the mountains again, begged me to stay back with the tribe for once, learn the white man's ways. Become a farmer. But I couldn't do it. So I came west for beaver again, as I had so many a time before, hoping to to earn a little money. I knew the mountains; I could take care of myself. On a trip last year I even brought my son along, our only child. . . ." He choked up then and couldn't continue. "But no," he said at last. "Thanks anyway for your offer."

Eight

———◆◆◆———

WE MADE TRACKS early the next morning for the Spanish Peaks. Actually, we did *not* make tracks, not if we could help it; Spy insisted that we wade the horses and mules up the river to the next convenient ford. When we left the water, breaking uphill to the west, he rode behind us brushing out our trail with a pine bough. Owen fretted at leaving the river, but when Spy pointed out that there were many streams, indeed many more great rivers, ahead, all draining from this same mountain system, he cheered some. They could prove richer in gold than the Gallatin. Still, his face grew long again.

We followed game trails up into the mountains, walking ahead of the animals more miles than we rode. The timber thinned quickly and soon we were climbing steep switchbacks through bare rock and heather, always trying to keep in the lee or shadow of the big raw rocks that studded the slopes. High above we could see the square dirty gray curl-horned forms of mountain sheep lying in the sunlight, with their lambs frolicking about them.

"Mutton for supper if we're lucky," said Spy.

"Won't the sound of a shot alert the Grovans?" Owney asked.

"I'll borrow Bar-che-am-pe's bow and arrows."

That lady rode easy, her shoulders only bunched a little now and then at the twinge of her wounds over the rough spots in the trail.

We skirted south of the Spanish Peaks, raising a lone mountain high to the south and what Spy said was Gallatin Peak to the northwest. "Our road leads between them," he said. "Then we'll drop down into the Madison basin. But I think we should spend the night up here in the high country so we can see any Indian campfires down below."

He killed a young ewe just at nightfall, and we broiled mutton chops over a fire we built in the dark lee of a sheltering boulder. It was fine-grained, sweet meat, juicier than deer or elk or even buffalo. The horses and mules had only scant forage, but they were fat enough to suffer a day of short rations with no harm done.

That night when I went to relieve Spy on watch, he pointed out many pinpoints of firelight far away to the northwest. "Indians camped along the Madison," he said. "A fairly big village; that means women and children. It's not a Blackfoot war party. I doubt they'd bring their whole band along with them this far south. Could be Flatheads on the way back over the pass from ther summer buffalo hunt."

"So where are those Grovans you fear?"

"Could be anywhere, but I am hoping the main party continued straight on up the Gallatin toward Targhee Pass. From there they could drop down to Henry's Fork of the Snake. Rich pickings for a war party, with lots of fur brigades working that country clear on down to Green River."

"You must have a map of this whole damn jumble, mountains and rivers and passes, all of them engraved somewhere in your brain."

"Well, I have been coming out here now for near ten years," Spy said. "The country has its way with you. I could not tolerate what was happening with my people back east, so I headed across the Mississippi on my own hook, came up from Saint Louis with General Ashley's expedition in 1824, along with James Clyman and Black Harris and Jim Beckwourth."

"You said back at the fort that Tecumseh was your uncle. Who was your father?"

"Tenskwatawa, they called him."

"The Prophet?"

"The very man. But he proved a false prophet. After Tecumseh was killed at the Thames River up in Ontario, the Shawnees disowned my father, stripped him of rank and title. The tribe decided to go the white man's way." He shook his head and laughed, a bitter laugh. "I guess I inherited my father's inability to see the future clearly. I sure didn't see the Rees coming to kill us in the Medicine Bows, and I surely did not see the future of this country here where we are today: beaver being trapped out from the Gila to the Columbia; buffalo killed by the thousands for their robes, even by the very Indians who depend on them for their lives. Next thing you know there'll be wagon trains of white farmers rolling west, heading out into this country to grow corn and wheat and cattle. They'll plant towns and cities out here, with churches, schools, libraries, banks, factories, dram shops. . . . They'll post a big sign in curlicue lettering just at the city limits: 'Welcome to Deadville.' Goddamn but I wish I had a swallow of whiskey right now. . . . Anyway, I'll leave no progeny behind me to suffer the outrage to come."

We were quiet for a moment, looking down at the faraway campfires. Off in the distance an elk bugled; early for the rut, but who knows what can happen in this high country?

"Tell me, Spy, you mentioned back at the Crow camp that you'd had trouble up here. What was it?"

"The other day I started to tell you about it but couldn't continue. Last spring the booshway Dade, traveling with a party of Grovan, caught me and my son trapping on the Buenaventura. Dade has some Delaware Indians traveling with him, cruel men but very efficient. You may have noticed them when they visited Beckwourth's camp. The Delawares killed my boy. I barely escaped with my hair. When I returned to my wife and told her, she left my bed. So I came west again, and that's how I met you and your brother."

Again a strained silence, then I said, "Maybe your wife was right. Maybe you should have stayed back east, learned the white man's ways. Sometimes I think this life we lead out here isn't, well, *normal.*"

He stood up suddenly and turned his back to me. From the stiffness of his spine I could see he was angry, enraged, and for a moment

I felt an icicle of fear hit my heart. Then he turned again, his eyes on fire.

"Is it *normal* for white folks to breed like rabbits so that they run out of land and have to move west to steal space from other people, my people? Is it normal to kill Father Beaver so that rich fops in London can look fancy in their tall shiny toppers? For that matter, is it normal for a man to work twelve hours a day behind a plow or in an airless mill or factory just to put a skimpy plate of greens and a sliver of sowbelly on the table for his wife and children of an evening, if the blight or the locusts or the goddamn hard times don't wipe him out first? Well, I have no wife and children anymore, but still, none of that for me, thank you."

He walked back to the campfire, leaving me there in the dark.

THE GROVANS DID not bother us; we'd given them the slip sure enough. Next day we crossed the Madison without incident, but no gold either, which made Owen even more sullen and anxious. Then the Jefferson. With the Tobacco Root Mountains to the north of us and the Gravellys to the south, we began a long, hard climb up to the Encantadas, and thence to the headwaters of the Garnet Creek. It took us two whole days to get there. The Garnet Creek, Spy told us, had been named by some trappers who found an abundance of those stones along its banks, at first mistaking them for rubies. "Though in the end they realized a small profit from the stones, they were sore disappointed to discover they were not the real item," Spy said.

"I hope that is not an omen," my brother said, his face as long as a gravedigger's.

The Encantadas were mean enough: abrupt, spiky mountains that looked like the teeth of a saw poised to rip at the sky's soft belly. Once across them, though, the going was easy. We followed the fast-rushing Garnet on down to its junction with the Buenaventura and pitched camp above a vast jungle of alders that filled a gulch draining down alongside the larger river. Without a word, Owen grabbed his pan and shovel from the pack and headed down to the gulch. His brows were furrowed, and I could swear he was trembling.

Spy and I had seen beaver sign aplenty on the small creeks feeding both the Garnet and the Buenaventura, so while the Daughters were cooking supper that evening we went out to set our traps. By the time we got back it was dark.

Owney jumped up from beside the fire, trying without avail to keep a big grin from splitting his face. Once again he was ablaze. He unwrapped a bandanna, and there nestled in its folds lay half a dozen nuggets, one as big as a wren's egg. It gleamed a rich yellow in the firelight like the eye of a wildcat.

"We're rich, Brother! I knew I'd find it sooner of later, I knew it was up here." He wrapped an arm around me and kissed me on the mouth. "Yahoo! All this in just three pans of gravel."

I looked at the gold. "Near a hundred dollars' worth I'd say. Couldn't have been salted, could it? Like those gravel bars down in North Carolina you read about?"

"To what end?" he said, bristling. "No one owns this land, so there could be no reason to drive the price up falsely. The land is free for the taking—first come, first served."

"The Blackfoot was here first, so he'll surely agree with you on that score," Spy said. "So, too, will the booshway Dade, who has the Grovans' permission to hunt this country, and who's warned us away from it in no uncertain terms."

"We'll worry about that when and if they find us," Owen said.

"We'd better keep a damned good guard of nights," I added.

"Oh, they'll find us, sure enough, one group or the other," Spy said, "no matter how close a watch we keep. And when they come, they'll have blood in their eye. Count on it."

THE FOLLOWING MORNING Owney and I, along with my girls, set to work cutting timber for the sluice boxes. Owney wanted at least a hundred feet of them, each section to measure twelve or fifteen feet long by some eighteen inches wide, built narrower at the downhill end so as to telescope neatly into the next one. There were blowdowns enough in the area—ponderosas and lodgepoles mainly—so that we didn't have to fell any trees, which was all for the better, since the sight and sound of them toppling might have attracted curious Indians to our campsite. We sectioned the downed logs to the proper lengths, then hammered in wedges to split them. The saw didn't make much noise, but the chink of the mauls on the iron wedges rang loud, and I could see Spy and the Pine Leaf, who were standing guard up on the rimrock above camp, flinch at each echoing blow.

We did not saw the split logs into board lengths; there was no need to if we built our trestles sturdy enough to support the half-logs, smooth side up, but we did work over the flat faces of the split logs with adzes and froes to smooth the wood as much as possible. Ditto with the splits that would form the sides of the sluice.

Then Owney cut riffle bars two-thirds the width of each box and nailed them alternately the length of it. Gravel is lighter than gold, and so would wash right over the riffle bars when we diverted water into the top of the whole affair; the heavy gold would sink to the bottom, catching on the riffles. We might lose some of the finer gold dust over the bars, it being washed down along with the gravel, but Owney planned to build a catch box at the very bottom of the rig to trap this runaway gold, and pan it out every little while.

"If we had brought boards to use, we could build removable riffle trays for each section of sluice," Owney said. "Then we could lift the trays out separately to remove the gold. But we don't have the time to saw out enough boards for the job. We'll have to scoop out the gold from the fixed emplacements themselves. Probably lose some in the process, where the fine stuff has sunk into the grain of the wood, unless we burn the sluices when we're finished here and then pan the ashes; but there seems to be an abundance of gold in the overburden. God only knows what we'll find down at bedrock, if we ever get that far. It could contain whole pockets of gold dust, as much as a pound or more."

By first dark that evening we had the sluice built and installed. Not enough light was left to start it working, you might think, but Owney shoveled a load of gravel into the topmost box and then swung the trough we had built to run water into the rig from a natural catch basin we found upstream. It went plashing and tinking down through the riffle bars, some of the water leaking out from the bottom to be sure, but the boards would swell as they got wet, and we could caulk the widest seams with moss and pine pitch in the morning.

Ayuh, I thought a bit uneasy, even nature herself seemed to be smiling on our get-rich-quick scheme.

But it had been a good hard day's work, to be sure, and my little Crow darlings were exhausted, their usually tough hands rubbed raw by lifting and shifting all those rocks and rough tree trunks. Pine Leaf had brought down a nice blacktail doe with her arrows, so we fried up some sliced deer heart and liver for our supper, and set a kettle of stew into which Plover had sliced some tubers and edible roots grubbed up from the hillside, to simmering over the fire. Spy and I went out to check our traps—in them were ten good-size beaver, which we duly skinned, stretched, and grained before sitting down to eat.

We all ate good and then I dossed down for a few hours of sleep until it came time for my watch. The Daughters did not bother me this night; they were too weary for the usual nightly frolic.

Owney was up at first light, working the sluice. By noon he couldn't stand the wait any longer and decided to "clean up," as he called it. That morning alone we had moved four cubic yards of gravel down the sluice. From the riffle bars he removed six ounces of fine gold, along with more than twenty small nuggets, a few the size of a pea, all of which he weighed carefully on the apothecary scales he'd packed along from Saint Louis.

"Fifteen ounces all told," he announced. "That will come to 200 dollars back in civilization!"

"Ayuh, provided we get it there," I said.

"Don't get all pessimistic on me now," he snapped back. "You're beginning to sound like that damn Shawnee."

"He knows this country; he knows the Blackfoot. And he is equally fearful of what the booshway Dade might do if he finds us in his country. Dade's Delawares killed his son up here last year.'

He looked up at me for a moment. Then he said, "So that's why he's so spooky. But you'd think he'd want Dade and his boys to show. You'd think he'd want to take revenge on them, wouldn't you? Perhaps deep down he does. Maybe it's only you who's yellow. Pine Leaf certainly isn't and those two girls of yours are too dumb to feel fear anyway. Well, we should stay—*we will stay*— and if Dade shows up we'll have it out with him."

"Now dammit, Owen. . . ." I rose to my feet with clenched fists.

"Do not even think of it, pipsqueak. You know what happened the last time you challenged me." Then he laughed and poured the gold into a doeskin pouch which he tucked into his bedroll.

"Now come help me on the sluice," he said. "There's a fortune to be made."

THE GULCH DIGGINGS proceeded rich all that week and the next, with Owney weighing in some 500 dollars' worth a day after cleanup. By now we were nearing the end of August and the nights had a nip of frost to them. In the mornings we found thin collars of ice on the edge of the catch pond and along the slower runs of the Buenaventura; the popples on the ranges across the way were yellowing high up. The beaver pelts were getting thick and heavy, and a black bear Spy killed had near an inch of sweet yellow fat under its hide and across the kidneys. It snowed a bit one night, that grainy light corn snow that spells winter coming on, and at sunrise the peaks around us wore caps of white that shone dull red in the early light. The Pine Leaf was all healed up now, but getting restless at staying in one spot so long. She said she was ready for the war trail.

"How much do we have so far?" I asked Owney one night around the cookfire. Spybuck was on watch, Pine Leaf busy down by the creek, steeping a buckskin in alder bark to tan it.

"Near on five hundred ounces." Owen replied. "About eight thousand dollars' worth, I reckon."

"There's your fortune right there," I said. "Why not clear out now, with winter just around the corner?"

"A week more and we'll have 12,000 dollars," he said. "A third of that belongs by agreement to your Shawnee. That will leave 8,000 for the two of us, enough to go anywhere in the world. New York, London, Paris, Venice, or, hell, *Constantinople!* Why, we could even return in triumph to Wales, buy us a lord's castle on the Wye, like that one Da always mooned about."

I studied the fire for a bit. A night owl hooted; the creek ran light-hearted over the rocks; then I looked up over our heads to where the stars burned hard and white against a cold black-velvet heaven.

"Are you going to bring Pine Leaf with you?" I asked him.

He thought about it for a moment and then laughed. "Can't you just see me with her in Milan, though, sitting in a box at La Scala awaiting the curtain of an opera premiere? Or gliding haughtily into the lobby of the Ritz in Paris? Dressed to the nines in the latest silks and satins, of course—with her lance and her tomahawk and her god-damned string of dried scalps? No, I think not. Better to leave her here, in her natural habitat."

"But, Owney, don't you love her?"

"Of course," he said. "*But in her place*, and I fear that place is not a town. Not even so mean a one as Saint Louis."

"That's where we differ, then," I said. "I love my girls, but I do not love a town, not even a so grand one as Paris. Nor do I love a castle on the Wye. These mountains have my heart now, along with the prairie and the game, but especially the people. No, I am not for the East."

He glared at me.

I said, "Perhaps we could split the gold back in Saint Louis. I wouldn't even begrudge you the lion's share. All I'll need is enough to buy me a new outfit. A string of horses, some more traps, a good rifle like that Hawken of yours, maybe a brace of pistols, powder and ball, some gifts to make friends with any Indians I happen to meet."

"Then you are a fool," he says sharp and angry. "You are young and romantic still, and it will cost you your foolish young life to remain out here. What is more, you have not yet reached your majority; thus I am by law your legal guardian. You *will* come east with me when we go."

"There is no law out here," I said. "How will you compel me to come with you? Will you bring the town constable down upon me?"

He stood of a sudden and dashed the dregs of his coffee into the fire, where it hissed and spit as eloquent as his mood. "You *shall* come back east with me, if I have to tie you to your horse and drag you there by main force. Now let's have no more of this rebellious talk."

He stalked away into the dark, back to his precious bags of gold. But the events of the next few days would prove this palaver to have been for naught. In the end, Owney himself would be tied to a horse and dragged away by main force, and then some. Our lives would never be the same.

NINE

MY GIRLS HELPED us at the sluice only when the mood struck them. They didn't like shoveling, so they usually busied themselves by picking out the larger rocks as they rattled down the flume and throwing them aside. But they could rarely stand even such easy work for more than an hour at a time, and the sluice was a demanding master, ever hungry for more gravel. Often the Daughters would wander away along the riverbanks in search of pretty garnets, or into the surrounding woods seeking small game for the stew pot, or into the hills to grub up tasty tubers with their elk-shoulder root diggers. On one of their excursions they discovered a grove of wild plum trees which, as autumn approached, yielded juicy purple fruit so sweet it would nearly dissolve in our mouths.

That following morning, though, they returned to camp with a surprising treasure. Around her neck Plover wore suspended on a rawhide whang a great shiny crucifix, while the Calf bore in her hands a golden chalice. They stood before me proud as peahens.

I dropped the shovel. "Where did you find those things?"

"Back in the alders," Plover said.

I called Owney over to us.

"Take us there," he said.

The Daughters led us deep into the alder jungle, along a winding deer trail ankle-deep in foul-smelling black muck, to an overgrown clearing at the face of a bluff. This was higher ground, drier as well; broken rocks, sheared from the cliffs above the river by the frost heaves of many a winter, had covered the base of the bluff to the height of a man. Veins of quartz glittered on the face of the cliff. Out about fifty yards from the rock pile was a shallow circular pit, curbed with a ring of loosely stacked boulders. It looked at first like the curb of a well, but there was no water down there; and why indeed should any men camped here require a well, with the river so close at hand? In the bottom of the pit, along with matted leaves and rotting branches, lay a big, round stone, from the top of which protruded the decayed remains of a log, probably pine, which had once been secured into a socket obviously hollowed out by the iron tools of white men. A deep, well-worn path circled the pit, a path that could only have been formed through months of wear from the hooves of horses or mules or perhaps oxen.

"I know what this is," Owney said. "The Spaniards call it an *arrastra*. It is an ancient method for crushing ore so that it can be panned to remove the gold. They must have had a mine near here, and threw the broken-up rocks containing the ore into this pit; mules turned this giant pestle—that boulder down there—and crushed them into workable gravel. Yes, there must have been a proper gold mine somewhere nearby, probably hidden now by that rockfall. It contains the mother lode that spawned the gold we are finding in the river gravel." He turned to the girls. "Where did you find the cross and the cup?"

They led us into a dense grove of popple farther along the face of the bluff. In among the trees we found the faint outlines of cabin walls, the pines from which it had been built rotted now into moss-grown pulp. Owney kicked the pulp; it crumbled to his moccasin. The ghost log was black inside, and the faint but acrid scent of ancient wood ash rose through the air.

"This place was burned down," he said. "Either by accident or on purpose."

We searched the interior of the cabin and found some shards of old pots, a rusted-out kettle with the wire bale still intact, and some strange black beads on which hung a small silver cross, gone dark now with age.

"A Papist rosary," Owney said. "The Roman priests pray upon it, one prayer for each and every bead."

Over in a corner I found something suspiciously round, all covered with moss. I scraped off the fuzz with my knifepoint. A human skull, the empty eye sockets staring up at me. We unearthed more bones, femurs mainly, along with half a rib cage, vertebrae attached. Then two more skulls, these bearing the char marks of fire. Plover rooted around near the fallen-down chimney and came up with a leather-bound book of some kind. The pages were stuck together due to dampness, but Owney pried it open. It was a Roman Bible. Written faintly in faded ink on the blank pages at the back of the book was something in French or Spanish; at first we could not make out many of the words. But then Owney found a handwritten date: *"21 Octubre 1753."*

"Spanish, it looks like," he said. "And from eighty years ago. In my reading up on the Spaniards and their mining of gold and silver in Mexico I found many references to secret mines owned and run by priests, Jesuits mostly. There were many laws passed by the Spanish king against this, one in 1592, another in 1621, again in 1703, but the priests persisted. I'll bet you anything that this was one of their mines. They probably followed the map made by those Dominican padres Captain Beckwourth mentioned. Escalante and the other one."

"Pretty far north for getting their treasure back to Mexico," I said.

"They might have taken it out by boat, going down the Missouri, then north up the Mississippi and the Illinois River, through the Great Lakes into French Canada, or straight down the Mississippi to New Orleans. Plenty of Jesuits both places. But whatever they did, they died right here." He picked up one of the burnt skulls and shook his head solemnly. "I wish this bugger could talk. I know there is a gold mine around here somewhere."

So nothing would do of course but we must find it. I went back to fetch the pry bars, and we started moving rocks from the face of the bluff. Later in the day Spybuck came looking for us. When we told him and showed him the skulls, he said, "Los Padres Perdidos."

"What's that?"

"When I was down in Santa Fe a few years ago, I heard tales of a lost Jesuit mine far to the north in the Shining Mountains, near the headwaters of the so-called Buenaventura River. The Mine of the Doomed Fathers. The whole shebang was wiped out by Blackfeet. That was supposed to have happened about forty-five years ago. One man, a peon serving as a muleteer, escaped, made it back to Santa Fe, and before he died told of the massacre. The Indians burnt the black robes in their chapel and sealed up the mine with big stones. The other peons, about twenty of them, they carried away to their camp so the rest of the band could share in the torture."

"Well, I'm going to reopen this mine no matter what," Owney said.

"I don't think that's wise," said Spybuck. "We'd best finish up here right quick now and get out of this country. Winter's coming on fast, and I cannot understand how the Grovans haven't yet found us. We have plenty of gold already from the river—enough for me, at any rate, and for Dillon as well if I'm not mistaken. It's only you who wishes to stay and risk our lives further."

"*I will have my gold!*" Owney says, reddening now and his eyes losing focus. "I will have it if I must remain here alone to get it!"

"You wouldn't want to do that," says Spy. "But how long do you think it will take to get those rocks cleared away and have a look at the old mine?"

"Two days at most," Owney says.

"Then let's give it another two or three days, no more. To speed things up, Pine Leaf can stand guard by herself and I'll help you move stones."

"Agreed," Owen said.

WE UNCOVERED THE mine entrance in only a day and a half. Owney said he knew right where it was behind that rubble, and he did. The Blackfeet had jammed big boulders into the mouth of the shaft, but we rolled them out easily with the pry bars. Inside, the shoring looked sound enough except for a few rotten timbers near the mouth of the mine, which we shored up with fresh logs. Then, about noon on the second day of work, Owney went inside with a pickax and a torch. He came out half an hour later with a lump of pure gold in his hand. It was the size of a baby's head.

"It's ungodly rich in there," he said. "They must have just reached the deep vein when the Blackfoot struck. The tunnel goes in about two hundred feet; at least I counted seventy paces coming out, slanting downwards all the way at a pretty steep angle. There are side tunnels leading off of it, but I didn't follow them. Then the main tunnel stops. All across the dead-end wall was this streak of gold, wide as a man's foot, running on and on, out of the bedrock and then back into it again. Now we must make a decision which way to dig next, to the left or the right. Or maybe both ways?"

"What are you talking about?" I said. "We agreed to get out of here as soon as you found the mine and had a chance to assay it. You have just done so, and now you start babbling about digging some more? We can always come back later with a larger party, Captain Beckwourth's Crow warriors, or even some engagés from the fort."

"But we cannot let anyone else know about this find. They'll steal it from us; mark my words. This is a real treasure here. Forget about that 12,000 dollars' worth of dust and nuggets we sluiced from the river. Chicken feed. This chunk of *oro* alone must weigh ten pounds, full twenty times the size of Da's far-famed Newfane lump; that's twenty-five hundred dollars' worth just by itself. If we work merely the exposed part of the vein, where I got this, we will have anyway 100,000 dollars. Maybe more. Go in and take a look for yourself."

"No thank you," I said. "I have no love for dark, tight spaces. Maybe Spy will go in with you . . ."

But he had no chance. At that moment I caught a sharp flash of sunlight smack in the eyes. We had equipped Pine Leaf with one of the looking glasses, telling her to signal us with it if she saw any intruders from her vantage point high on the rimrock. This was her signal.

But it was not Grovan she had seen. It was worse by far: Lafe Dade and his band of free trappers.

* * *

THEY RODE INTO camp late that afternoon as the sun was slanting down over the Gravvelys to the southwest. Before they arrived, at Spybuck's urging we had built a hasty fort of sawlogs and boulders back of our campsite, well stocked with powder and ball, water and meat, in case there was trouble.

There were a dozen of them in the party, as mean a crew as ever forked saddle leather. Eight whites, including Dade, and four dark, hard-eyed Indians dressed in trappers' clothes that Spy said were Dade's Delawares. I had counted fifteen men in the band when they appeared in the Crow camp earlier that summer. Five of these current arrivals were sore wounded, fresh wrappings around their heads or arms or legs, in some cases with the blood still seeping through.

"Damn your eyes, you greenhorns, you must be the ones that put the Grovans on the prod!" yells Dade as he rides up. "You are the boys I met back at the nigger Beckwourth's camp, ain't you? Did I not tell you at that time to stay out of my country, that I enjoyed a special relationship with the Grovans? Well, I do not have it any longer, thank you. They shot us up good and proper, rubbed out three of my best men, and wounded a lot more. Now explain yourselves, if you can! Or, by God, I will kill you right here and now."

"Cool off some and stand down from your horses," says Spy. He has his fuke over his elbow, hammer cocked, finger on the trigger guard, and the muzzle pointing straight at Dade's belly. "We do not know what you're talking about. What Grovans?"

One of the Delawares knees his horse up alongside Dade and mutters something into his ear. I notice the Delaware looking at Spy.

"Spybuck is it?" Dade yells. His eyes are crossed more than usual, his face beet red behind the carroty beard. He looks at Owney. "I will talk to a white man if I may. And do not deny that you killed four of the Grovans who preceeded you up the Gallatin last month. Your Crow bitch left her arrow in one of them, which they fished his body out of the river where you dumped it. The Grovan know this Bar-cheam-pe of old. But they mistook my new Shoshone bride for her, and before we could explain things they was shooting. Then, by God, they cut my woman's throat!"

"Yes," Owney says, "we did indeed kill those Blackfeet, as you say.

But only after they attacked us; it was in the heat of battle"—a black lie, which was unlike my brother—"and we could not but protect ourselves from their onslaught. We're terribly sorry about the loss of your wife. Now stand down from your horses and join us at the campfire for some fresh-brewed coffee. We have some lovely plums as well."

Well, the soft word turneth away wrath, as they say, and in this case that word was *coffee*. They climbed down and for the moment, at least, the crisis seemed past.

TEN

I N ANTICIPATION OF our departure, Spy and I had pulled our traps and bundled the beaver plews we had taken into two full packs, which we placed in the big leather tent where we all slept. It was not long before a Delaware named Thomas poked his big nose in there and saw them. He immediately informed Dade. Owney had told the booshway that we were here collecting garnets, hence the sluices; and, indeed, to prove so he produced a big burlap bag full of those semi-precious stones. These were the stones my girls had collected, of course.

"I have got no use for garnets," says Dade, "so you are free to take them with you when you clear out of my country—within the hour, I might add. . . . But my man Thomas tells me you have also been col-lecting beaver for me. Two full packs of prime plews. Very considerate of you, and I thank you kindly."

"Those are our own plews," I say. "This is not *your* country, either. It belongs to the United States of America and all the citizens thereof. No one man can stake out any part of it for his own exclusive pur-poses."

"Like hell," says he. "Sonny, you do not know the rules of the mountain trade yet. First man into a new beaver country, it's his to trap until he chooses to move on or grows too weak to defend it from those who'd supplant him. Mister J. J. Astor of New York City learned that to his dismay over to the Oregon country when he tried to muscle in on the Britishers. The North West Company and the HBC drove him out of business. By the same token, my partner Mr. Johnston Gardner found a big party of Limejuicers under Peter Ogden trapping the Snake; that was not six or seven years back. Ogden's boys was bent on killing every beaver in that drainage, creating thereby a fur desert to force us Americans back east of the divide. Well, Johnston Gardner rode right into Ogden's camp and declared he would buy every beaver pelt on the premises for three dollars a pound. The HBC was paying its trappers less than a dollar a *plew!* More than a hundred free trappers changed loyalties that day. By God they did!"

"Well," said I, "then we will be glad to accept three dollars a pound from you for our peltry."

"But I am not *paying,* sonny. I am *taking. For you are in my country.*"

Now Owney called me and Spybuck over to where he sat, for a secret palaver.

"Let 'em have the dratted plews and maybe they will clear out of here," he whispered. "They don't yet suspect we've found gold. If they get wind of it, they'll just build a big bonfire and throw us all in, like they did those Rees. And nobody back in civilization will be any the wiser. As you so rightly pointed out the other day, there is no law west of Missouri."

"Where do you have the gold hid?" Spy asked.

"In the tent, under my bedroll."

"Well, that infernal Delaware is heading over for another look-see right now."

And indeed he was. Owney yelled, "Hey, keep the hell out of our tent, you red devil!"

"I am only looking for to bring out the beaver," Thomas said. But he put his hand on the butt of one of the horseman's pistols he carried stuck through his scarlet sash.

Sitting off to one side during this whole sequence of events, Pine

Leaf had been quiet. Now I noticed that she had nocked an arrow to her bow.

"The business of the beaver is not yet decided," Owney said.

"The hell it ain't," said Thomas. He drew his pistol.

Pine Leaf shot him through the throat. With a great cry of rage and joy, Spy leaped to where Thomas stood reeling, the arrow through his neck, and with his knife ripped open the Delaware's chest to cut out his still-pounding heart. . . .

And where are we then, my lovelies? It is all a great rattling bellow of blue smoke and rifle balls, a horrid blend of sounds and sights momentarily glimpsed disappearing and emerging again sharp and clear through the gun smoke. Dade grabs for his rifle, but another arrow sends him ducking low behind the fire; others in the party run to the shelter of the sluice. Spybuck's fusil bangs buckshot, and three of Dade's trappers yowl, stagger; one of them drops but crawls to safety.

Out of the sudden pall of smoke a Delaware came at me with a hatchet; I swung the barrel of my fuke and knocked him sprawling into the fire.

"Run to the fort!" Owney yelled.

Spy grabbed the pistols from Thomas's belt sash. We scrambled for cover, but I paused to look back for the Daughters. One of my girls was down. It was the Calf. The back of her head was blown off.

I yelled, "Goddamn you all!"

Running back to the creek, I flopped down on my belly and fired the fuke under the trestles of the sluice. A big load of buckshot ripped into the boards: two men dropped out of the shadows, gutshot, and fell thrashing and cursing into the spillway. One trapper raised up in the open and aimed his rifle at me. Bloom of bright smoke from the muzzle! The bullet threw dirt in my eyes. I got up and ran and dived over the log parapet into the fort. Not till I was crouched safe behind the wall did I notice that two of my fingers were missing, shot off by that last close bullet. The whole of the little one on my left hand was gone, clear back to the knuckle, along with the top two joints of my left ring finger. I was bleeding some. Plover ripped a chunk of moss from the logs and wrapped it tight around them.

"Reload fast," Spy says. "We must always keep at least two guns charged in case they try to take us by storm."

Oh, damn those swine for killing my Calf!

HERE WAS OUR situation then: The sawlog fort stood about ten rods back from the sluice in Garnet Creek where Dade's gang was hidden. The Buenaventura flowed deep and swift at their backs, about another eight or ten rods away. As the afternoon wore on, the sky had grown overcast, and now a thickening fog was rolling in from the river. Our position was slightly higher than theirs, so we could fire down into them whenever one or another man showed himself to shoot at us. Thus we had them pinned down. But this would no longer be possible when night or the fog obscured them. Plover had grabbed up one of the Delaware's rifles before she ran for the fort. She did not know how to shoot it, but the Pine Leaf, though she preferred bow or lance, was a fair shot with a rifle, as she proved on her first squeeze of the trigger, provoking an angry yowl from one of Dade's men.

Spybuck had taken our animals back into the hills before Dade showed up, but Dade's horses still stood hobbled or tethered off to one side, out of the line of fire, yet well within our range. We debated whether or not we should kill their horses, finally deciding to spare them in hopes a truce could be worked out and Dade induced to decamp.

"We have killed at least one of them, the Delaware Thomas, for which I thank you, Pine Leaf," Spy said, "and wounded perhaps five more, some gravely. But that still leaves us even up with them in number of warriors, though we have fewer guns."

"We cannot let them come out from behind the sluice," Owney said. "They'll find the gold in the tent, then follow our trail through the alders and discover the mine itself."

"Worse things than that may happen," Spy said. "Let's keep our perspective. If only one of them gets above and behind us with a rifle, up onto the rimrock, he'll be able to pick us off singly from afar, like so many roosting turkeys, or at least drive us out into a crossfire."

"Perhaps one of us should sneak around behind the ditch and kill them off one by one," says Pine Leaf. "Or perhaps, better yet, we might charge upon them direct, leap over that sluice, and fight them man to man. That's what the Bloody Arm did to those damn Blackfeet holed up in the Rock Fort one time."

"No, it was Five Scalps who did that," Spy says. "Mister Edward Rose."

"You are wrong," Pine Leaf says sharp. "*I was there!* It was the Bloody Arm, the Enemy of Horses, who did it: Captain Beckwourth himself. . . ."

"Oh, stop this damn yapping about which Negro did what to whoever," Owney pipes up. "We must figure us a strategy to get out of this pickle and retrieve the gold."

"Quiet!" I said. "They're moving around down there now; something's up."

One of the sluice boxes had been pulled down, I noticed, and withdrawn behind the remaining ones. Now we heard the chopping sound of hatchets and the hammering in of nails.

"They're building shields," Spy said. "Get ready."

We saw to our weapons.

Suddenly what seemed like the whole damn Dade gang came swarming out from under the sluice, firing their guns and charging up toward us behind man-sized walls of thick pine boards, all shrouded ghostlike in a pall of their own gun smoke.

"Shoot low, for their legs!" Spy said.

We fired, reloaded, fired again . . . and through the smoke I saw a couple men fall. The rest seemed to hesitate a moment. Then one of the downed men crawled aside, into our tent, to get out of our direct fire.

Owney saw him wriggling and pegged a quick shot but missed.

"Goddammit, he will find that gold!" he yells. He takes up the pistols, checks the locks to ensure they are capped.

"So what?" I say.

"So what? So *what* you say? The gold is everything! It's my whole damned life! If I don't come back, make sure you hide the entrance to the mine. We must not let Dade find it."

"Don't go down there, Owney," I plead. . . .

Then he is over the parapet, charging down the slope toward the sluices. Pine Leaf leaps after him, battle-ax in hand. They disappear into the swirling cloud of fog and gun smoke. Pistols bang; someone screams; then silence.

As we waited for a renewal of the charge, Plover slapped Owney's rifle into my empty hand. She'd reloaded it. I looked down at her crouched there behind the sawlogs. Her jaw trembled, but her eyes were as dark brown, as calm, as those of the kit beaver that day we first met. I wanted to fire down into the fog of battle but reconsidered when it occurred to me that the ball might strike my brother or Pine Leaf. I stayed my hand and saved the last bullet for Plover. She was brave enough, I guess.

By the time the smoke cleared, they were back behind the shield of the sluices, taking their wounded with them. They had torn down our tent and dragged it back to cover with them. Owney and the Pine Leaf were nowhere in sight. Then someone raised a tattered strip of white cloth on a stick and Dade yelled up to us, "A truce to talk things over?"

Spy looked at me and the Plover. We nodded.

"Go ahead then!" Spy yells back to him.

"We have Owen Griffith and the Crow bitch," Dade says. "We also have your peltry, your traps, your horses, and those bags of what I presume is gold, both dust and nuggets. You have, quite unprovoked, killed three of my men and sore wounded half a dozen more. I call that even up, a fair exchange. What I propose is this: You shall allow us to get to our horses and clear out of here. We will take Owen Griffith and the bitch with us, hostages, until we are safe away from this place, then leave them unharmed on the trail."

"What about the gold and the furs?" I yell.

"They shall serve as reparations for the injuries you have done us."

"But you killed my woman, the Yellow Calf!"

"And the Grovans killed *my* woman, thanks to what you-all did to them over on the Gallatin!"

"Goddammit. . . ."

Spy grabbed me and slapped me across the face. I was too weak from pain and the loss of blood to protest much. "Its a standoff," he hissed. "Don't be a fool! You can always get another Indian girl."

AND SO IT was done. We watched them mount and ride back up the river, my brother sagging in the saddle with a rough bandage wrapped around his neck and Pine Leaf bound head-down over the back of a mule, but alive and kicking nonetheless. Our packs of peltry and the bags of gold jounced along on a third mule. They trailed off out of sight into the high country to the south.

But Owney never came back to our camp there in White Hart Hollow, by Garnet Creek; nor did the Pine Leaf. After recovering from our wounds and burying our dead, we followed up Dade's trail for three days, hoping to discover some clue to the fates of our comrades. At last we found it: the remains of a huge bonfire, in the ashes of which lay the charred remains of two corpses, one male, one female. The lipless skulls grinned up at us out of the dead coals. To the leg bones of the man adhered the charred remains of a white man's boots. I examined one more carefully. Sure enough, tacked into the heel were my brother's initials: OG. He had studded them that way for identification on the trip up the Platte.

"Christ!" I said. "He burned them alive, just like he and Gardner did those Rees!"

But Spy had doubts. "Mebbe not," he said, poking at the bones with the haft of his hatchet. "These skulls both look Injun to me— long-headed, like Shoshones. Mebbe he caught a couple and burned 'em to put us off his trail, hoping we'd think it was Owen and Pine Leaf and thus give up the chase. He could have stuck your brother's boots on the man to make it look more convincing. Or mebbe your brother and the woman escaped but were later caught by Grovans— or, hell, even those damned Rees we fought with—and the Injuns burned 'em for sport. We don't rightly know who done this here"— he spit in the ashes—"and following up this trail any farther will prob- ably just get us killed."

"What's your damned point?" I said, hot at him for his lawyerly ways. "Whoever done it, and whoever's dead here, we must follow Dade—to the ends of the earth, if necessary—and exact revenge from him. He's the bastard that caused all this woe."

"Spy's right," Plover said. "We're too weak to exact any vengeance on anyone right now. Too few guns, too few horses, for a long chase. Better we head back to Crow country. Dade will show up sooner or later, and then we can settle matters with him—from a position of strength, not mere rage."

"Well," I said, "you two can go back to the Crows, but I'm going on after Dade. I must avenge my brother."

But that night it snowed—the first of the onrushing winter: eight, ten inches of the stuff. In the morning Dade's trail was totally obscured. He had nearly a week's start on me, and I didn't know the country ahead.

So there we left it and returned to Crow country and the hospitality of Captain Beckwourth.

PART II

OWEN'S STORY

1

THREE DAYS DOWN the trail to the south, Dade's Delawares captured a pair of Digger Indians, man and woman. They were the sorriest-looking redskins I'd ever seen: dirt poor, dressed in ratty skins, they'd been surviving on bugs and aspen bark and were making their way over the mountains to the Humboldt Sink, where the balance of their people lived. Dade had the Delawares build a huge fire of pine logs. When it was at full blaze, he came over to where I was tied against a lodgepole and pulled off my boots.

"What are you up to?" I asked him.

"Sharing the wealth," he said. "That poor Digger over there's got no boots. His moccasins are made of bark. He's got a long way to go 'fore he gets back to his people. We're going to help him on his way."

He went over to the Digger and pulled off the ragged moccasins, threw them in the fire. They flared into smoke and ash in an instant. He drew my boots on the Indian's splayed, horny feet.

Then the Delawares grabbed the Diggers and tossed them into the maw of the fire. They rolled the flaming logs atop.

"Bon voyage," Dade said.

"Christ!" I screamed. "You heartless devil!"

He smiled down at me. "Not heartless at all. I'm thinking of your brother and his friends. They'll come after you, of course. They'll find the remains of this fire and also those of our late wayfaring acquaintances. They'll find what's left of your boots as well and give up the chase. Or so I hope. That way I won't have to kill them when they catch up with us. I should think you'd be grateful to me for my foresightedness in sparing their lives."

LAFCADIO DADE, AS I might have suspected, had no intention, on leaving the hollow, of releasing either Bar-che-am-pe or myself. Instead he carried us with his party to Nuevo Méjico, there to sell my warrior-woman into slavery at the hands of the Apaches. I was delivered over to the Spanish authorities and falsely convicted of trapping in Mexico without a proper license.

My sentence: life imprisonment in the copper mines of that province.

The cozy little mining town of Santa Rita del Cobre lies in a valley of the Mimbres Mountains west of the Río Bravo del Norte and not far from the headwaters of the Gila River, about three days' hard journey by horseback to the south of Albuquerque. Indians of the region— Navajos, Pueblos, Zuñis, Apaches—had known the area to be rich in copper long before the Spaniards first came, late in the sixteenth century, to what they would name Nuevo Méjico.

The native copper of Santa Rita, for which the town is famous, can be found in the form of small lumps scattered through a matrix of tough granodiorite, a crystallized form of granite that lies just inches beneath the topsoil; but more commonly, at least in those early days, the soft red metal occurred in flakes, leaves, and tabular masses, some of these latter of great size. The native metal emerged from the earth in large outcroppings, called *bufas*, and it is said that masses of copper weighing up to a ton were found there in the first few years of Santa Rita's exploitation by the Spaniards. These they cut up into manageable loads, which were wrapped in thick felt blankets, loaded on pack animals, and sent off in long *conductas*, or mule trains, to Chihuahua, 300 arduous miles to the south.

In their day, the Indians had hammered this "free" copper into crude ornaments and bowls, but the metal was too soft for the manufacture of tools or weaponry, so they held it in low esteem compared with flint. The Spanish, however, knew its true value: beginning in 1804, when Don Francisco Manuel Elguea, an enterprising merchant of Chihuahua, acquired the mine from his friend Col. José Carrasco, who had had it in turn from a drunken Indian, Santa Rita provided the government of New Spain with most of the copper employed in its petty coinage. The common copper coin of Mexico was the tlaco, which was an eighth of a reál, itself the eighth part of a peso.

I spent four years digging and hauling this metal from the earth, four years of dawn-to-dusk labor with pick and shovel, ore basket and wheelbarrow, down in the airless dark shafts of Santa Rita, or else up in the whip-cruel sun of a dust-filled world. In the winter it was cold as Christ's tomb down there in the *criadero de cobre*, with a foot of snow and more covering the scarred soil of that once-verdant valley floor, and the wind whistling day and night down from the sawtooth crest of the Mimbres Mountains, a forbidding parapet that served our Spanish keepers far better than a prison wall.

Not a day went by during my captivity that I did not contemplate escape, not a night without dreams of it. But flight was impossible. Our guards, armed with rusty flintlock *escopetas*, were a lackadaisical lot for the most part, country boys like the prisoners themselves, only too glad to gossip with us during their long dull watch tours and always willing, for a small "bite" of bribery, which they called *la mordida*, to smuggle in delicacies from town if we could afford them. They would be no problem to a man determined to escape. The question was what to do after leaving Santa Rita. Except for a few well-guarded trails, the Black Mountains and the Mimbres range barred passage to north or east, and even were one to evade pursuit in crossing those mountains, he would only find himself in a more heavily populated part of New Mexico, where recapture, and subsequent torture in punishment for the attempt, would at best be but a matter of days. Worse still, the country beyond the Río Bravo belonged to the Mescaleros, cruelest and most warlike of a dozen or more Apache bands. A classic frying pan–to–fire situation, I am sure you will agree.

Southwest and northwest of Santa Rita lay more mountains, the arid Hatchet range and the awesome Mogollóns. But my only hope of escape lay to the west, through the valley of the Gila River, whose fierce rapids ran down through gorges walled, it was said, in half-mile-high cliffs of granite and cactus. The Gila emptied eventually into the Río Colorado, and thus to the Sea of Cortés, but wild Apaches ranged all the intervening country, only too eager to flay alive any white man they captured, or broil him head-down over a slow fire until first his eyeballs, then his skull itself burst open and his brains dripped sizzling onto the coals.

When not working the mines, we were kept chained under close watch in the donjon of a tricornered *castillo*, or fort, which had been built of sturdy adobes by Don Francisco Manuel Elguea in the early years of the century. The walls were full fifteen feet high and topped with shards of broken glass that gleamed like the fangs of a rattlesnake when the morning sun illumined them. Martello towers, manned day and night by sentries with blunderbusses and swivel guns, guarded all three corners of the castillo.

My fellow *mineros* were mostly Indians and *mestizos* from Mexico City or the provincial capitals, illiterate brutes convicted of petty theft, mayhem or apostasy, et cetera. Yet it was from them that I learned the modicum of Spanish which I now possess. They were for the most part simple men, who had been lured to the big cities of Mexico by dreams of wealth, only to be exploited or disdained by the Puros, the pure-blooded Spaniards, who ruled that society at all levels. Unable to return to their tribes or rural villages, as much due to pride as to fear of the contumely they would face from their neighbors when they crept back home in defeat, they had turned to crime merely to put food in their bellies. One mestizo, a cutpurse named Jorge Guaymas, became a particular friend of mine. He came from a small fishing village on the Sea of Cortés, near the town that gave him his surname, and told me wonderful tales of his life there: of days at sea on the rolling blue waves, with dulcet breezes stiffening the sail; of whales and great shoals of tunny and gigantic fishes with swords on their snouts, leaping high in the sun at the bite of a hook; of palm trees and lobsters and juicy pitahayas; and of nubile young *indio* girls who would gladly spread their legs for a tlaco. . . .

Yes, the common daydreams of a prisoner, I will grant you, fed thin on a year-round diet of sour tripe stew and the gritty cornmeal porridge they call *socorro*, with only his fist for a bedtime companion, but they kept me thinking of Bar-che-am-pe and swearing vengeance on Lafcadio Dade.

She had weathered the long trip south quite well, I thought, given her wild, warlike nature. Only once did she try to escape, but when the surviving Delawares caught her after a half hour's chase through the midnight sagebrush along the South Platte River and she felt the bite of the bullwhip for the first time in her life she seemed to lose heart. I had taken a pistol ball low in the neck in our fight on Garnet Creek, so was hors de combat at the time of her abortive escape. Yet she seemed to resent my failure to assist her.

During the first few days of our captivity, I had harbored hopes that my brother and his friends might somehow, miraculously, come to our rescue. I dreamed of them swooping down at night on the sleeping camp, perhaps, shooting arrows and bullets and swinging their tomahawks, and thus effecting our escape. With the help of the kindly Captain Beckwourth and his Sparrowhawk braves, I dared hope, we might yet throw a *cordón militaire* around the White Hart gold mine and extract from it a suitable treasure. But how much treasure would I find suitable? I realized then that I had fallen victim to what is referred to in the literature as "Gold Fever." We had clearly overstayed our welcome in the White Hart country. Had we but left when Dillon and Spybuck urged, I thought, we might now be safely back at the Crow camp, preparing for our return to the East and delights of civilization.

And yet . . . and yet I could not but hope that Dillon had heeded my last request, closed up the mine and hidden it well, before clearing out of that vile country. For Dade, having found the alluvial gold, would surely return to the spot later and build his own sluice, then scour the sands of Garnet Creek for more of it. But if Dill and the others had sealed the mine shaft well, leaving it as we found it, Dade might never find the true treasure. Perhaps he would leave the country entirely, content with what wealth he secured from the creekbed, and establish himself in trade with the capital gained at my expense. Then when I managed to make my way back north . . .

Ah yes, I see now that the Gold Fever still had me in its grip.

I WAS NOT allowed within the walls of Bent's Fort but kept incommunicado under guard in Dade's camp half a day's ride to the west, under the guard of the Delawares. From the Arkansas we proceeded through low mountains, fording the Río de las Animas, or Purgatoire River (which Dade called the Picketwire), then the Río Canadiano; and then southwest through some heartless stretches of desert which the Mejicanos call *jornadas de los muertos*, or Journeys of the Dead, to the village of Socorro, where we recruited our livestock. In that somnolent, fly-plagued town the men amused themselves with strong drink and inexpensive women, both of which seemed plentiful. I of course remained in chains. We turned south again. After an arduous trek through malpais and mountains we arrived at the camp of the Mimbreño Apaches, hard by the mines of Santa Rita del Cobre on the Mimbres River.

Because they are a nomadic people, delighting in murderous hit-and-run raids on their neighbors, the Apaches live simply: their dwellings, called jacales, often consist of no more than a blanket or a buffalo robe thrown over a cluster of bushes. We had been spotted long before we were close enough to the camp to make it out as such. As we rode up, an imposing figure emerged from one of these rude tents to greet Dade: an Apache who must have been six and a half feet tall, with shoulders nearly half that broad, a head that would fill a wash basket, and the cruelest, most intelligent face I have ever seen on any man, savage or European (though perhaps that is an unnecessary distinction).

This was the Indian known to the Spanish as Las Mangas Coloradas, or the Red Sleeves. You may have wondered how he came by that florid name. Like your common Mexican peons, Apache men often wear a loose cotton shirt, or *camisa*, with long sleeves; Mangas Coloradas was said to have killed so many Mejicanos and steeped his hands in such quantities of their hearts' blood that the cuffs of his shirts were permanently stained with it. I saw no evidence of this during our brief meeting.

Mangas was only too happy to purchase Bar-che-am-pe from Dade. She would serve as a slave to his many other wives. Dade's price for her was 100 pesos, which Mangas paid from a large clay *olla* standing outside his jacal. When last I saw her, Pine Leaf's wrists were bound with rawhide; she was being led away by half a dozen shrill harpies, all wives of Mangas, who took great delight in beating her with cudgels every step of the way. Yet even as they thrashed her she turned back to look at me, her face impassive. Then she raised her bound hands to her breast and with her fingers, to my utter surprise, flashed me a quick message in the Plains sign language: "Keep strong heart; I come to you when I can."

With gleeful cries the harridans forced her to stoop low and clubbed her into the fetid jacal which would be her home from then on.

I was delighted at the message.

Bar-che-am-pe had merely been shamming in her shows of docility. Waiting a chance to make another break for freedom, taking me with her this time. Perhaps she would eventually escape from the Apaches, find me, and together we could return to the north. That faint hope sustained me for many months through the next few years until finally it faded entirely, leaving me in despair.

Dade's pretext for selling me into captivity at the mines was that he had caught me trapping on Mexican territory *sin guía y sin permiso*—without guide or license. This was a mortal sin in the eyes of the authorities. Mining operations at Santa Rita were, at this time, leased to an absentee American named Robert McKnight, who apparently spent all his time hobnobbing with the rich *hidalgos* in Santa Fe; the prison's colonel-commandant, a dapper Puro named Gaspar Luis Ortega, was only too happy to take me off Dade's hands. He even paid that scoundrel a reward for my "capture"—five tlacos in Santa Rita copper!

"Your true value," said Dade, his mouth twisted in what was meant to be a wry smile. "Now, Griffith, I bid you farewell. Perhaps this will teach you not to trespass on the lands of Don Lafcadio Dade. I am sure you will profit from the experience of the coming years. After all, you are a man in love with the bowels of the earth, and the riches to be found within them. Vaya con dios, compadre." With that he slapped me across the face, turned on his heel, and walked out the door, scattering the reward money to the urchins who waited without.

2

THE *CALABOZO* TO which we were confined when not working in the mines bore an elegantly written sign over its door: DESTINACIÓN DE LOS CATTIVOS. That was the most civilized thing about the place. Windowless and floored in dirt, lit only by a guttering oil lamp, it provided no bunks or latrine. We prisoners, about half a hundred of us, relieved ourselves in the far northwest corner of the communal cell, the coolest part of that Stygian pit, on the theory that the smell would be less offensive emanating from that quarter. Once a month, perhaps, the guards issued shovels and a wheelbarrow so that we might "muck out the stable." Otherwise the ordure would have smothered us. At night and often during the day those prisoners who had serapes or blankets wrapped them tightly around their heads to muffle the stench. I had neither.

Though the temperatures outside the prison walls could reach or exceed 100 degrees in the summer and fall, the nights were cold regardless of season. With a dozen other unfortunates who had nothing in which to wrap themselves I huddled for mutual warmth in a rank, louse-ridden knot of misery—a snoring, coughing, farting, wheezing hillock of filth.

My motive in first befriending Jorge Guaymas was because he had a blanket: a large, thick one, woven of goats' hair. It had been sent him by his mother when she learned of his imprisonment. I have no idea what kind of *mordida* he paid the guards to actually acquire possession of this gift, but that blanket was big enough for two. Jorge was a small man, not very assertive; larger prisoners were always stealing his porridge or elbowing him into the dung heap when he crouched to relieve himself. I, on the other hand, was the tallest man in the *calabozo*, and, if I dare say, the most adept at fisticuffs. One afternoon, shortly after Jorge's arrival at the jail, a prisoner named Candelário Guzman, a poor-box pilferer from Las Cruces, grabbed the water ladle from Jorge's hand just as he was about to drink. I stepped in and hit the man with a quick right hand beneath the ribs, a short, twisting little liver punch I had learned in the ring at Swartsburg. Usually this blow is so painful as to render its recipient incapable of further aggression. Candelário bounced back, however, all the more enraged at my effrontery; he came bulling in wide open, whereupon I hammered him with a facer which flattened his nose, and my, how the claret flowed! That finished the fray, of course. All of this was done quickly, surreptitiously, so the guards might not see and retaliate with their ever-ready bludgeons.

Jorge's gratitude for my intervention was immediate and effusive; in short order we were sharing his blanket.

AND THUS DID those first four years crawl by, though we scarcely had need to keep track of them in that place. Yet with each day, each month, each season, the hatred I felt for Lafcadio Dade grew more intense, more measured, more venomous, etched deeper and more bitterly into my soul. Occasionally through the guards we would pick up bits of news from the outside world: Apaches had raided a *conducta* coming up from Chihuahua with supplies for the town; Yaquis or Comanches or Kiowa Apaches were killing and thieving and burning their way through the countryside between Santa Rita and Socorro, then disappearing again into the mountains or the llanos to the east; whole parties of Anglo trappers had been wiped out by *indios* along the Gila or the San Juan River. I prayed each time that one of the names mentioned in these massacres would be that of Lafe Dade; but no.

Finally, in 1837, the people of Chihuahua had had enough of these Indian depredations: a junta took control of affairs in the provincial capital and proclaimed a Proyecto de Guerra against the Apaches and their allies. This cunning "Scheme for War" offered the citizenry a reward of $100 for the scalp of every adult male Apache brought to the capital, $50 for every squaw's scalp, and $25 for that of each Apache child.

In no time the vultures were descending, most of them Anglos, I'm sorry to say. After all, the beaver trade was about played out, due mainly to that change in men's fashions Sam Tulloch had mentioned to us at Fort Cass. All the haut monde were now wearing silk hats rather than felt. By the late 1830s the West was full of hard, ruthless, proficient white men, Americans, British, French Canadian, who had learned the wiles of the Indian warfare the hard way, whether from the Blackfeet or the Sioux, the Pawnee or Comanche or Kiowa. What difference did it make to them if the hair they now sought came from a beaver or a red man? Indeed, Indian hair paid far better, with beaver bringing barely two dollars a plew these days.

The first to take advantage of Chihuahua's generous bounties was, of course, our old friend Lafcadio Dade. He arrived at the presidio of Santa Rita del Cobre on a fine spring day in 1837, soon after the Proyecto had been announced. He had a proposal for the *alcalde*. Up until now the Mimbreños had confined their raiding to areas far south of us, down around El Paso del Norte and Chihuahua; they still maintained a careful peace with the Santa Ritans, and their main village remained on the banks of the nearby Mimbres River. From a friendly guard we learned that Dade planned to invite all the Mimbreños to a great fiesta, celebrating the continued, nay eternal, friendship between Santa Rita and the Mimbreños. There would be *musica* and *danza*, games of chance, cut-rate prices on the goods in all the *tiendas*. An entire herd of steers would be roasted on spits, along with flocks of chickens, goats, and turkeys; the women of the town would provide tamales, tortillas, *arroz*, et cetera. *Ay, por Dios—mescál* would flow like the Mimbres River in spate; a mountain of the finest, sweetest *socorro*, a veritable Popocátapetl of the stuff, would rise from the town *zocolo*, or plaza, for the delectation of all . . . higher even than the towers of Palácio de Méjico itself. To ensure that the Apaches might feel completely safe, even the threatening cannons mounted atop the martello towers would be removed for the occasion.

"Won't the *indios* take advantage of this generosity to attack us?" asked Jorge of the guard.

That man winked a slow wink. "It is not to worry," he said. "El Capitan Dade has considered all eventualities. Wait and see what happens."

The Sunday of the Fiesta Granda broke cool and clear, the sun beaming down from the crest of the Mimbres like a fat, warm, benevolent uncle. Brave music filled the streets of Santa Rita: trumpets, flutes, castanets, tambours, guitars, drums; bells pealed from the squat adobe tower of the Iglesia San Pedro Martír; even a sweet-voiced choir of schoolboys was at hand, clad in flowing white robes and under the direction of Fray Bartolomeo, a young Dominican friar who administered Last Rites to dying prisoners. All the *damas* and senoritas of the town had donned their most colorful dresses; the plaza was a riot of reds and gold, blues and greens and purples.

The Mimbreños entered the plaza through the Puerte del Rio, and their women, too, were wearing their finest: supple deerskin shirts bleached white in the sun and cryptically patterned with elaborate beadwork, colorful skirts of dyed reeds or bark or reworked Navajo blankets; around their necks dangled baubles of native gold and silver from the secret places in the mountains which the Apache guarded so tenaciously. Even the children were carefully washed and scrubbed, their customary nakedness covered with loincloths.

We prisoners had been allowed out of the *calabozo* for the morning, under heavy guard to be sure. Colonel Ortega himself ensured strict attention to duty in this matter with a keen and threatening eye. We would be allowed half an hour at the fiesta, during which time we might eat as much as we could hold; then it would be back to the mines. I scanned the Apache crowd carefully, in hopes of spotting Pine Leaf among the women. I could not find her, neither did I see Mangas Coloradas among the men, most of them elderly, who accompanied the *indio* women and children. Nor could I spot the other war chief of the Mimbreños, Cuchillo Negro, the Black Knife, a villainous-looking Apache who had been pointed out to me on other occasions during one of his rare visits to Santa Rita.

Well, perhaps they were off on a raid, I reassured myself, and Bar-che-am-pe with them. But I knew that was not so. She was dead. Suddenly I felt it in my very guts, and with that realization my hatred for Dade boiled up in bitter bile from my stomach, and I vomited onto the stones.

"Que pasa?" asked Jorge, alarmed. "Are you ill?"

"No," I said, shrugging his arm from my shoulder. "I'm only hungry."

Yes, hungry beyond belief, beyond starvation, for Pine Leaf's strong arms, her warm naked body pressed against mine beneath a buffalo robe, somewhere up there in the cool mountains of the north, hungry above all for vengeance on Dade. . . .

And then at that very instant I saw him, for the first time since he had sold me into this Hell on Earth. He was standing well away from the crowd, smoking a long black *cigarro,* his back to a pile of pack saddles stacked against the wall of shrubbery which grew at the western end of the *zocolo.* On the bushes behind him hung many empty grain bags in which the *socorro* had been brought to the fiesta.

I searched Dade's face carefully for . . . for what? Evidence that he had found my gold mine? What could I detect if he had?

Some indication of self-satisfaction, of cupidity fulfilled, of course. The same look I had seen on my own face in Bar-che-am-pe's looking glass, back there in White Hart Hollow, the day I discovered that the creek bore abundant alluvial gold.

I detected no such glow in Lafcadio Dade's eye—rather, a shifty nervousness behind his usual cocksure smirk.

By now the Apaches had swarmed to the big trestle tables laden with food at the center of the plaza. The feasting had begun, but still our guards held us back with the threatening muzzles of their *escopetas.* The Mimbreños wolfed down meat and *socorro* as only Indians can eat; men, women, and children filling their bellies as fast as their hands could stuff it in their mouths, then washing it all down with great drafts of mescal from the gourds provided for that purpose. Jorge lamented, "At this rate there will be no *comida* left, not a crumb for *nosotros. . . . Pobres cattivos!*"

Then I saw Dade gesture with his hand, the most subtle of signals, and the Santa Ritans at the serving tables sidled clear of the *indios*.

Dade stepped back to the edge of the shrubbery. Some of the sacking that draped the branches was pulled aside by hands within the thicket. Dade himself toppled the pile of pack saddles. Now from within the leafy shadows I caught a quick glint of brass. The ugly belled muzzle of a six-pounder, one of the very cannon whose removal from the martello towers had been meant to reassure these Indians, poked out of the brush, aimed straight at the feasting multitude. Dade took a deep pull on his *cigarro*. The coal sparked bright red; he reached down and applied it to the touch hole.

A brazen, clanging roar; a great tongue of fire flashed out at the Apaches, quick as a snake, and a double charge of grape, chainshot, nails, scrap metal, and stones tore through them. Some of the balls reached the far side of the plaza, pocking the adobe walls and felling half a dozen burros secured at the rail in front of the presidio. As the smoke cleared, a great writhing mass of Indian bodies lay revealed. Big chunks of meat, some of it roast beef, some human, dangled from the trestles and the surrounding ornamental plants; a cloud of cornmeal blown from the tables mixed with the gun smoke and settled to cover the scene of slaughter like some pale, diaphanous shroud. Strangely, there were no cries, no curses, no groans or ululations of grief. Not even the dying children would cry out in pain, such was their tribal stoicism. Apaches.

Now Dade's men and a detachment of *soldados* from the presidio descended on the dead and wounded, most with scalp knives in hand, or with cocked muskets to finish off the wounded. I later heard that 243 Apache scalps were taken that day, mostly those of women and children, which fetched Dade and the town fathers of Santa Rita del Cobre the equivalent in pesos of more than $16,000.

When all the hair had been lifted, Colonel Ortega gave a signal; our guards at last raised their *escopetas* and told us to "dig in." The rest of the food was ours for the taking. Sad to say, most of the prisoners dashed down to that horrid scene of mutilation and commenced stuffing into their mouths whatever they could chew: cornmeal, beef, tamales, chicken, and even, in their haste, I'm sure, some gobbets of Apache flesh. But that was the condition to which we had been reduced.

3

THE DAYS IMMEDIATELY following the slaughter of the Apaches were ones of loud exultation for the citizens of Santa Rita. Masses were offered up at the Iglesia, praising the Lord for his aid in bringing off this great triumph over the hated enemy. Dade and his crew, along with two members of the *ayuntamiento*, had departed for the capital soon after the massacre, bearing two burlap sacks full of Mimbreño scalps, to collect a fortune in reward money, some of which would be shared with the townsfolk. Another communal fiesta was bruited, this time to celebrate the famous victory, but supplies were low in the *tiendas* and storehouses, thanks to the lavish outlay for the feast that had baited the trap. Still no one was worried. Not yet. A large *conducta* was expected momentarily from Chihuahua, and it was decided to put off the celebration until its arrival.

But then, as the thrill faded, some townsfolk remembered that a few of the Apaches had escaped the massacre, fleeing town as fast as their legs would carry them. What kind of vengeance would they plan in the wake of this betrayal? The names of Mangas and Cuchillo Negro flitted ominously through the collective mind, along with those of such other well-known young Apache raiders as Delgadito (the Slim One), Poncé, Coletto Amarillo (the Yellow Tail), Pedro Azul, and, the most murderous of all, Victorio. These were names that would ring down through the sad history of the Southwest in coming years, along with the countless funeral bells they caused to toll. When scouts returned from the Mimbreño camp with reports that the ashes in the fire rings were cold, the jacales empty of all but garbage, not an Indian in sight, people began to sleep uneasily at night.

Dade and the *ayuntamiento* members failed to return within ten days, as had been promised, with the reward money. Nor did the supply *conducta* appear, though it was now a week overdue. The *alcalde* posted watchmen on the summit of a natural *torreón* near town called the Needle, with orders to report the first sign of a dust cloud from the approaching supply train. Rations had grown quite short, and people tightened their belts. We prisoners simply went hungry, subsisting each day on a handful of cornmeal per man and all the water we could drink. We drank plenty but soon were too weak to work. Some of the Indian prisoners caught locusts, beetles, ants, and songbirds, picked up what carrion they could on the march to and from the mines, ate this, and were the stronger for it. Finally, though, the mines were shut down, pending arrival of supplies.

Sometimes at night from the adobes in town we could hear the wailing of hungry children, mingled in an atonal counterpoint with the song of coyotes on the mountains all around. It struck me as oddly affecting. Sometimes I wept.

At last the *alcalde* could wait no longer. He issued an official *pronunciamento*: the *conducta* was not coming. His town was dying. Santa Rita's 320 citizens, men, women, and children, were to pack only the most necessary of their belongings and prepare for a long march to El Paso del Norte. The presidio's fifty valorous *soldados*, those noble heroes who had so roundly defeated the treacherous Apaches in the recent Battle of Santa Rita, would in consort with the *castillo*'s twenty-five trustworthy guards provide an armed escort sufficient to ensure the safety of all. The sturdy prisoners from the *minería* had volunteered to serve as additional transport, two-legged, strong-backed burros and mules to carry the town's scant burdens. This would allow the brave officers of fort and presidio, as well as the gallant caballeros of the citizenry, to remain mounted in case of trouble from the *indios*. Clearly the Apaches were on the warpath; ambush was always a slim possibility, but these brave soldiers and gentlemen would ensure a safe trip for all. Every due precaution would be taken.

The following day we departed, heading southeast. Beyond the village walls we passed the long, low mound in which were buried the hairless victims of Santa Rita's treachery. Townsmen averted their eyes. A day, two days we marched through rocky hills and arid flats gray with sagebrush. Behind us accumulated the litter of a people in flight: furniture at first, chairs and tables and bedsteads, then cook pots and chamberpots, mattresses, family portraits, utensils, finally dolls and other toys of the squalid children. Then the youngest children themselves began to die, some of hunger or sheer exhaustion. They were buried in hasty shallow graves while coyotes looked on. Axletrees broke; mules and burros died. By the fourth day out of Santa Rita, we were all bone-weary, our nerves frayed by the constant sense that we were being watched from the nearby hillsides, and not only by four-legged vermin. There were Apaches up there. We could feel the vengeance in their hearts. It was palpable, fiercer than the sun.

On that day, in a narrow, winding arroyo, we came at high noon upon the remains of the *conducta* on which we had relied for succor. Buzzards flapped up from the tattered skeletons of mules and men. Coyotes slunk away into the boulders that studded the sides of the gulch. Empty crates, burnt wagons, overturned carts lay on the hillsides as if tossed there by the hand of an angry giant; ripped sacks that had once contained cornmeal fluttered on the slopes, snagged in their haphazard flight by the teeth of cactus. The dessicated corpse of a man, burnt nearly black by the sun, stood in the center of the road, impaled on the shaft of a Spanish lance planted butt-first in the sand. The *alcalde* recognized the dead man as his brother, Coronel de Milicia Rodrigo Mondragon y Carrabal, commandant of the El Paso militia.

We prisoners were detailed to remove the body from the spear and bury it. Jorge chose to work with the gravediggers. I helped with the corpse. The body was crisp as a popover after its days in the pitiless sun, but do not believe that a mummy does not stink. This one stank plenty. After laying Colonel Mondragon to rest and listening to fulsome prayers from Padre Terrazas, followed by a seemingly endless elegy from the bereaved *alcalde*, we set to work digging a pit in which to bury the other victims of the Apache attack. Every moment we spent with pick and shovel down in that long trench we harbored fear of ambush: each shovel load might be our last; and each man's back, I am sure, itched and twitched as mine did with fear of the bite of a silent, plummeting Mimbreño arrow. It did not come to pass, though, and late in the afternoon the refugee column moved a mile or two farther down the road to a more defensible piece of ground before encamping. Our sentries were doubled that night, but no one, I am sure, slept well.

Ahead of us lay the final *mal punto* on our march to El Paso del Norte: a chain of bald sandstone *cerros* eroded into grotesque shapes by the wind and rain of centuries, through which the road wound in sharp switchbacks and a series of ever narrower, ever steeper canyons toward the open plain beyond. We were now near halfway to El Paso; if only we could survive the passage of this last treacherous outcropping of hills we would be relatively safe for the rest of the journey. However, as Jorge informed me, the guards called this section of the trail La Carretera de Acecho, or Ambush Highway as it were; and that it certainly proved to be.

The *alcalde, ayuntamiento*, caballeros, and *ricos* of the town all rode in the van of the column, accompanied by the entire force of soldiery from the presidio; then came the poor people, and finally the prisoners, with our hapless guards bringing up the rear. These last could be relied upon, I knew, to drop their muskets and flee at the hiss of the first Apache arrow. The privileged persons ahead, along with their escort, would bolt ahead on their fleet steeds, hoping to outrun *indio* pursuit. That would leave the rest of us at the mercy of Mangas.

Once again I found my mind veering toward memories of Bar-che-am-pe, her long black hair reaching nearly to her toes, her breasts firm beneath the doeskin shirt. But no, with bitterness this time: She had promised to come to me, to free me from this fate. Instead the fickle vixen had left me to this fate. But no, perhaps she'd died at the hands of the Apaches in trying to fulfill her promise, the vow expressed by her sinuous fingers at our last interiew, there in the Mimbreño camp. What if . . .

But even then I would blame her. After all, she'd failed us both, me most of all.

THE KILLING GROUND: Mangas had chosen well. The trail wound through a narrow slot, in shape like the letter Z; sheer walls of unscalable sandstone rose to either side; above us, at an elevation of perhaps fifty feet, ledges followed both sides of the canyon walls, studded with boulders behind which Apache marksmen could easily conceal themselves. By now the sun stood directly overhead, its light reflecting and refracting from the pale yellow of the rock to create a blinding glare when one sought the sky.

We were well into the canyon when the attack finally came: no yells, no drums or whistles or war whoops, just a faint hiss through the air, the silent, sudden fall of iron-shod arrows.

There were no screams at first, not even from the women. All up and down the column, Santa Ritans fell in place or toppled from the spines of their burros, arrowshafts sprouting from backs, breasts, and bellies like the wild shoots of a storm-pruned apple tree.

The troops and *ricos* and bold caballeros charged ahead, as I had predicted. They disappeared on their tall horses, around a lefthanded bend in the rock, into another ambush I am sure. Beside me, a panic-stricken *soldado* loosed a shot from his musket though he had no visible target. The boom of the explosion echoed down the canyon and I heard the ball whine as it caromed off the wall. Again only the hiss of arrows. . . .

Then I saw Mangas himself. He stood on the knife-edged ridge of sandstone directly before us: tall, wide, black against the hot white sky, his lank black hair framing that sad, cruel face. Watching, watching . . . I grabbed a musket from the hands of a stupefied prison guard, cocked the hammer, raised it to my shoulder, dropped the sights squarely on the Apache chief's face: fired . . . *click, spark, boom* . . .

And Mangas seemed to yawn: opened wide his mouth to catch the bullet, chewed it to a pulp, and spit it back at me, laughing. . . .

*   *   *

I WOULD LIKE to tell you how Jorge and I escaped from that death trap. Oh yes, I would: how we found behind a screen of cactus a narrow adit in the sandstone wall, slithered into it; how it opened out to the height and breadth of a man; how we ran barefoot down a long, cool, dark tunnel, its walls veined with gold and silver, deep into the heart of the stone, pursued at first by bowlegged Apaches; how at each turning I killed them one by one, crushing this Mimbreño's throat, ripping that one's heart from his breast, but running, running, running all the while; how suddenly, dreamlike, our old dog was at my side, bold Thump, long dead now I know, but in this dream of mine young again, and the size of a lion; how she turned and rent with her fangs those who would kill us, her wicked growl, her jaws filled with steaming meat, all of this in silence save for the hiss and thwack of arrows; and how that tunnel opened out onto another world: green glades, cool ponds, songbirds, and butterflies . . . Vermont! Or was it the Welsh otherworld, the Uffern?

But that is not how it happened. What happened instead was Bar-che-am-pe.

4

At first I did not recognize her. She was dressed as a man, her hair bobbed to shoulder-length, her nose strangely different. She came up the canyon at the head of a phalanx, riding a black horse, leading two others. Death itself, I thought—that hard, cruel face. . . . But as the other Apaches charged ahead, their lances atilt, spearing those last few Santa Ritans who still lived, grabbing up frightened infants and dashing their brains out against the stone walls, she reined in her horse before me and told us to mount, in the *Crow* tongue. Then I knew her at last, by her hard voice and the heat of her eyes.

And we rode back out of that butcher shop. Behind us, spurring us forward, came the first high screams of the torture victims. No Apaches were yet in pursuit of us, but certainly they would follow. We rode north, then west, then north again. All the rest of that day we rode hard, and on through the night. By dawn we were nearing the Mogollóns. Far behind us I could see vultures wheeling in a tall column, over the sandstone hills. We could not afford to rest our mounts, time was of the essence, and now the horses were failing fast. They sweated a foul white foam, tongues lolling, cracked and dry, until their eyes rolled back in their heavy heads and they foundered, one by one.

Pine Leaf cut the throat of her mount and we drank the hot, sweet blood. She cut out the horse's backstraps; they would serve us for supper. The horsehide we rolled into a dripping package which I carried over my shoulders; it would serve us later for moccasins. Jorge and I were barefoot, and soon our feet would be bleeding. Then we ran, ever upward toward the snow peaks, until we had reached the height of land from which the Gila descended. By now it was near dark of the second day.

"Into the river," Bar-che-am-pe signed. And in we plunged.

Ah, the blessing of cold water: rolling downstream with the currents, *agua fría*, drinking even as we swam, down through the long dark green pools, then onto the shingle, then running knee-deep through the shallows over gravel, trout flirting out from beneath our heavy feet; and again into deep water. Finally at dark we emerged onto a sandy bar beneath sheer granite cliff topped by piñons and scrub oak.

Cold and wet as we were, I took her in my arms and kissed her. It was every bit of what I had hoped and dreamed these many years: release at last! I wept.

NO, I CANNOT account for the weakness that swept over me that day and persisted for such a long time thereafter. Perhaps four years of prison life had unmanned me; perhaps it was too sudden an exposure to the light of freedom, the bright vastness of the Great West itself, when what I was accustomed to was the dark of mine pit and despair. Physically I was strong enough, though underfed to be sure, but four years of swinging a pick and shovel, of dragging baskets of ore up those steep tunnels, pushing heavy barrows over broken ground, had given me muscles like steel cable. The weakness was surely in my soul. I felt, as I lay there in Pine Leaf's strong embrace, like a babe in the arms of its mother: content to lie there forever; yes, let her feed me and rock me and sing me a lullaby, let her teach me to walk and to talk. . . . But not yet, not yet.

*　　*　　*

SHE TOLD ME then of her life among the Mimbreños. She had been too bold in her speech for Mangas Coloradas, too hot to handle as a wife. After many whippings, Mangas had given up up on her. She was an outcast then, too fierce to kill, too strong to die, wandering from jacal to jacal begging scraps from the women, fighting the dogs for leftover guts and bones. On her own one day, using a riata fashioned from the skins of rattlesnakes she had stoned to death, she captured a wild horse on the prairie and broke it to bit and saddle.

Yes, the very horse whose throat she had just cut, whose blood we had drunk, whose bloody black hide I carried across my shoulder. She was tough all through now: Crow tough, Apache tough.

From ashwood she had hewn herself a bow, from reeds and knapped flints a supply of arrows, fletched with the feathers of vultures she slew with rocks. These long, light, hollow-shafted arrows had a short piece of hardwood inserted at the forward end, on which was mounted the inch-long, razor-sharp arrowhead. Soon she was following the war parties on their raids into Mexico. The Apache soldiers made fun of her at first, but when one of them tried to rape her she put a knife into him and defied the others to avenge their brother. Impressed with her valor, the warriors set her many tests of courage, endurance, and skill with arms, finally accepting her as a warrior.

"Many Mejicanos are dead to my arrows," she told me, "many Spanish hearts skewered on the point of my lance." The Mimbreños gave her a new name: Tats-ah-das-ay-go, the Quick Killer.

"Why didn't you head back to Crow country as soon as you could?" I asked her as we sat huddled together at the base of the cliff. "It would have been a simple matter once you had become a soldier."

"I promised you I would come for you," she said.

"But how could you know I was still alive, after all these years?"

"I found out where you were from the women who trade in Santa Rita. I watched you from the sagebrush when I could," she said. "Going to and from the mines."

"But if you could observe me that closely, why did you not try earlier to free me from the Spanish stronghouse?"

"Too many soldiers," she said. "Too many guns. I could get no Apache warriors to help me. 'Why should we risk our lives to liberate a filthy White Eye?' they asked. Besides, until the killing of the Apaches in Santa Rita, Mangas and Cuchillo Negro were content to remain at peace with the town. There they could trade gold and silver, taken on their raids down in Mexico, for powder and lead, blankets and knives and coffee, even pulque or mescal at times, though they manufacture those kinds of Strong Water themselves. Only after the slaughter did they vow vengeance on all of Santa Rita. You have seen what they do when their hearts are bad. Now we're free of them, both the prison and the Apaches, and we have to make good time. I'm afraid your compadre from the *calabozo* won't be able to keep up. His eyes anger me. They are soft, like those of a doe before the flight of the arrow."

She rose to her feet and drew her knife.

"What are you going to do?"

"Kill him. Then fill his belly with stones and sink him in the river."

"No," I said, shocked at her brutality. "Wait, please. . . . He's my *amigo*; can't you understand that? He's just a harmless, gentle, simple mestizo from far to the west of here. And he knows the country we're headed into, the language of the people. Spare him."

"Then let me at least cut his eyes out. I can't stand those Spanish eyes, and I will not have them on us, not when we make love."

"Christ, you're a hard woman," I said. "All right, I'll send him away. I'll tell him not to look at us, on fear of death."

"Then do so at once," she said. She shook her head. "You white men and your *amigos*. Captain Beckwourth was always going on about personal loyalty, honor among friends, and he's not even white."

I hurried over to Jorge and explained the situation. His eyes filled with fear.

"I should have let the Apaches kill me," he said. "At least in battle they do it swiftly."

"Now goddamnit, stop that," I said. "Get over to the far end of the sandbar, behind that pile of driftwood, with your back to us, and stay there until I tell you. Don't you *dare* look back at us. Otherwise you'll end up worse off than Lot's wife: with your guts ripped out and a belly full of rocks for supper, swimming with the leeches at the bottom of this river."

"But I—"

With that I cuffed him across the mouth, spun him around, and kicked him in the direction of the driftwood.

LATER, AS PINE Leaf and I lay wrapped in the stiffening horsehide, all passion spent, we heard Jorge creeping up the shore. In the morning he was nowhere in sight.

"The Apaches will get him," Pine Leaf said. "It would have been swifter if I had done it."

Heartless as it may sound, I was nonetheless relieved to be shut of Jorge.

That day, after she cut and sewed me some moccasins, we made our way farther down the Gila, traveling swiftly now on the bluffs that lined the river. Our aim was to follow the Gila down to the San Francisco River or perhaps even the Colorado, then by swinging north and well west of Apachería make our way back to Green River by mid-July. There we could join the American fur traders during their customary summer rendezvous. Perhaps Captain Beckwourth would be there, and my brother with him. And maybe even that bastard Lafcadio Dade. . . .

Pine Leaf said that during the Mimbreños' march to the canyon where they avenged themselves on Santa Rita they had cut Dade's trail, heading north from Chihuahua. He had many men with him: Mexican peons for the most part, along with offscourings of the city's jails and slums: *borrachóns, ladrónes, matricidios,* et cetera. I thought little of it at the time, but later the problem began to eat at me. Why would he bring a small army of unskilled men to the Rockies? Certainly not to trap, nor yet to serve as cannon fodder against the Blackfeet. Then the answer came: *of course,* to work the gold mine in White Hart Hollow! He had found it at last, perhaps with the aid of his allies the Gros Ventres, and was planning to develop it: extract from the depths of the hardrock all the hidden treasure . . . *that rightly belonged to me!*

On the instant my temperature rose five degrees. Yes, Gold Fever is like malaria: it recurs without warning.

*   *   *

AS WE DROPPED down the Gila over those next few days, the landform and vegetation changed. Pine, piñon, aspen, and juniper gave way to sycamore and ash; lower still grew vast stands of scrub oak, which the Mejicanos call an *encinals*. Cottonwoods leaned craggy and crooked along the seasonal feeder streams. Then we were into a treeless country where everything had teeth. We began to see forms of vegetation and cactus peculiar to this increasingly arid region: the big *biznagas*, the sap of which the Mejicanos made into tasty candy; stately *pitahayas*, which bore a tart, luscious fruit; tough mesquites whose aromatic beans we crunched as we hiked, and whose gum was pleasant to chew; *mescál, palmillo, palo verde*, and the wicked Spanish bayonet.

FROM TIME TO time during that long traverse I smelled gold or silver in the rock of our passage. Good leads they were, too, quartz and black sand in abundance all along that greasy green river. But none of them as rich as what I had found on the Buenaventura. Dillion never went into the padres' mine, did he? No, we had no time. It was wonderful in there, a shelf of pure quartz in which was marbled the gold vein itself, like the fat in a buffalo's hump. I felt I could reach through the rock and dig it out with my bare hands, smear it on my face like butter. Oh yes, we had a treasure within our grasp that day. Then Dade came along. . . .

THE HEAT OF the days grew fiercer, more oppressive, the river water increasingly alkaline as we descended. It griped my bowels and left me thirsty even after I'd glutted myself on it, but Pine Leaf fashioned a leather bucket from our horsehide, filled it, then sliced some small plates from the sides of a *nopal* cactus and immersed them in the water. The mucilaginous juice clarified it immediately, removing the bitter taste as well.

We had left the highlands of the elk and mountain sheep behind us; now we saw only blacktail deer with their long mulelike ears, along with countless coyotes, jackrabbits, gophers, polecats, and a few ratty-looking badgers waddling across the flats. The ugliest creature we met with in that wasteland, though, was the *escorpión*, a black venomous lizard up to three feet long, known also as the "Gila monster," which dwells among the sun-heated rocks along the riverbank. Pine Leaf said they bite fiercely and are loath to release their poisoned grip even after their heads have been severed.

One day, crossing a prairie of thick grama grass, we spied a small band of antelope in the distance, standing still as statuary, watching us in our progress. Pine Leaf quickly dropped to her knees, motioning me to stop but remain standing. She broke off a stalk of yucca, removed her red bandanna, and tied it to the tip of the pole. Then she told me to resume walking.

This prairie was flat as a billiards table, with no cover whatsoever, yet when I looked back over my shoulder to where I had left her I could see nothing of Pine Leaf, only the lone yucca stalk standing there in the grass, its red flag winking in the breeze. As I proceeded, the antelope began moving cautiously but with great curiosity toward the flag. I stopped perhaps a quarter-mile farther on to observe. There stood the antelope now, clustered around the flag, staring at it, transfixed at its movements. Then a prongbuck suddenly dropped into the grass, next another, and finally a third. At last their companions grew frightened, flashed their white rumps, and ran away. Pine Leaf emerged from where she had buried herself in the grama and proceeded to dress out her victims with the knife that had slain them. Quick Killer indeed. "We will make camp up in those rocks ahead while the meat dries," she said. "It should carry us through to the Colorado."

5

STILL CONFRONTING US was the great northward bend of the Gila, which is crossed regularly by war parties of Coyotero and Sierra Blanca Apaches on their raids into Sonora. Beyond that, and north, was the country of the Navajo, cousins of the Apache and equally murderous. Pine Leaf redoubled her caution. At night we would camp without a fire in the rimrock high above the river canyon. She would scan the sky and the surrounding peaks and ridges intently. I could see nothing out there but clouds, with now and then a distant plume of smoke which I assumed from its steadiness marked the campfire of a Pima or Maricopa hunting party. These tribes were friendly to both Mexicans and Americans, so I had no worries about what might transpire should we cross their paths. Certainly I knew that the various tribes of wild Indians used smoke signals to convey their intentions one to the other, but believed that the puffs employed in this crude form of communiqué, through the purposeful interposition of a blanket or buffalo robe, would be broken into rhythmic patterns.

"That smoke you're watching, it's from a cookfire, isn't it?" I asked her one evening.

"No," she said. "Mangas is out there. He is signaling to another band for cooperation in setting an ambush. Single puffs of smoke rising, widely spaced from each other, mean that the man who started the fire has seen something suspicious, maybe dangerous: enemies. Many puffs mean the strangers are well armed and numerous. A steady smoke spells ambush."

"How do you know it is Mangas?"

"I know him. I was his slave."

"How long has he been on our trail?"

"Four days now. Your friend is with him."

"Jorge?" I was startled. "How do you know all this, from the smoke alone?"

"No," she said. "Remember the other day when I went back along our trail to brush out those footprints you left in the mud? Not far behind us I saw the tracks of Mangas, along with the crooked toemarks of your *amigo*. Mangas has six men with him. One of them is Delgadito, another Poncé. The others are young, of no consequence."

An unsettling thought. . . .

"Who's Mangas signaling to for help in the ambush?"

"Coyoteros, I think. He has friends among them. See that fireglow out there, far ahead of us downriver?"

I stared but could not see it. Darkness was falling fast now, and the sky to the northwest was dark.

"Look for a glow on the rock, up high, along the ridgeline," she said.

Then I saw it, just a faint, flickering smudge of reddish yellow.

"The Coyoteros are signaling their agreement," Pine Leaf said.

Now suddenly I felt a stab of fear, and with it of course resentment at the woman's aplomb.

"Why didn't you tell me this when you learned of it?" I snapped at her.

She laughed. "Owen, you have enough to worry about just putting one foot before the other, without having to watch over your shoulder. You march like a crippled old woman. Besides, had I told you of your friend, you might have insisted that we free him from his captivity."

"Why didn't Mangas kill him right off?"

"He probably wants to crucify the three of us together. Apaches are very superstitious, all of it mixed up with the magic of the padres.

I believe he is thinking of your Christian god Jesús y Maria and the thieves who were nailed to those trees beside him. Apaches love that story. Three is a holy number."

I considered that for a moment. "If you know where he is, then he certainly knows our location. Why hasn't he hit us already?"

"Mangas has a hard rule of warfare: 'Sin ventaja, no salen.' Without a clear advantage, he will not attack."

"Six against two seems advantage enough."

"But I am one of the two," she said.

AT MIDMORNING THE next day Pine Leaf spotted a column of dust rising far south of the river but heading our way. The country along here was treeless, open but for the sage. Crouching low, we ran toward a pile of red rocks well away from the gorge. She scampered quickly to the top and stared hard, a long time, at the approaching dust cloud. Then she came down.

"Mejicanos," she said, smiling. "*Soldados*—how do you call them, *dragónes?* Dragoons. It must be a reprisal for Apache raids down in Sonora. They ride up here now and then, when their honor finally goads them to roust themselves, and burn a few jacales, kill some women and children, then prance back triumphant with scalps on their lances. Usually they strike the Pimas and Maricopas, though. A scalp is a scalp."

"Maybe they will take us with them," I said. "Save us from Mangas and the Coyoteros."

Pine Leaf looked me up and down. My hair, tangled and filthy, hung past my shoulders, my beard halfway down my chest. I was dressed in rags, the cotton clothing I'd acquired in the *calabozo* stained red with Gila dust and ripped to shreds by cactus. She didn't look much better. "They will spear us for *vagabundos*," she said, "or at best merely laugh and spit upon us and go their way. No, we'll trail them; tonight I can steal a gun and some horses. They have good taste in horses. Mounted and better armed, we'll stand something of a chance against Mangas."

"Where is he now—Mangas?"

She pointed to a low line of sage-grown hills behind us. "He was closing on us before he saw the troops," she said. "I had not seen them yet, but when I looked back to see how soon he would be upon us, I noticed him looking across the river, then turning his horses away toward those *cerillos*. He'll wait now until dark to move again. The soldiers would see his horses otherwise."

"What would you have done if he had attacked us?"

"Fight him." She smiled to herself and shook her head—to ask such a question! "Sometimes, Owen, I think you are *medio tonto*, half addled."

The dragoons turned downriver when they reached the gorge but did not cross over. They seemed to be looking for a ford; the bluffs were too steep here to reach the river with horses. We followed on our own side, keeping low in the man-high sage. I could scarcely keep up with Pine Leaf, who was moving as fast as a walking horse. By nightfall I was exhausted, legs turned to lead, eyes blurred from too much sunlight. She brought me some bitter water from the river in a *huage*, or gourd, which she'd hollowed for that purpose, handed me the last few strips of dried antelope meat.

"Refresh yourself, *caro*," she said. "With luck we won't have to walk anymore. The *soldados* are camped just across the way, with two *mozos* watching the herd. Can you shoot a bow?"

"Not very well," I said.

"Que lástima. I'll leave it with you anyway, in case Mangas comes up while I'm gone. My knife will be enough for these Spaniards."

I heard her go down through the rocks, the riffle of her body sliding into the water. . . . The moon was just rising, fat and red on the horizon. . . . I dozed off.

Next I knew, horses were stamping near my head. Vague shouts in Spanish came from across the Gila, along with scattered shots from carbines and pistols. "Quick, mount up," said Pine Leaf, standing over me. Her face was streaked with mud. "We must ride fast."

The moon stood straight overhead. I swung up on the back of a horse, Pine Leaf slapped it on the rump, and we galloped away from the river. All night we rode, trot and gallop, north and west, Pine Leaf leading the way on a finely speckled *alazan* with two blacks in tow; I on a chestnut. No saddles, only bits and bridles, but I was still a good horseman after four years: you never forget that balance. Bitter alkali dust rose from our horses' hooves, obscuring the trail ahead, but I noticed Pine Leaf looking skyward from time to time, where the dust cloud was thinner, to check our route against the stars. Toward morning we stopped at a fetid spring to water the mounts. Pine Leaf carried a Spanish cavalry lance and an *escopeta*, along with a powder horn and bullet pouch. As the light strengthened, I noticed blood caked black on her knife hand.

"Are you injured?"

"No," she said, noticing it for the first time. "The second *mozo* struggled when I cut his throat. It spurts a lot, you know. I had no time to take their hair."

Of a sudden I was weeping again, the weakness I had felt since the rescue turning my heart to water. I grabbed her and hugged her to me, all the fear and hope and waste of the past four years, all the confusion of emotions, self-contempt, vengeance, love, despair . . . flooding forth from the red holes of my eyes. Her hard, hot, rank body: the smell of woman and dust and blood.

How in the hell had I come to this?

We dropped down onto the dried mud, and there among the rattling reeds and the sound of horses sucking water, their bellies rumbling with it, we made love. For what would prove the last time. . . .

"Medio tonto," she murmured, not unkindly, when we were done.

MANGAS CAME THAT night.

He had his *ventaja* now; the Coyoteros were with him, at least a dozen of them, from what we could determine as they approached us over the plain through the dusk.

We had found another rock pile' for our fort, a hillock that rose from the plain like a fresh smallpox scar, wealed around the edges with huge but strangely light boulders of a dead gray pumice. We piled rocks around the hollow to form a low breastwork, then brought our horses down into the shallow depression thus formed and hobbled them to feed in the sparse needle grass that grew there. Mangas's marksmen would have no easy time in killing or driving them off.

I now took time to examine the leather-cased musket which Pine Leaf had taken, and found, to my amazement and delight on removing it from its buckskin sleeve, that it was a double-barrel rifle. A fine one, too: a slim, elegant English flintlock in .45 caliber made by Joseph Manton of London and converted only recently to fire by means of percussion caps. Despite its two barrels, the rifle was only marginally heavier than my old Hawken; it balanced perfectly as I threw it to my shoulder. The erstwhile owner had cared for it well: no rust on locks or barrels, no serious pitting on lands or grooves, thus no worry on my part that the gun might throw wild or, worse, rupture if I happened to double-charge it in the heat of battle. The leather bullet pouch was full. Plenty of fine-grained French powder in the horn. From the rifle's sling hung a separate spring-loaded charger which carried the percussion caps, two dozen of them, ready to be snapped on the lock nipples whenever I reloaded. I found a tin container in the bullet pouch which held more caps.

"Where did you get this rifle?" I asked Pine Leaf. "It's far too expensive to have belonged to a mere *mozo*. Too well cared for, as well."

"I took it from an officer," she said. "He came into the remuda just when I'd finished with the others. A nice-looking boy, and brave. He tried to draw his saber as I stabbed him."

From a *ciénega* we'd passed that afternoon Pine Leaf had plucked two dozen long, straight reeds, which, even as she rode, she busied herself converting into extra arrows for her bow. An outcropping of chert provided her with arrowheads. It was fascinating to watch her knap them, *chip chip, finished*. They were wicked-looking little bits of stone, with sharp fluted edges that could slice the toughest horsemeat. She bound them to the reeds with thongs from her supply of sun-dried antelope hides. Then, as we awaited the enemy's approach, she found a dead pelican near the rock pile and from its malodourous feathers fletched her shafts.

As the Apaches drew near, we noticed something strange: behind them two of the horsemen were dragging what appeared to be heavy bundles. One of them consisted of lodgepole pine trunks; the other proved to be poor Jorge. "No trees out here," Pine Leaf said. "Mangas has brought the makings of his crucifixes with him. He prides himself on thinking ahead."

Jorge was naked, his body now little more than a hunk of raw meat after being dragged across miles of cactus, volcanic rock, and alkali flats. When they stopped, just out of rifle range on the prairie before us, I saw that Jorge could not stand upright. They had hamstrung him and his feet flopped limply below his ankles.

I counted twenty Apaches in the party. Half of them immediately on halting set to work chopping the lodgepoles to appropriate lengths, then notching the uprights to accommodate the crossbars. Soon they had the three crosses planted in the loose, rocky soil. With the remainder of the wood they built a large bonfire directly behind the crosses, so that the firelight illuminated them from the rear. Now Mangas and a slim young Mimbreño rode toward our rock pile.

"That is Delgadito with him," Pine Leaf said. " 'The Skinny One.' Very brave, very cruel."

"Tats-ah-das-ay-go!" Mangas yelled. "Quick Killer!" He had a strangely high voice for so large a man. Then he continued in Spanish, no doubt so that I, too, could understand his ultimatum: "You have transgressed against the People once too often. Now you must die, and the others whom you helped to escape will die with you, in the manner of their cowardly god Jesús y María. I know you will make a fight of it, and a good one, for you have learned the arts of war from me, Mangas Coloradas, the greatest general in the world. You cannot escape. We have you, and we are too many for you. But hear me: for every arrow you throw at us, for every bullet you fire, you and your white-eyed lover will suffer the more before you die. I make you this offer: Surrender now and I will kill you each myself, swiftly, with a single stroke of the knife. Fight us and you will pay for it in pain. I will give you some time to discuss this offer between yourselves. Meanwhile my men shall provide you with some light amusement." He reined his horse around and rode with Delgadito back out of rifle range.

"I believe I could have hit him from here," I told Pine Leaf as they galloped back. "This rifle is capable of it."

"Perhaps you should have," she said.

"What will they do now?"

"Have some fun with your friend."

"What will we do . . . when they're done?"

"He will come out again and ask us for an answer."

"I'll shoot him then."

"Good."

I WILL SPARE my gentle reader a description of the torture that followed. Suffice it to say that, though Jorge was half-dead already and, one would think, beyond feeling any further pain, he was not so fortunate. His screams tore my heart. Finally, when the red devils grew bored with their games, they pulled down one of the crosses, hammered Jorge's hands and feet to it with thornwood spikes, and elevated it again. Delgadito then fetched a firebrand and applied it to the dying man's feet. Jorge's head came up from where it had been resting on his breast. He stared wide-eyed, wild-eyed, into the dark, his gaze directly on me I swear, and screamed in a loud girlish squeal, "*Owen! I beg you! Kill me!*"

With that I could take no more: I broke. Vaulting over the breastwork, I crawled down through the cactus toward a sagebush that I knew would provide me cover within rifle range of the *indios*. By now it was dark enough that I could hope the Apaches hadn't seen my movement. But of course they had. In an instant, half of them were spurring their ponies toward me, no war whoops, dead silent, lances at the ready. As they approached, I heard an arrow whistle over my head and one of them reeled in his high-peaked Mexican saddle. Then another arrow, another man down. I raised the rifle and with two quick shots dropped another pair. The remaining Apaches split off to either side of me, and a lance thudded in the sand at my feet. I ran back to the rock pile.

"You *are* a damned fool," Pine Leaf hissed. "Do I have to explain everything to you? That's precisely what they wanted you to do! That's why they tortured your friend, to lure you out and kill you! Now reload quickly; they'll come again."

By now it was dark as Erebus. The Apaches scattered their fire, which had provided the only light on that gruesome scene. The moon would not rise for another hour or more, though already we could see a faint graying along the rim of the eastern horizon. I had read, in our schoolboy storybooks, that Indians were always reluctant to strike in the dark. They were said to be too fearful of Night Spirits, those evil demons that snatch away the souls of the righteous, to risk mortal danger after the sun has set. Do not believe it, not of the Apaches: No, for they, those sons of darkness, they revel in it, for only then can their full stealth be exploited to the maximum. Darkness concentrates their evil, so that they move more silently after sunset, strike more swiftly, bite more fatally than the serpent in your bedroll. They themselves are the Night Spirits!

Barely had I recharged my barrels when the first Apache was over the wall and into our fort. I had the impression of a heavy-bodied cat pouncing silent into our midst. Only the hot stink of man sweat and wood ash announced its humanity. He writhed away before I could shoot, then sprang at me. Pine Leaf's lance caught the warrior through the throat just as his knifepoint touched my belly. She thrust him away before he could gut me. "Be alert, *tonto!*" she said as his body wriggled on the spear. Reaching over with her knife, she plunged it into his heart.

Then three more were among us, naked save for breechclouts and moccasins, their hard, slippery bodies slick with bear grease, knives slicing the darkness. We wrestled there in the sand behind the wall. Grunts and whistling breath through flat noses, punches, the hollow thwack of elbows on skulls; I felt a hot wire burn across my chest and bicep, grabbed a fist, twisted, and stuck the Apache's knife into his own breast. The next, I broke his neck. Pine Leaf had killed the third. Blood dripped down my arm, into the sand. In the darkness it looked black.

"Can you still see to shoot?" she asked.

"Barely."

"Get back closer to the horses." She pulled loose a white breechclout from one of the dead and wrapped it around her head like a bandanna, pirate style. "You'll recognize me by this. Shoot all others who come over the wall."

I ran back to the ponies. The *alazan* stamped his hooves, nickering with fear. One of the blacks tried to kick me. I saw the pale flash of Pine Leaf's bandanna against the gray of the pumice-stone wall; then more Apaches were into the fort. I aimed as best I could and fired; flame lancing from the muzzle illuminated the scene for an instant and gave me enough of a sight picture to fire again. As I reloaded, an Indian came at me. I clubbed him with the barrels, then smashed his skull with the brass-shod butt.

Now Pine Leaf stood and stepped back from the wall, her lance butt planted in the sand, the head tilted forward a bit, and a horse came fast out of the dark, clipping the pumice with its hooves; Pine Leaf's lance took it in the belly as it passed overhead. The pony fell screaming, and from it tumbled Delgadito. She was on him in an instant with her knife. . . . Then I looked to my left and Mangas stood there, tall, it seemed, as the stars themselves. He swung a hatchet at my head. I blocked the blow with the Manton, the ax edge taking a great ugly sliver from the fine checkering of its oiled English walnut forearm. . . . I felt a pang of regret at that, but as you know, I have always loved fine tools, especially rifles—perhaps more than the people in my life. . . .

One barrel was loaded and primed. I thumbed back the hammer, placed the muzzle against Mangas's chest, and fired. He disappeared in a welter of smoke and blood. I could smell burning meat. . . .

"Run, *tonto* . . . to the horses!"

I followed Pine Leaf into the pony herd, saw her swing up on the back of the *alazan*. I grabbed at the mane of a black, but he kicked me loose, kicked the wind out of me and what little sense I still had left. . . .

Bar-che-am-pe, the Pine Leaf, was gone, out into the night.

6

HOW I ESCAPED from that place I do not know. Probably I held onto the black gelding's mane, maybe his tail, and he dragged me out into the night where, curiously enough, the Apaches chose not to follow. After all, I still had the rifle, and their leader lay dead or dying (or so I thought at the time. In point of fact, my ball had barely penetrated the heavy muscles of his upper chest, missing both heart and lung; he recovered in short order, much to the sorrow of many a Mexican and Anglo household in that sad territory). They probably decided to track down Pine Leaf, I thought, figuring they could always find me, a mere white man. Or they may have felt their medicine had suddenly gone bad. Quién sábe? The mind of the Indian is always a mystery.

I discovered the truth of the matter later that day.

At first light I found myself deep in the desert. Pine Leaf was nowhere in sight. Though I still had the rifle in hand, powder horn and bullet pouch slung across my shoulder, a knife at my hip, I was thirsty, exhausted, and bruised blue-black from navel to sternum thanks to the hoof of my horse. The knife cut across my chest and arm was no longer bleeding, but it still hurt a lot. Moreover, three or four of my ribs felt cracked, and I spit frequently to reassure myself there was no blood in my sputum. Had there been, I don't know what I might have done to remedy the matter. But the most pressing need, I realized when I sat quietly for a few minutes in the shade of a rimrock ledge, was for something to drink. Remembering the spring where we'd watered the horses the previous day, I headed south and east hoping to find it. A low range of hills in the hazy distance looked green. Perhaps there was water in them, a spring or one of those brief rivulets that quickly sinks into the sand once it's left its source. I made for it on my flagging horse.

As we neared the hills the horse's head came up, his nostrils flared, and he put on a burst of speed that even a cruel Spanish bit could not curb. When he stopped he began digging in the sand with his forefeet. Water bubbled up into the hole thus excavated. We both drank from it at once, grit, froth, and horse saliva be damned. I walked him closer to the hills, and sure enough, we found the spring which fed this "sand river." As I filled my canteen, though, I heard what sounded like gunshots from the far side of the hills. I picketed the horse away from the water, for I did not want him to founder from drinking too much too fast, then made my way, rifle in hand, over the ridge.

In the desert beyond I saw Pine Leaf's horse lying dead. Half a dozen Apaches had wrestled her to the ground. Among them I recognized Delgadito, badly cut by Pine leaf's blade, but still alive—still raging. As the others held her down, he drew his own knife. He was less than two hundred yards from me. I raised the Manton to my shoulder, laid my sights on the Slim One, cocked the hammer . . . and then, even as his knife slashed Pine Leaf's face, thought, *But I only have two shots. The Apaches will be on me before I can reload. . . .*

I did not fire. I could hear Delgadito yelling down at her in Spanish. He ripped her shirt open and lay bare her breasts. "Puta! Esposa infiel!" As his knife flashed downward into her chest, I slipped away, back to my horse. I mounted and we sped back into the wasteland. Yes, I was scared senseless, more frightened of those devils than of Hell itself. Only later did I feel the shame of my sorry performance. I should have killed Delgadito and then, with the second barrel, Pine Leaf herself. Anything to spare the woman I loved that ignominious death. I should have offered myself to their slow, skilled knives.

*   *   *

BUT I WAS a coward.

FOR HOURS THAT morning we plodded over an empty gray prairie that stank of sage, through flats of alkali or black sand, threading our way past wind-shifting dunes as tall as circus elephants, until at last, with the sun directly overhead, I had to admit I was lost. Utterly, inconsolably lost. We climbed a dune, the horse slipping two steps for every three he accomplished, and I looked out at the country.

Bleak . . .

Dry . . .

Nothing. . . .

A hot, hard blue sky with the sun slashing down like a madman with a razor.

Only then did I realize that, in my funk, I had left the canteen behind, soaking in the rivulet. Again we were without water.

Toward late afternoon I spied movement against the blue shimmering haze: black dots at first, tilting and circling, which resolved themselves at last into a kettle of *sopilotes*, turkey buzzards, turning high over broken ground, a volcanic *malpais* by the look of it, in a direction which I took to be the south. I rode toward it.

As I neared, I saw black figures standing motionless, with outspread arms, against the background of gray and black rock. Men! But were they Apaches, waiting to kill me? Well, so what? Maybe they'd give me a drink of water before Delgadito's knife fell. But still they did not move. Only when I had closed to within a quarter-mile did I realize, and bitterly, the truth of the matter: they weren't men, but rather the very crosses which Mangas had erected for our crucifixion. I had ridden all day in a circle, only to arrive at my point of departure. Laugh if you must at my greenhorn stupidity. . . .

At least the Indians were gone. Jorge's body still hung from the thornwood spikes, the blood from his wounds gone black in the heat of the day. Flies buzzed around his mouth and nose. I could not bear to look at him. Instead I dismounted and went over the wall to see what I could find in the fort. The Apaches had removed their dead and wounded; only a few pools of sun-caked blood marked the scene of that desperate fight. I picked up some broken arrows from the barrage which had opened the combat, thinking that perhaps the steel arrowheads might come in useful should I survive the day. The Apache pony Pine Leaf had speared lay bloating in the sun; vultures flapped at its torn belly, turning away from their feed only to hiss at my approach. For a moment I thought of opening the dead pony's veins to drink some of its blood, anything to quench my burning thirst. But blood is salty; it would only make matters worse. I slumped to the ground in despair, my eyes roving wildly over the scene of desolation, hoping, hoping still . . . Then from a tumble of pumice boulders I saw protruding the rounded neck of a familiar *huage*: one of the gourds we'd filled with water at the spring yesterday, the spring where we'd made love.

God bless you, Pine Leaf. . . .

I drank my fill, then drank it again. The water was lukewarm, green, thick as pea soup, but to me it was nectar. . . .

Of a sudden from behind me came a faint croaking voice: "Owen, por Díos . . . agua!"

Jorge was still alive. His red eyes stared at me from a black, blistered face; blood welled from cracks in his lips. I went over to him, stunned, and raised the gourd to his mouth. He finished what was left, then smiled his gratitude. His teeth were amazingly white in that ruin of a face.

How could he still be alive after all Mangas and his men had done to him? You might well ask it; I know I did. But of all the tribes in the West, the Apaches are the most adept at the fine art of torture: they will keep a victim alive as long as possible, so that even after they depart the scene they know he's still suffering.

With no small effort I removed the wooden nails which pinned Jorge to the cross and lowered his maimed body to the sand.

"I'm finished," he said at last. "Maybe I'm dead already and this drink of water is merely my first taste of Heaven. But I think not. Promise me . . ."

He fainted for a while. I moved him to the shade of the pumice-stone wall.

"Promise me," he continued when he regained consciousness, "before God, that you will go to Guaymas and seek out my mother. Senora Josefina Diaz, for she remarried after my father was lost at sea. She used to live near the waterfront, where the fishing boats haul out. Tell her of my fate, and that my last thoughts were of her. Ask her to pray for my soul in Purgatory."

I said nothing.

His eyes opened wider, black as coal, black with reproach and the threat of retribution from the grave. He raised himself to his elbows.

"Promise me now," he said. "On your *honor!*"

"I promise."

Jorge died at sundown. I scraped out a shallow grave in the sand at the foot of the cross on which he had hung, laid him in it faceup with his hands folded over his chest, covered him with logs from the other crosses, then piled rocks atop that to keep coyotes and vultures from his body. With my knifepoint I carved on the cross these words:

JORGE GUAYMAS
KILLED BY APACHES
SUMMER, 1837
REQUIESCAT IN PACE.

I will not recount my further adventures on that awful *jornada del muerto*. Suffice it to say that I made my way with no mishaps back to the Gila, followed it down to the Colorado, turned south, and continued down into the lush delta of that river. There was plenty of game to sustain me along the way, so I fed well. The Yuma Indians were peaceful that year, at least when I came to their village on the Colorado, and I passed safely after paying a "toll" of the peltry I had accumulated along the way. Some very primitive Indians who call themselves Co-copos occupy the delta. They treated me kindly. A Mexican fishing boat trading with them for ocelot and jaguar pelts took me aboard and carried me at last to Guaymas, where I located Senora Diaz and apprised her of Jorge's final words. Then, my promise redeemed, I sought gainful employment.

Across the Sea of Cortés, near the town of Mulege, I heard from a French engineer of a silver mine at San Ignácio, the owners of which were seeking a skilled Anglo overseer. Applying there, I was promptly hired, and here I remained. The work was simple and straightforward, allowing me abundant leisure time to explore the mountains hereabouts for precious metals or stones. During these excursions, which have rewarded both my employers and me with several new finds, I find myself putting into practice all the Indian arts Pine Leaf taught me during our escape from Mangas. As you know, I have always been a good shot with a rifle. Now I have added the spear and the bow to my repertoire. Bandits and *Indios Broncos* infest these mountains, but where once they stalked me now they flee at the first sign of my presence. It is reassuring to be feared. . . .

ONCE OR TWICE a year since my arrival here I have made journeys with our *conductas* to the seaport of La Paz. There, a month ago, I met an English sea captain who had left the United States only last September. He provided me with newspapers from New York, Baltimore, and Savannah, from which I learned of the rise to sudden fame and fortune of our old friend Lafcadio Dade. It seems that since the American conquest of New Mexico he has managed to purchase, for an unstated price in gold, the Hidalgito mine in the *cerillos* south of Santa Fe. This, as you doubtless know, is one of the oldest and richest gold mines in the entire territory. How Dade, a mere fur trader, managed to accumulate the wherewithal—in bullion—to make this grand purchase the writers of the articles said they knew not.

But I know.

He got it from *my* gold mine, in White Hart Hollow.

He got it at the expense of *my* suffering.

He got it at the cost—to *me, and to me alone*—of my only male friend in this cruel Mexican world and the only woman I have ever loved.

I buried Jorge with my own hands. I saw Pine Leaf die beneath the blade of Delgadito.

*   *   *

THIS BITTER KNOWLEDGE has not rested easily on my soul. I wake at night from dreams of Lafcadio Dade, laughing uproariously and running his fingers through mountains of gold dust. . . .

Thus I have made a vow.

I am returning to Nuevo Méjico to exact a vengeance on this source of my woe. Just what form it will take I cannot tell. But rest assured that however it should fall, Lafcadio Dade will be compensated in full for all the pain and loss and suffering he has caused me.

PART III

WHITE HART HOLLOW

CHAPTER I

―――◆―――

Hidalgito, May 5: Special to the Santa Fe Republican.
Word has just arrived of a dreadful mining disaster at the gold-
fields south of here. At three minutes past two o'clock Monday
morning, an explosion rocked the Number Three shaft of the
Minería de Hidalgito, some 30 miles south of the capital. The
subsequent collapse of the shaft killed 96 miners and half a
dozen overseers. Another 20 or 25 men managed to escape by
scaling a ladder leading up from the shaft.

"It was a moment of sheer hell down there," said Ephraim
Ings, 48, the Missouri-born supervisor of night operations at the
mine. "A great tongue of flame came roaring toward us from
the depths of the tunnel, carrying with it the severed appendages
of men and mules. Men on fire staggered every which way.
Those of us who could got out of there as soon as possible.
And well that we did, for we had scarcely reached the top of
the ladder when the whole mine caved in."

The mine owner, Mr. L. R. Dade of Santa Fe, when apprised
of the calamity said he could not understand how an explosion
of such force could have occurred, barring a mishandling of the

gunpowder used in mining operations. "My powder men were all well versed in safety procedures," he said. "Mr. Ings, the supervisor, was an artillerist with Colonel Price in the late affair at Taos, and his entire powder crew was American."

Spy was out tracking some Kiowa horse thieves over toward Sandía Peak, and Jim was due back any minute now from the La Fonda hotel, where he'd gone to pick up the mail, so I was holding the fort by myself that day, the fort being our small 'dobe office on the Calle Don Pablo García near the Misión San Miguel in downtown Santa Fe. Usually Plover sat up at the front desk, interviewing prospective clients, but that morning she'd stayed home—the baby had the croup and the older children had had to go to school, so they couldn't look after the young-un—thus I was sitting there alone, having finished the newspaper and now nodding off over the chapter on torts in *Blackstone's Law*, when Dade came stomping in.

Of course I'd read of the dreadful blast in one of Dade's subsidiary mines, not just read of it but heard the boom itself that night. It rattled the glass in the bedroom window, and Plover said she could see the red flash of the explosion. She'd just come back to bed from nursing the baby. Close to a hundred men had died when the mine roof came down on them. Mostly Mexicans, sure, but they're people, too.

"Damn your lights and liver, Griffith, your brother did this!" Dade yelled as he came through the door. His face wore a high color, higher even than its normal brick red, and his hair leaped out from beneath his sombrero like flames in a hayrick. Through the door behind him stepped his bodyguard, Lenny LeNapier, the sole survivor of that band of murderous Delawares who once accompanied him on his rambles through the Wild West.

"Now easy, Lafe, easy does it, or you'll have a syncope for sure. You know my brother is dead. What did he do, come back from the grave to haunt you?"

"He blew up my most productive mine," said Dade. Of course, he made no mention of the men who died in it. . . . "Take a look at this."

He reached inside that cute little blue velvet don's jacket he favors and pulled out a folded paper. "My *secretário* here"—he flicked a thumb at Lenny—"just picked up this letter at La Fonda with the morning's post."

The new post office wasn't completed yet, and all the town's mail was still being delivered to La Fonda, the old inn that marked the end of the Santa Fe Trail. I unfolded the letter and read it.

Don Lafcadio Dade
Hidalgito Enterprises
City

Sir:

For too long you have rode roughshod over the innocents of the West, *indio*, Mexican, and Anglo alike. Your cruelties are legend from the Three Forks of the Missouri to the Plains of Chihuahua. It is unfortunate that so many miners had to die in the recent explosion, but I blame that on you: for making men work round-the-clock. *This is just the first taste of my vengeance.* By my count you have half a dozen *minerías* in New Mexico alone, three in Colorado, and another, perhaps the richest of all, somewhere to the north. Which will be the next to go?

Owen Glendower

"That is not my brother's hand," I said, though it did look familiar. "As you've told me often enough, he was captured by Rees after you released him years ago in the northern mountains. We found the fire in which they'd burned him. His bones and boots as well."

"Isn't your brother's name Owen?"

"Yes."

"Isn't this letter signed 'Owen'?"

"Owen is a common name among both the Welsh and the English. His last name, in case you've forgotten, is Griffith, not Glendower." I didn't mention that Owen Glendower was a famous Welsh hero, a rebel against the English. If Dade didn't mention it, why should I?

"Then how does this 'Glendower' know about the mine 'some-where to the north'? If your brother is in fact dead, that leaves only you and me, your wife, your Shawnee pal, and Beckwourth who know anything at all about Los Padres Perdidos. And I have had your word that you would say nothing to anyone about that place. God knows I paid enough for your discretion. No, I believe your brother escaped from the Rees and for some unbalanced reason has now decided to raise hell with me."

It was true that Dade had set us up in this business of tracking stolen horses and indeed threw a lot of business our way simply be-cause he was the wealthiest, and thus the most influential, man in Santa Fe.

"You're forgetting about Lenny here," I said. "He was there; he knows about the Padres mine. Maybe . . ."

The Delaware looked over at me and smirked.

Dade said, "Lenny couldn't have done this. He's with me all day and sleeps outside my door at night. Nor could he have told anyone about the mine. He can't write, and the poor fellow hasn't uttered a word since the Yaquis cut out his tongue back in '38."

"Look, Lafe," I said. "I truly believe my brother is dead. Wouldn't I have heard something from him otherwise? It's nearly ten years since the massacre. All right, I'll grant you there's a slim chance that perhaps he isn't dead after all, but this letter could be from anyone. There are enough boozers and losers around here these days who'd love to take credit for any noteworthy deed, whether good or evil. Anyway, what could I do about the matter even if the man who blew up your mine *is* my brother?"

"Beckwourth and Spybuck are among the best trackers in the Southwest," Dade said. "Get out there and track him down. Keep him from blowing up more of my properties. I'll pay you plenty if you do—enough to buy you that rancho in California you're always dream-ing of."

He was right. There was an *estancia* near the mission in the Valle de San Fernando, north of the sleepy little Pueblo de Nuestra Señora de los Angeles de Porciuncula, a town with more letters in its name than it had citizens, where Jim and I had once stolen some horses.

The hacendado was a decent man, a tall, courtly Spaniard named Ventura who had entertained us most hospitably during our stay. He had a splendid wine cellar, stocked with vintages he had cultivated, pressed, and bottled himself. The main house was furnished with tables, chairs, bedsteads, and cabinets that the don had commissioned to be carved from black walnut and oak grown on his own property. Groves of oranges and lemons surrounded the house, watered from a crystalline stream that descended from the surrounding hills. Herds of blood horses ranged the grasslands, intermixed with long-horned kine. We killed two grizzly bears which had been raiding the don's swine pens, and in gratitude he opened his casa to us. We reciprocated by stealing 200 of his best mounts. In the midst of many a mountain winter I have thought of that lovely rancho, so yearningly that I could smell the blossoms on the cool breezy patio while sipping a large glass of orange juice of a morning. . . .

PERHAPS NOW IS the time to explain what had transpired since that day Dade and I went our separate ways at Garnet Creek. He had left us afoot, with only the guns we carried to see us safe back to the Crow country. We buried the Yellow Buffalo Calf in the manner of the Plains Indians, anointing her body with ocher and wrapping it in cured hides, they laying it faceup on a platform we built in a tall pine tree on the mountainside. It was a sad day. After finding what we thought were the charred skeletons of Owen and Pine Leaf in the ashes of the bonfire, we headed back down to Wind River. Spy and Plover managed to steal some horses from a band of unwary Shoshones, so we made good time. There was plenty of game en route. We found Beckwourth's people hunting buffalo on the flats near the Popo Agie. When I told him of our misfortune he shook his head.

"If I had a buffalo robe for every similar tale I've heard," he said, "I could retire to Saint Louis along with General Ashley. No, to New York with J. J. Astor. It's catch as catch can in the mountains, and you got caught."

Hard words, but the truth nonetheless.

Jim said that with luck Owen would effect an escape from Dade's boys. He knew Lafe Dade and doubted the man would murder my brother in cold blood. Pine Leaf was another matter: to Dade, as to most white men in the West at that time, Indians were vermin who deserved rubbing out. I suspect Jim's feigned indifference to Pine Leaf's fate stemmed from hurt feelings at being rebuffed by the woman.

Spybuck left us that fall, heading back to the Kansas Territory, where he had heard his tribe had been relocated from their ancestral lands east of the Father of Waters. Plover and I wintered over with Jim, up in the Absarokas, and a fine winter it was. We had plenty of dried buffalo meat to eke out the fresh elk and deer we killed from time to time. The tepees were snug and warm, abundant wood for the fires, water and grass for the animals, and indeed we never had to resort to feeding the horse herd on cottonwood bark, as was the need of less fortunate tribes. Each night Jim regaled us with tales from his heroic past. Splendid stories: all blood and battles, loves and losses, " 'scapes i' the imminent deadly breach." Indeed, they were Shakespearean in their scintillating scope. For Jim was a mighty reader as well as a champion yarnspinner. He loaned me books from his "traveling library," as he called the brass-bound trunk in which he kept them: the works of Chaucer and Shakespeare, Montaigne and Rabelais, along with more modern tales like *Robinson Crusoe* and *Gulliver's Travels*. He recommended a well-thumbed copy of Adam Smith's *The Wealth of Nations*, but I never got into it, perhaps because the plot unfolded too slowly.

In the spring we resumed the ageless cycle of Plains Indian life: hunting, raiding, stealing horses and women, making fur and babies, living and dying. This is how we survived for the next two years, which in retrospect seem the happiest of my life. Then in July of 1836, during a routine visit with Mr. McKenzie at Fort Clark down on the Yellowstone, Jim suddenly found himself out of work. The king of the Missouri said Jim was spending too much time stealing horses and fighting the Blackfeet, not enough collecting peltry. I was off hunting buffalo at the time. When I returned to the Crow camp Jim was gone.

Plover, who'd remained with the band during the final months of her first pregnancy, after presenting me with a fine son whom we named James in honor of our benefactor, informed me that Captain

Beckwourth had headed back to Saint Louis. There, I later learned, he had joined the Missouri Volunteers as an express rider, master teamster, and assistant wagon master, bound for the Seminole War in Florida. Such were the vagaries of mountain life in those days that I did not meet up with him again until the fall of 1842, at a trading post on the Arkansas River called El Pueblo.

A bustling little town stands there now, but in November of that year El Pueblo consisted of a mud-walled fort some sixty yards square surrounded by the shacks of some fifteen or twenty trappers and their families. Jim ran the cantina and the subtler's store, guided by principles he'd gleaned from Adam Smith's book—which is to say at a considerable profit. Mexican traders up from New Mexico traded the raw whiskey called Taos Lightning for furs and buffalo robes, and I'd heard that the doings at El Pueblo could get rather rough. I rode into the scruffy little settlement from the Bayou Salado one blustery autumn evening just minutes ahead of a howling blue norther. After stabling my horse with the *caballerizero*, I went into the cantina to wet my whistle. It was a low-ceilinged room, lit by guttering oil lamps, the air thick with the pungent smoke of *cigarros*. The bar consisted of a rough-hewn slab of mountain mahogany perhaps twenty feet long with a shelf lined with many bottles of mescal, aguardiente, and red whiskey.

Four men were playing cards at a table in the corner. One had his back to me, but from the width of those shoulders and the curly black hair that fell from beneath his flat-crowned hat he seemed familiar. Across from him sat a figure I clearly recognized: Old Bill Williams, a legend in the mountains at the time. Skinny and tall, stooped and weathered tough as whang leather, he spoke in such a high, whiny, cracked, thin voice that you never could tell whether he was laughing or crying: "Do 'ee hyar now," he was saying just then, "you danged crittur, 'ee can't play *cyards* thataway, not by drawin' from the bottom of the dang deck."

Williams, born in the Tarheel State, raised on the Missouri frontier, and a parson among the Osage Indians before he grew disillusioned with preaching and traded his Bible for beaver traps, never used bad language.

His opponent answered him in words too low for me to follow.

But I noticed him shift himself on the rickety chair and elbow his unbuttoned capote clear of the haft of knife which was sheathed on his belt. The handle of the knife was wrapped in dirty white silk. . . .

"Do 'ee hyar now?" Williams skreeked. " 'Ee're a low-down half-breed nigger *Frenchman*. . . ."

Jim Beckwourth drew his white-handled knife and lunged across the table, but Williams skipped away from the blade and crashed a swift left hook to the other man's jaw. The knife dropped to the packed dirt floor, and Jim soon followed.

I went over and picked up the knife, then Jim himself. Led him over to the bar and ordered a Taos Lightning. He looked at me with woozy eyes.

"I always was a sucker for a left hook," he said. "How the hell are you, Dillon?"

Later, after a couple of drinks, Jim took me to his quarters in the fort and introduced me to his new bride, "Miss Louise Sandeville," a dark-hued beauty whose real name was Luisa Sandoval. She hailed from Taos, where Jim had had a trading emporium before setting up this "renegade" post in competition with Bent's Fort, farther down the Arkansas. He invited me to work with him there at Pueblo. I went to Arroyo Hondo, a little town in the sheep country north of Taos, to fetch Plover and the children. There were two of them by this time, a bubbly, bright-eyed little daughter having joined our family the previous year. We named her Gwenivar, Gwennie for short. Over the next couple of years Jim and I trapped together, made a few horse-stealing raids into California, had some wicked fights with Utes and Digger Indians, visited the missions to refresh ourselves on the padres' beef and brandy, joined Juan Alvarado's army and fought against Governor Micheltorena's forces at the Battle of Cahuenga in 1845, and generally had a high old time of it. When word came to us that the U.S. was about to go to war with Mexico, we stole 1,800 more horses and headed back over the mountains to join the fun.

It was there that I met up with Lafe Dade again. I spotted him on the street in Taos one evening and my heart went cold, followed him into a cantina, determined to gun him down. He was standing at the bar drinking a shot of Taos Lightning. Must have felt my eyes boring into him and turned. He went white. My hand was on the butt of the revolver at my hip. God only knows what my face looked like.

"You," he said.

"Goddamn right. Dillon Griffith. Finish your drink and say your prayers, Dade. You're going to die right here and now." I drew the Colt.

"Why?" he blustered, trying at once to look guiltless and indignant. He was neither. He was just plain scared.

"You killed my brother, you scum. *You burned him in the fire.*"

"I never!" he bleated, his eyes wide and bright with fear. "I let your brother and his woman go, just like I promised. But there were Rees in the country; we'd seen their sign all over the place. Still, your brother insisted. So I honored my word—swear to God—even gave him his pistols back. Shortly after we separated, we heard gunfire behind us. I sent one of my men back and he saw the Rees. They had both Owen and the woman. He came back at a gallop to fetch us. But we were too late. The Rees had already tossed them both into the inferno, then decamped. It was awful." He gulped down his drink. "I swear to you on my honor as a white man and a Christian, I didn't kill your brother."

I hesitated. Around me I heard the low muttering of voices—the other drinkers in the saloon, all of them white men, all of them armed, many of them, I suddenly realized, Dade's friends and associates.

"Put the gun down, Dillon," came Jim's voice from behind me. "It wouldn't do to kill him now. Too many folks have heard what he said. It'd be murder, partner. You'd hang."

He was right. I holstered the pistol, bellied up to the bar, and ordered a shot of Lightning. My hand was shaking.

Dade and his pals cleared out in a hurry.

I HAD NEVER gone back to White Hart Hollow after our flight in the fall of 1833. Plover had no desire to go there, for the place bore too many sad memories for her, what with her friend the Buffalo Calf's death, and I certainly agreed with my wife on that score. If nothing else, my missing fingers reminded me of that sorry business every day.

Besides, the Blackfeet were still a great danger in those parts. It was not until 1837 that the tribe was reduced, by a mysterious smallpox plague, to a less aggressive state.

But from reports by various Indians and mountain men over the years I knew Dade had brought a workforce of Mexican prisoners up to the Buenaventura to develop the mine. He'd even built a sturdy fort-cum-prison compound at the site and named it Dadeville. When he began throwing money around in Santa Fe, buying up mines and stamp mills in the name of Mexican "owners" who were merely front men, Jim and I knew very well where the money was coming from.

"He's probably lying," Jim said as he stood beside me in the cantina that night. "But we can't prove it, and now that we're in what passes for civilization, we can't just gun him down without paying for it by trying on a hemp necktie for size. Our best recourse is the law, either Spanish or American. What Dade's doing up north is technically illegal. The country where the mine is located was first discovered and mapped by a couple of Spanish priests, Sylvestre de Escalante and Francisco Dominguez. Under Spanish law, any precious metals found in the course of such explorations had to be split fifty-fifty with the Crown, whose share, since the revolution, now rightly belongs to the Republic of Mexico."

"Let's turn the bastard in before the U.S. Army arrives," I said. Gen. Stephen Kearny's Missouri Legion was still weeks away from Santa Fe, but already the governor of Nuevo Méjico, Manuel Armijo, was loading wagons with all he could steal in anticipation of a swift departure for Chihuahua. "Armijo will confiscate everything Dade owns and then throw him in the *calabozo*. Hell, he might even hang the skunk."

"No, he won't," Jim said. "He'll just take a big *mordida*. I've got a better idea."

The next day, Jim bearded Dade in his lair, a big hacienda just out of town, and made a proposition. In return for a large interest-free "loan" to establish us in the stock detective business, along with a promise to send us as much business as he could in the future, we would not tell the governor of Dade's transgression, nor would we breathe a word of it to the American authorities who would soon be in control of New Mexico, and who could be just as corrupt and greedy as any Mexican, while at the same time wrapping their peculations in an odor of blue-nosed sanctity. Since the "loan" was much less than Armijo's *mordida* would have amounted to, Lafe Dade readily agreed.

Thus was established the firm of Beckwourth, Spybuck & Griffith, Stock Detectives. Since the arrival of the Missouri Legion in New Mexico, an outfit that largely consisted of border ruffians, rustlers, horse thieves, cutpurses, and runaway murderers, you can bet there was plenty of work for us.

CHAPTER II

"W<small>ELL</small>," I <small>TOLD</small> Dade on the morning after the mine blew up, "since I'm still convinced my brother is dead, I suppose we might take the case. However, I'll have to consult with my partners."

"You've been reading too much goddamn law," Dade said, thumping the tome that lay open on the desk before me. "By God, though, you're getting windy enough to play the lawyer's role; that's for sure. All right then, if your partners agree to take on my 'case,' get your hinders on out to the mine as soon as you can and start sniffing. I'll send Lenny along with you, to keep you out of trouble."

"Lenny can stay at home. Spybuck is due back any minute now from the Sandías, and he cannot abide a Delaware. I could not guarantee Lenny's safety if those two tangle."

Lenny uttered a chortling gargle, made the uglier by the wobble of his tongue stump in that wide, reptilian mouth.

"Lenny can take care of himself," Lafe said. "Stop by the hacienda and pick him up on your way to Hidalgito."

With that they took their departure.

No sooner had they gone than Jim appeared from the back office.

"I saw them through the window from across the street," he explained. "Didn't know how it would play, so I came round the back way and listened at the door." He stuck a .44-caliber Colt's Dragoon back into his belt. "By the way, your brother *is* alive. And Dade's right: Owen's the one who blew up the mine."

With that he withdrew a thick packet from his coat pocket and placed it on the desk. It was addressed to me in Owen's handwriting, care of General Delivery. There was also a small envelope containing a covering letter.

"I read this note while I was eavesdropping at the door just now," Jim said, "and got the drift of what Dade was telling you. Sorry."

"Dear Dillon," it read. "The enclosed manuscript is an account of what became of me after we separated at Garnet Creek many years ago. I wrote it during a long stay in Mexico to explain to you, and to whomever else it may concern, why I must follow the course of action which I have just intiated. I'm dismayed to find you on friendly terms with Lafcadio Dade, and have thus hesitated making my presence known to you. Perhaps we will meet again somewhere down the trail. Owen."

I was flabbergasted, of course, and for a moment my head spun. He was alive!

And he was a killer.

It took Jim and me the rest of the morning to read Owen's manuscript.

"Jesus," I said when we'd finished. "Well, clearly I can't do what Dade wants. Bring in my own brother for the hangman's noose?"

"Who says we have to bring him in?" Jim said. "We've known Dade's a rotter from the beginning. We've only been using him to keep a close eye on him. Now we can set it up so it looks like we found Owen and had to kill him."

"Lenny will be with us."

"Yes, but so will Spy. He'd be only too delighted to arrange a fatal mishap for our traveling companion."

I must have looked dubious, because he continued more reassuringly: "And after all, who knows whether we'll ever find Owen? If your brother's learned to evade Apaches, he'll probably give us the slip without half-trying."

*   *   *

AND SO IT was agreed. Spy returned that evening from Sandía. He had the horses, thirty of them, but not the thieves.

"They fell off a mountain," he told me. "No survivors."

"All three of them?"

"They were Apaches," he said. "Jicarillas. You know how clumsy they can be when they have to walk. I couldn't let them ride, even in chains, for fear they might escape a-horseback."

Spy had returned to the West from Kansas in '46, as a scout for Kearny's Missouri boys. His wife still wouldn't have him back, he said. Things hadn't worked out on the new Shawnee reservation, either. All the old warriors had either died or turned into businessmen. The young ones were farming, just like proper Americans. He told me all this after I happened upon him one night in Taos, after the suppression of the Indian rebellion which had cost Charles Bent his life. Bent had succeeded Armijo as governor and spent most of his time in the Palacio at Santa Fe, while his shy Mexican wife and children stayed at home in Taos. He was taking a short vacation there when the uprising began. One of the house guests during that holiday season was Josepha Jaramillo Carson, the seventeen-year-old wife of the well-known scout Kit Carson, who lived in Taos when he wasn't out killing Indians. These Indians knocked on Bent's door at six in the morning, came in, shot him with guns and arrows, scalped him while he was still alive, cut off his head, then, oddly enough, sat down and cried. Bent had been a popular governor. Still, he was an Anglo, and for that he died. Near two dozen other Americans, men, women, and children, also perished in the uprising, which left the Pueblo Indians and their Mexican allies in control of the town.

This was on January 19 of 1847. By February 2, Col. Sterling Price with 350 men and four howitzers had marched up from Santa Fe. Jim and I were with them. The Indians holed up in the mission church, whose thick adobe walls they hoped would save them. Not so. We started shooting at dawn, and by midafternoon the howitzers had battered gaping holes in the mud bricks. The artillerymen wheeled a twelve-pounder loaded with cannister up to the door and fired it straight into the *iglesia*. The Missourians fixed their bayonets, spit on their scalp knives, took another swig of aguardiente, and quickly stormed the church. Only seven gringos died in the assault. Later we counted 150 dead Indians sprawled in the smoke-wreathed rubble.

The leaders of the revolt were duly tried in a court of law, and hanged.

I found Spy lying drunk and half-naked that very night, in a gutter outside Estis's cantina in San Fernández de Taos, singing old keelboat songs in the stagy accents of, well, a drunken Indian. That's how I recognized him. When I picked him up and slung him on my horse, he opened his red eyes. "Paleface brother heap kind to no-good red-skin," he slurred with a horrid smile. "Here, have a scalp." He fumbled the grisly thing out of his shirtfront, then vomited all over himself. I got him to our camp on the outskirts of town, where Jim had a good fire going, coffee bubbling, and hump ribs popping hot and fat on the flames; we sobered him up by morning. He'd been sober ever since, and more murderous than ever. Though he will kill another Indian without blinking an eye, it preys on his soul to see them perish at the white man's hand. A contradictory fellow indeed.

"You've got to be more circumspect in your disposal of prisoners," I told him now. "Anglo law is a lot stricter than the Mexican variety. One of these days some sheriff or lawyer is going to wonder why so many of the men you capture never make it back to town."

"I didn't kill those Apaches," Spy said. "We were coming along a narrow trail through the mountains, the prisoners chained at the ankles in single file. I followed with the horses behind me. A boulder fell from the cliff above, knocked two of the Indians over the precipice, and of course the rest followed. I think the rock was pushed down on them by the Tats-ah-das-ay-go."

"What was that name?"

"You've heard it before," he said. "Remember, I told you about it last time I was down there, in the fall of last year. The Mexicans say it's a hobgoblin or ogre or wicked witch of some sort who preys upon the Apaches. Been at it for the last ten years at least. Sort of a bog-eyman, or woman actually, for some say the Tats-ah-das-ay-go is of the feminine gland. I always figured it for a spook story, you know, the kind mothers frighten their children with. 'Be good or Tats-ah-das-ay-go will get you!' That sort of thing. Now I'm not so sure but she's real."

"Yeah, I remember now. But I feel I've heard or seen it somewhere else recently. What does the name mean in English?"

"Quick Killer."

"Damn! But it can't be. He says he saw her die. . . . Plover, show Spy my brother's letter if you're done with it."

She took off her spectacles and handed Owney's pages to the Shawnee. We were seated in the study of the big, ruined old *casa de campo* that Plover and I share with Captain Beckwourth and Spybuck up in the hills above Santa Fe, rent free, of course, courtesy of Don Lafcadio. When we'd returned from California with that big herd of horses, back in '46, Jim found that the fair Luisa Sandoval had flown the coop, run off with a Missourian named John Brown, and remarried. He was mopey for a while—usually *he* left *them*, not vice versa—but now seemed resigned to the rejection. On this particular evening, all was snug and happy in our new abode. Logs blazed in the big fireplace, the children were finally asleep, and Jim was out at the stable watering the horses. While Spy read the letter, I topped off our coffee mugs. He sipped his absently from time to time, turning the pages swiftly. He looked up at us after coming the part about Pine Leaf's name change, raised his eyebrows, then continued.

"It could be her," he said when he'd finished. "I thought I saw a figure darting away from the clifftop just as the boulder toppled. Of course it might have been another Indian—Pueblo or Comanche or Tonkawa, all of them sworn enemies of the Apaches."

"Did it look like her?" Plover asked.

"Everything happened so quickly, I didn't see more than a flash. Couldn't tell if was a man or a woman, or a bear for that matter. Later, after picketing the horses, I went up there and checked for footprints. Found some. Human all right, and they were the right size to have come from a tall woman. Bar-che-am-pe was big enough to fit them."

"It sounds like Pine Leaf," Plover said. "At first I was certain, after reading Owen's story, that the Apaches had caught her and killed her, or else she would have returned to Crow country. But now I can see

I was wrong. She'd be much more likely to stay on at the fringes of Apachería to count more coups, take more scalps, make life hell for her enemies. She was never like other women. Vengeance is her life."

"Did you track her out?" I asked Spy.

"The footprints disappeared once they reached bare rock. It would have taken a while for me to find where the trail resumed. Night was falling and I wanted to get clear of those cliffs before making camp, so I wouldn't suffer a fate similar to that of my late captives. Next morning I headed for Santa Fe. But if it hasn't rained or snowed up there since I left, we could go back and find them, if you think it worthwhile. Tracks last forever in this dry country."

"Let's see what we find at the mine tomorrow," I said, getting up from my saddle-frame-and-steerhide easy chair. "I'll go out to the stable and tell Jim about this 'Quick Killer' business."

WE LEFT BEFORE dawn for Dade's *estancia*. I didn't know how long we'd be out, so we brought two remounts apiece, a canvas Sibley tent, sleeping robes, a few long ropes of dried beef (they dry their jerky by the yard out here), plenty of cornmeal *masa*, chilis, and frijóles, a big can of lard, and appropriate pots and pans. Plover had to stay home with the children and to keep the office open, but Spy was a splendid chef in many languages. He had taken to Mexican cooking and loved to experiment with the chilis, the hotter the better, which made for great meals but frequent stops along the trail afterward. His *menudo norteño* could wake up the dead.

We were, as usual, armed to the teeth. You never knew what you'd meet on the trail in those days: it could be *bandidos* or Apaches or maybe a rampaging grizzly. I still preferred my brother's old .54-caliber Hawken, which I'd learned to shoot with some long-range skill after I inherited it, but now also packed along a pistol, in this case a brand-new Walker Colt. This was a ponderous beast, weighing nearly five pounds. Its nine-inch-long half-octagon barrel threw slugs accurately out to near fifty yards, six of them in a cylinder load, and when it was empty you could always use it as an admirable shillelagh at close quarters. Jim, in addition to his heavy Colt Dragoon six-shooter, carried an improved Colt's ring-lever rifle, like the pistol a repeater, equipped with the same newfangled revolving cylinder, but containing eight loads in the rifle rather then the six available to the handgun. The Colt's browned octagon barrel was only thirty-two inches long, which made it stubby-looking compared to the Hawken, but the rifle made up in firepower what it lacked in range. Curious, when you think about it, that Jim, the old-timer, carried the most modern weapons. Spy still preferred his venerable smoothbore fuke, though he, too, had added a brace of handguns to his armory, in his case a pair of Whitneyville Colts, a couple of inches shorter in barrel length than the Walker but very fast out of the holster. His pistols were also in .44 caliber, so we could replenish each other's pouches at will. When we ran bullets at night, one man could run the same size for all.

Lenny was waiting for us at the gate to the *estancia*. So, too, was Dade, though it was barely past dawn and of late he had become a late riser, as befit a man of his standing, I suppose.

"I decided to come with you," Don Lafcadio stated as we came up. "My business can wait, and this is far too urgent a matter to trust to underlings."

"Well then, boys," Jim said, turning to Spy and me, "why don't we just reverse course then and ride back home? The hunt seems to be in good hands, what with the master of hounds in the saddle and his best pooch trotting along with him."

"Don't get sassy, Beckwourth," Lafe said. "I knew you way back when."

Spy and the Delaware eyed one another. As we rode on toward the diggings, I noticed that each took every opportunity to lag a step or two behind the other. Soon they were trailing the rest of us by nearly a hundred yards. Of course neither Indian wanted the other behind him, in position for a back shot, but this was ridiculous. Finally I reined in and rode back to them.

"What are you fellows up to?" I said, fixing Spy with a stern glance. "Is this some kind of a woodland redskin backwards race? Pretty soon you'll both have lagged your asses clear down to Santa Fe if you don't start moving forward. Why don't you both ride ahead of the rest of us? That way you wouldn't have to worry about backshooters. Don Lafcadio will watch Lenny's and I'll watch yours. Now let's make some tracks."

It would be a long trip, I feared.

Chapter III

THE MINERíA DE Hidalgito consisted in those days of three major diggings. What Dade called Shaft Number One had been discovered and begun by a vagabond Mexican *minero* up from Durango in 1829, who sold his claim to Governor Armijo soon afterward for the less than munificent payment of 3,000 pesos. Digging had immediately intensified, thanks to the governor's unlimited access to free labor in the shape of *prisoneros* and peons, and the first shaft was now some 1,400 feet deep. Of the 2,500 men employed at the mine, fully half worked this tunnel.

Shaft Number Two was on the far side of the mountain, about half a vertical mile distant from Number One and directly opposite it. This adit, Dade said, had been blasted out of the bedrock with gunpowder poured into holes driven by steel screws, which in turn were hammered by men swinging ten-pound sledges. The shaft now penetrated horizontally into the hard rock some eight hundred feet, where the tunnel hit the ore-bearing ledge and then followed it—or was in the process of following it—out to the left, or south. Dade had built a tramway up the far face of the mountain and down the Shaft Number One side to facilitate the movement of ore to the stamping ground, which was located near the main shaft. The patio of this Hacienda de Beneficios, as it is politely termed by the Mexicans ("The Estate of Profits"), measures some thirty-two thousand square yards in area. Through a portion of it, more than two thousand mules march in circles day and night, sometimes shoulder-deep, through a huge, thick mud puddle consisting of crushed ore, copper, and salt. Water from a leaky wooden aqueduct leading down from the surrounding peaks kept this paste at the right consistency, and from it, through some arcane porphyritic process I haven't the science to explain, much less comprehend, the gold is extracted: some hundreds of thousands of dollars worth to date, or so Dade told us.

The whole place was mutt ugly. Mules staggered blind through their endless circles caked in corrosive muck, their hides worn bloody by their harness. The men who worked the hoists bringing baskets of ore up from the pit each wore the hollow mask of defeat. A shift was changing when we arrived, and I watched the miners emerge from the *entrada*, skinny, naked save for loincloths, their dark, flat Indian faces smeared with blood from the shards of rock that rebounded from their picks. Guards armed with shotguns watched them line up to await the refastening of the chains which fettered them together. All of the supervisory personnel, I noticed, were Americans, border ruffians from Missouri to judge by their twanging voices. I followed the ongoing workers into the tunnel, past a great clanging steam engine which sucked water from the mine in a continuous gray-green gusher, and watched them descend the rickety ladders into the depths. It was black as the proverbial Pit down there, save for the golden glints of occasional lanterns. Now and then a hollow roar was followed by a blast of hot air rising from the shaft, a weak, subterranean fart whose fetor was compounded of blown gunpowder, man sweat, the perfume of shit and piss, and the stench of stale water. One of the prisoners looked up at me from the dark as he climbed down the ladder. Was his visage writ in despair or merely Indian stoicism? For a moment I had an image of my brother descending into this pit, or one very like it. Four years on the ladder. . . . If he was the man who had blown up part of this mine, at the cost of so many lives, perhaps he was doing a good deed after all. Putting men like these out of their misery. . . . I certainly would prefer death to such a life.

Perhaps the racket of the engine had addled me, but for a moment

I had a clear vision: If this is what wealth meant, this gutting of the bowels of the earth, this rendering of men into mere shit so as to replace the shit that was extracted with silks and crystal and carriages and foofaraw; if getting rich meant putting men to this kind of labor, forcing mules to walk these endless miles through a foul-smelling slurry, their hides rotted through with salt and chemicals; if it meant having your ears assailed day and night with the ceaseless yammer of steam engines, the clang of heavy hammers on steel spikes, of picks in rock, *then I wanted none of it.*

"Where did the blast take place?" I asked Dade when I came back out.

"Shaft Number Three," he said. "We'll go over there now, but I wanted you to see what I have at stake here. And in other places as well."

SHAFT NUMBER THREE lay half a mile west of the Estancia de Beneficios, on a barren slope composed of scree and cactus. Another steam pump stood at the *entrada,* cold and dead for now like the men entombed in the mine. A guard tower had been erected to cover the entrance to the shaft, with a platform atop it which could support half a dozen armed lookouts. Apache or Navajo raids were always a possibility in these mountains, and even the normally docile Pueblos were capable of skulduggery in the wake of the Taos suppression, Dade said, but the watchtower was mainly manned to prevent any prisoners from escaping. The guards had strict orders to turn away any unauthorized visitors.

"What was the weather like up here the night of the explosion?" Jim asked. Dade turned to a short, stocky Missourian who had joined us at the shaft. This was Ephraim Ings, the night supervisor, a fellow Welshman judging by the shag of his eyebrows.

"Overcast," he said. "Chilly. Raining a bit, as it sometimes does at this time of year. Just a thin mist of a rain, with fog rising from the creekbeds. Black as the pit of a jakes, it was. I remember thinking, *I hope no Indians show up tonight, for the guards might find it hard to keep their powder dry.*"

Spybuck was checking the ground around the entrance for unusual footprints. Now he came over to where we sat our horses.

"The barefoot tracks are those of the prisoners," he said. "I notice your boot prints there in the mud, Mr. Ings. How were the night guards shod?"

"In boots as well," Ings said. "They are all of them Americans, horsemen born and bred, and do not favor city shoes, nor yet heathen moccasins . . . er, beggin' your pardon, Mr. Spybuck."

"Did anyone here that night have a dog with him? A small dog, maybe fifteen pounds in weight, with long toenails?"

"Not that I recollect," Ings said, scratching his stubbly chin in thought. "Do you see such tracks down there? Might they not perhaps have been left by a coyote?"

"Too small," Spy told him. "But a dog was up here that night."

"What the hell is this?" Dade broke in. "I want a man, not a dog, unless it was some trick circus mutt that knows how to set off a keg of gunpowder."

"Dogs stick with their owners," said the Shawnee. "There are also a set of tracks made by moccasins. A Indian's tracks, toed inward. He's heavyset, I'd say, about 180 to 200 pounds."

Jim and I dismounted and walked over to the adit with Spybuck. A stench of rot wafted up from the shaft, along with the putrescent odor of tainted water. Nothing had been done to retrieve the bodies of the dead. Spy pointed to the sign in question. "They aren't Apache or Navajo moccasins," he said in a low voice, "nor Pueblo either. I've seen this style only once before, during a hunt I made with Ewing Young's brigade down in the Sierra San Pedro Martír."

"Where's that?" I asked.

"Below La Puebla de San Diego, down in Baja California."

"Owen for sure. That's where his letter came from."

"They don't have to know that," Spy said. "Let's let on that they're Coyotero Apache or some such tribe, one they know little about."

"These tracks look older than the boot tracks," I said. "Look how they're crumbled at the edges."

"They were made just when it started to rain that night," Spy said. "Probably during the changing of the guard, just before the night shift came on. But I don't think Owen went into the mine entrance. He was probably just scouting. Notice that the man and the dog went over toward the corral. I followed them out, and they disappear. He had a horse tied over there, in the dark, a good one to judge by how little it shifted while he left it there. He picked up his dog, and they rode on out. The hoofprints are indistinct, so he probably had wrapped them in hide or burlap to muffle the sound. But no, he didn't go into the mine from here. He must have found another entry to the mine to plant his bomb."

He'd been casually scuffing out the moccasin tracks as we spoke, very cool and indifferent. This was in case Lenny LeNapier decided to check the tracks for himself. But that blockhead had not yet bothered to stand down from his horse.

"Let's find it," I said.

"Not now," Spy advised. "For the moment let's lay it on heavy about the Coyoteros."

Which we did. But Dade was not taken in.

"Do you think I was born yesterday? Lenny can read sign as well as Spybuck. He told me, in sign language, that these tracks were made by a gringo. It's your brother all right. And if you want to stay in business in this territory, you won't try to dupe me again. We'll find him, rest assured."

THAT NIGHT DADE chose to sleep in the quarters provided for the mine supervisors, a spacious adobe structure near the Estancia de Beneficios. We pitched our tent near the corral, and while Jim went over to the adobe with Dade for a drink before dinner Spy and I headed up into the hills, ostensibly to hunt up a herd of *carneros cimarrones*, mountain sheep, which we'd seen on the ride back to the *estancia*. Once out of sight of the others, we circled back to Shaft Number Three and began casting for Owney's horsetracks. Spy found them on a reverse slope, perhaps a hundred yards from the adit but invisible from the watchtower.

Behind a little tuft of *palmillo* we found what we were looking for: the low, narrow mouth of a cave in the side of the hill. Dried scat indicated that black bears had used it for their winter quarters in years past, probably up to the time the digging and blasting at the mine had made them search out a quieter residence. Both man sign and dog tracks disappeared into the cave, the man crawling on his belly and dragging a heavy sack behind him. I dropped to my hands and knees and slithered in. Ten feet inside the hole it was utterly dark. I felt the hair rise on the back of my neck; my breath came short, gasping. I felt I would suffocate in there. Yet Owen had always felt at home beneath the earth, exploring deep into the caves we found in the Taconic Mountains or the Alleghenies. He didn't need his eyes underground, he once told me: the earth and the rocks themselves told him which way to go.

A faint current of air moved along the tunnel, colder and wetter than the air outside, and bearing with it the smell of moldering meat. So the cave must in some way be connected to the mine shaft, probably through a natural crevice in the rock. Once Owen had discovered this cave, and with his instinctive feel for subterranean formations, the hidden geography of the Uffern, that would not have been difficult; he could have crawled in here with his bundle of gunpowder, lit a long fuse, and dropped it down into the mine shaft from its ceiling. Even if the bomb lodged partway down the chute, fire from the subsequent explosion would have reached the mine shaft; the shock of the blast would loosen the rock enough to make the whole tunnel collapse. Even the mountain would settle, rearranging itself. But by that time he'd be well clear of the cave and on his way.

With that thought, I decided to get out of there. The cave itself might collapse at any moment.

"This is the place all right," I told Spy when I'd regained the open air. "He dropped his bomb right down into the mine. You can smell the dead in there. Let's forget about that sheep for supper. Tortillas and chilis will suit me fine."

Spy said, "The sheep are gone anyway, spooked off. Someone is down there in that woodline, watching us."

"Owen?"

He shook his head. "It's not your brother. While you were in the cave I faired out his track from here." He pointed to the northwest, where an entire horizon of long, square-topped, snow-clad pyramids of rock flared red in the sunset. "He headed up there, toward the Sangre de Cristos. No, it's someone else down there in the woods."

"Who?"

"The Quick Killer, I'd say. She must have seen me down at Sandía, maybe recognized me, and followed me up here. I've had a feeling for some days now that someone was watching us." He shook his head again. "She's good, damned good. Best not to go after her. She'll approach us when she's ready."

CHAPTER IV

T HE FOLLOWING MORNING we began running Owen to ground. Dade and LeNapier came with us. "Jim likes to track fast," I said. "Sure hope you fellows will be able to keep up."

Dade snorted. "Don't you worry about me, sonny boy. I was criss-crossing the mountains of the West while you was still in swaddling clothes."

Oh, yes, I thought, *but you're a lot older now, Don Lafcadio. You've gotten fat and soft from too much lying around your estancias counting your money. All that aguardiente has robbed you of your wind. Let's face it: you're an old fart.*

Frankly, I hoped he would have a syncope right then and there, and from his color it looked like he might. But he sputtered on for a while about the old days, so I picked up the pace. Soon he was too busy keeping his seat on the hard-trotting blood stallion he rode to say any more. But he knew I was right. Yet even though it might kill him, he tried to keep up.

We rode north and west through increasingly rugged hills, alter-nating a trot or a canter with a few minutes of walking. On the steeper slopes we dismounted and led the horses, to allow them to recoup. Jim was older than Dade but still fit, both from our horse-stealing expeditions to California and from the many trips he'd made up and down the Santa Fe Trail in recent years, escorting trains of trading goods from Independence. There was talk in town of establishing a stage line between Santa Fe and Independence or Kansas City sometime next year. It would carry light freight and mail by contract and make the round-trip twice a month. But there were still plenty of wild Indians along that route, Cheyennes, Arapahoes, Kiowas, Comanches, and Lipans, and I wondered how long such a civilized innovation would last if it ever indeed got rolling. No, the best way between the two points was still a strong, slow, well-armed wagon train, led by a knowledgable scout like James Pierson Beckwourth.

Spy had ridden off to the west a ways, hunting some meat for our dinner, but also for sign of Quick Killer, of whom we had as yet said nothing to Dade. Jim and Lenny rode ahead, following the trail left by Owen and his horses, for he had two of them, a tall stallion (Jim said) and a shorter, heavier pack mare. "I can see how you arrive at the tall-short distinction," I said, riding up to join them, "from the differing lengths of stride. And the weight difference is clear from the depths of the hoofprints. But how in the hell do you know one's a stallion?"

"Look there," he said, pointing to a damp spot in the sandy trail. We reined in our mounts. "The horse stops to stale. The piss splashes down between or slightly ahead of the rear hooves. That's a stallion or gelding. A mare stales backwards a bit, and the wet is behind the hooves. I say it's a stallion because he got restless, see?"—pointing to a tattoo of hoofprints in the sand—"when the mare started making water. They'll do that, you know."

"Mountain man lore," I said.

"No, just common sense. Watch them sometime when you've got a minute."

Every now and then we saw the dog's tracks running alongside those of the horses. Then they'd disappear again for a while, just plain vanish. Finally I figured it out: Owen was carrying the dog with him on the saddle but allowing it to run a ways whenenever it got too squirmy. The paw prints, I saw, were similar in size and shape to those of our old terrier, Thump. Owen always loved that dog more than I did. He must have gotten himself another terrier somewhere along the way, out of sheer sentimentality. Only a terrier, after all, would follow him so eagerly into that bear cave. It was strange, I thought: Here's a man so vengeful that he'd blow up a mine full of innocent souls, prisoners at that, without a second thought. Yet still so soft-hearted as to carry a small dog with him, a-horseback, to spare it from running itself to death keeping up. A man of mixed priorities, this brother of mine.

Spy rejoined us during the afternoon. He had a spikehorn mule deer buck draped over the back of his packhorse. "Found him munching piñon nuts up in the hills," he said. "Should taste sweet."

"Any sign of our watcher in the shadows?"

"Didn't see her, but she has three horses. Traveling light. She can move if she wants too, a lot faster than we can."

I looked back at Dade. He was riding better now, his muscles firming up after two days on horseback. He looked better, too, a lot of the pallor giving way to a brassy gleam of fresh sunburn. Only trouble he had was in mounting and dismounting: his thigh tendons must be aching something fierce by now, but that, too, would pass. He rode up to join us.

"Where do you think he's headed?" he asked.

"He's tending toward the east now, probably going to leave the Sangre de Cristos on his left hand, I reckon," Jim said. "Looks like he's aiming for Colorado."

"Damn. I have two new mines up there, up near Pike's mountain. Both of 'em damn promising. Silver. The Spanish used to pack lead out of there, and usually where there's lead there's silver as well."

"If it's any comfort," Jim said, "I think we may be gaining on him a bit. That stallion of his has been limping some, and he's switched over to riding the pack mare. Doesn't have too much in the way of gear with him, and it's easier on the stallion that way."

"Does he know we're following him?"

"He's been riding up to a height of land every now and then, I imagine to spy us out, or at least our dust cloud. If he has a glass with him, he'll know how many we are."

"So he's not all that far ahead," Dade said.

"Ten or twelve miles. We can close with him tomorrow if we put on a turn of speed."

"Why not today? Our horses are healthy, fresher than his."

"Be dusk by the time we caught him up. Night's not a good time to fight a desperate man. All this is good ambush country. I've seen him shoot. He'd knock your eye out at 300 paces."

Dade scanned the sky, judging the height of the sun above the western horizon. Three hours to sunset, another hour of twilight after that.

"I want to get this over with," he said. "I'm going to send Lenny ahead on our fastest horse, that tall bay he's been holding in reserve. If my Delaware can't kill a damned white man, no Injun can."

"He's your boy," Jim said. "Throw him away if you must."

A few minutes later Lenny LeNapier galloped ahead, warbling his Death Song with that truncated tongue. He had stripped down to a breechclout and carried with him a Hawken rifle, a sinew-backed bow of Osage orangewood, a quiver of arrows, a two-foot-long bowie knife, and a wicked-looking Delaware war club with a six-inch spike mounted in its face.

"Loaded for bear," Jim said, watching him go. He spit in the dust. "Well, as they used to say in Virginia, some days you eat the bear; some days the bear eats you."

He didn't get far. An hour later, as we skirted a dense stand of scrub oak, Jim spotted the bay horse grazing absently on acorns in the shade of the thicket. Riding up, we found Lenny dead, naked and nailed to one of the low, thick-trunked, knotty-limbed trees by three of his arrows, one each through his hands, the third through his lower abdomen. His scalp had been ripped off, and big, slow blue flies fed in snarling clusters atop his raw skull. His chest cavity had been slashed open with his own bowie knife, and when I peered inside I saw that his heart and liver were gone, too. The bear fed well that night, I reckon.

We scraped a shallow grave for him there in the rocky soil of the oak thicket, covered it with slabs of sandstone against the wolves, and camped well out into the prairie that night. Dade was unusually silent as we supped on *biscoche*, the hard, sweet bread of the country, and *venado con chilis colorados*. "He'd been with me a long time," he said at last. "Since '25, that's what, twenty-three years? Came out here from Missouri with about two dozen other Delawares, best damn trappers I ever worked with. But too much in love with war. Slow but sure they went under, six kilt by the Blackfoot, another three by the Snakes. Apaches took off yet half a dozen more. One of them, a fellow named Darby Earnshaw, got et by a griz' up to South Park. Only one of 'em went bad—the one they called 'Big Nigger,' who stood with the insurgents in the Taos *iglesia*. His real name was Edward Chambers. He'd married a woman of the Taos pueblo, but still he had no call to side with the rebels in the rising. Oh, he made a lot of Missouri boys come that day. Some say his rifle, with his squaw reloading for him, accounted for most of the American dead. Was he kilt there or what? I hear it both ways."

"His woman was killed, but he got away," I said. "He's up in the mountains right now, I heard, hiding out till the fuss blows over. Up in the Bayou Salade." I'd met Ed Chambers in '43 or '44, at Pueblo. He was a tough cuss.

"Well, good for him, though he oughtn't to have raised his rifle towards his own countrymen."

Jim laughed at this last statement. "Don't expect patriotism from any Indian," he said. "After what's been done to them, why should they feel brotherly toward the white man? Lands taken by force, whole woodland tribes cast out of their ancestral homes and sent across the Mississippi to a prairie country they've never hunted before, set down cheek by jowl amongst the wild tribes who deem them subhuman, worthy prey for their arrows and lances. Some of them have even been enslaved by unscrupulous whites."

Dade thought about this for a moment. His color heightened. I readied my revolver, for I thought he might explode after the reference to slavery. After all, his mines were worked in large part by New Mexican Indians who might as well be slaves, since their trumped-up prison sentences were interminable. But he must have counted the odds: three of us with ready Colts against only one of him. "Then there was Thomas Gray," he said at last. "Your friend the warrior-woman did for him up on Garnet Creek. But she paid for that murder when I gave her to Mangas Coloradas. I hope her bones are bleaching even as we speak, somewhere up in the Mogollóns."

I wanted to tell him right then and there that she was still alive, and especially when, later that evening, Jim told me that it hadn't been my brother who killed Lenny LeNapier. All the sign indicated Pine Leaf's hand.

IN THE MORNING we came acropper. Descending into the flats east of the Sangre de Cristo Mountains, we followed Owen's track to a point where it intersected with the fresh trail: apparently a mass exodus of vehicles, horses, mules, oxen, burros, men, women, and children. To complicate matters, dogs of all sizes were traveling with this band, making it more difficult to isolate the tracks of Owen's companion from the others. The entire party must have numbered two to three hundred people, on horseback, driving, or walking. They had at least one hundred carts and wagons with them.

"What is this," I asked Jim, "the flight of the Israelites from Egypt?"

"Ciboleros," he said. "Mexican meat hunters. It's a bit early in the season for them, but every year the villages around here sent out bands of buffalo hunters to the Llano Estacado, in groups large enough to defend themselves against the Indians. Women and kids come along to help with the skinning and butchering. They ride down the *cibolas*—buffalo—and lance them to death, Indian fashion. Then they dry the meat, pack it in their carts, and head back across the Pecos, their commissary supplied for the year. It's quite a sight to behold. Usually they hunt in the fall, when the buff' are their fattest, but last winter was a hard one, and I suspect they were having to tighten their belts a bit earlier than usual."

All four of us combed the morass of tracks for the distinctive hoofprints of Owen's horses, but the ground was so crosshatched with wheel marks and hoofprints that it took near an hour to find even a doubtful sign that he'd traveled with them. The *ciboleros* were headed east and a bit south, toward the Pecos River.

"The bastard is traveling with these people to throw us off," Dade said. "Well, they can't be moving too fast, not with wagons. We'll ride them down and have our man."

Spy and I rode at a quick trot along the northernmost edge of the *cibolero* trail, looking for a place where Owen might have broken away from the train. We did not find it until midafternoon.

"Here he goes," Spy said, indicating the prints. "His horse for sure. Still favoring that off hind leg, though not quite so much. He's headed back north again."

"Wait up a minute," Dade said. "His horse is lame. Why would he stick with it? Maybe he swapped it to the Meskins for another, sounder mount, then paid a man to ride the lame one north so's to fool us. Where's his packhorse? Where's his dog? No, I'll bet he's still ridin' with the *ciboleros.*"

"How do we know for sure?" Jim said.

"Let's split up," Dade said. "Me and Griffith will follow out the *ciboleros;* won't take us long to catch them up now. You and Spybuck keep on the tracks of this lame horse. We'll find out from the *ciboleros* just where he's at, and maybe what he's up to. Could be the bastard's heading back to Santa Fe to blow up the rest of the Hidalgito."

CHAPTER V

―――――◆◈◆―――――

Iᴛ ᴡᴀs ɴᴇᴀʀʟʏ sundown by the time Dade and I caught up with the *ciboleros*. They had come upon a small herd of buffalo, perhaps 100 animals, and were in the process of running them. While the hunt went on, the wagons drew up in a rough circle, covering altogether about ten acres, and prepared to make camp for the night.

The spearsmen had ridden out to the herd and driven them into a circulating "surround," the buffalos loping counterclockwise in a thick black mass. Dust towered into the darkling sky. From time to time a rider would dash into the herd, his ten-foot-long lance braced against a leather strap secured to the high-cantled saddle, and drive its two-foot-long blade into a cow buffalo's shoulder just behind the crease. They avoided the bigger bulls: too hard to kill, and the meat was too tough. Sometimes, if the lancer hit bone, his spear broke off short, but most often they struck true. The blades, forged as we later learned of strong Toledo steel, were unbarbed, and as soon as a rider had stabbed one buffalo to the heart, he was out and dashing at the next. We saw one *cibolero* kill six in a run that could not have lasted more than two minutes. These men were skillful. One would not have wished to meet them on the field of battle.

We watched from a rise above the killing ground. When the lancers had made enough meat for the day, they allowed the remaining two dozen buffalo to escape and rode back to the encampment. The lancer who had killed the six buffalo, and whom I had been watching, spotted us on the hilltop. He must have descried us as whites, for he called over two compadres and rode up to meet us without hesitation. He was an older man, tall and gray-haired yet lean as a hungry wolf. Like the others, he was dressed in leather and wore atop his head a low-crowned, flat-brimmed sombrero of finely plaited straw. His lance was bloody halfway down to the tassels that danced gaily near the grip of the shaft.

"Hola, gringos!" he said as he rode up to us. "Como 'sta ustedes? Dónde va?"

This man proved to be Don Tómas Griégo, *alcalde* of the small pioneer village of El Rosario, a fledgling settlement located in the Blue Mountain country north of San Fernández de Taos. After we had introduced ourselves, he escorted us down to the camp. Already the wagons had been wheeled into a defensive circle; guards armed with bows and arrows and a few ancient flintlock *escopetas* were posted against the Indios, and while some of the women built cookfires and prepared the evening meal, others were out ripping hides from the dead buffalo and slicing off thin sheets of buffalo meat. Rawhide lines had been stretched between the wagons, and over these the meat was draped. Don Tómas told us they would camp here tomorrow, which promised to be a typically hot sunny day, during which time the meat would dry, whereupon it would be packed down tight in layers into the meat carts for transport onward. In this fashion the village would replenish its commununal *cocina*. The Mexicans pulverized this dried buffalo meat into a fine powder, which was then liberally mixed with tallow and a sizable dose of *chilis calientes* to form a spicy meat paste, which was stored in glazed *ollas* of great capacity. Tonight, though, we dined on *biscoche*, frijoles, and fresh buffalo hump.

After we'd eaten, a few of the villagers produced their guitars and began singing *canciónes de amor*. The women rolled plump cigarillos of corn husks and the sweet, pungent tobacco of the country and offered them around. We lit them from an ingenious form of lighter made of cotton cord, bound in calico, and run through a slender tin tube no thicker than a goose quill, the women igniting the cotton with deft blows from their firesteels, puffing them to life, then extinguishing the flame by drawing the cord back down into the tube and snuffing it with their thumbs. When one of the women noticed me admiring the device she offered it to me. I refused it as politely as possible, but she insisted. I took it. Who knows? It might come in handy someday.

"Have you seen another gringo traveling in this vicinity recently?" Dade asked the *alcalde*.

"Sí, only yesterday morning," Don Tómas replied. "At first I took him for a Mexican, his Spanish was so good. Just a slight accent. Perhaps an *alemán*—you know, a *germánico*—for there are many of that persuasion in this country since the revolution began in Europe. They come for the mining. But I think now he was a countryman of yours, a *norteamericano*."

"Which way was he traveling?"

"Porqúe?"

"He's a friend of ours. We were supposed to meet him in the mountains but were delayed, and when we reached the rendezvous, alas, he had already gone on. But whether he continued north, as was our plan, or returned to Santa Fe we know not, having lost his track among your many."

The *alcalde* looked at us skeptically. "Your *amigo* rode with us today, senor, then departed."

"Judging by his track when last we saw it," I said, "his horse was going lame."

"Sí." He was wary now, reluctant to say more.

"Did the hoof improve enough while he traveled with you for him to continue his journey?"

"It was not all that lame to begin with."

"Perhaps he purchased another horse from your *caballada*?"

A long pause.

"Quizás."

"Did he?" Dade asked.

"Excuse me, senores," Don Tómas said, rising from the blanket on which he'd been seated. "I must consult with my *ayudantes*."

"Your brother must have paid them plenty," Dade said when he was gone.

"Offer him more."

Dade put ten pesos on the blanket. When the *alcalde* returned, he looked at the silver with ill-concealed distate. He picked the coins up and handed them to Dade. "I believe these must have fallen from your purse, senor. They are not mine."

"Where did our friend go?"

"It is true your friend purchased a horse from us. He then proceeded northward, toward the Río Huerfano. Now if you will forgive me, there are matters of importance I must attend to. I assume you will be on your way . . . *north* . . . in the morning. I will say my farewells now. Buen viaje, senores."

He was a proud and honorable man: having taken money from my brother, he would not sell him out. I was sorry to learn, some weeks later, that the entire party from El Rosario had been wiped out by Comanches on the Llano Estacado. No survivors.

As we prepared to leave camp the following morning, Jim and Spy came riding in from the north, escorting a shamefaced young Mexican on a lame bay stallion.

"Caught up with him last night," Jim said. "Nice enough fellow. Owen paid him twenty pesos to divert us. That's more money than this kid has seen in his whole life."

"Which way did Owen go?" I asked.

"Southwest, the lad said. Probably to Santa Fe."

"God damn it, I was right. He's heading back to the Hidalgito," Dade said. "He led us on a wild goose chase. Let's make tracks!"

We rode hard all that day and half the night on Owen's trail, but he had too great a jump on us. From time to time along the way, checking our backtrail, Spy caught sight of a lone rider: Pine Leaf, the Quick Killer. She was trailing us at a distance just out of rifle shot. I saw her, too. When she noticed me watching, she reined in her mount. We sat our horses, near half a mile apart. But I felt her eyes boring into my brain. I pulled a spyglass from my saddlebags and twisted her into focus. Her face was hard as obsidian, longer, it seemed, and thinner. There was something wrong with her nose. It looked too wide, shiny down the middle. Her black eyes, staring down the tunnel of the glass, had the same mad intensity as those of a buffalo wolf preparing for the kill.

"I think she's lost her mind." Spy sat his horse beside me. "Wilderness will do that. We can't live alone too long. Maybe some small wrinkle in her soul is telling her to rejoin the human race. She could have killed at least one of us anywhere along the trail, or anyway taken our horses. We must give her more time. The decision must be hers."

When we arrived at Santa Fe in the early-morning hours, Dade proceeded straight through to the mine, with Jim and Spy accompanying him. I rode up to the *casa*.

Lamps burned in the kitchen, and when I went to the back door I found it locked and barred. I knocked. The muzzle of my old fuke poked out through a slot in the adobe wall beside the door. "Vamos," came Plover's voice. "Or I shoot."

"Hey, it's me!"

"Válgame Dios! Dillon! Thank God you're here. He has kidnapped Jaime!"

Plover and the two girls were in the kitchen. Gwen was now seven, a tough little tomboy who loved to ride the pinto pony I'd given her last Christmas after "retrieving" it from horse thieves up on the Picketwire. She named it Jocko. The baby was another girl, just over a year old, named Esmeralda for the green of her eyes. We called her Esme for short. She'd recovered from the croup.

"He followed me home from the office yesterday," Plover said. "I didn't recognize him at first—he has a white beard now and white hair down to his shoulders. He was dressed all in leather like a *cibolero*, his coat was a wolfskin, and he wore a big dark sombrero of felt. He had a little brown-and-white dog trotting at his heels. I figured him for some bummer from Missouri, looking for a handout. He rode behind me, about a hundred yards back, all the way home. I wasn't worried, for I always carry my scalp knife. But when I dismounted at the stable, he was standing beside me. All of a sudden. Poof! As if he'd appeared from thin air. 'Plover,' he said in Crow. 'Why is my brother working for that devil Dade? Why is he pursuing me?' Then I knew him."

She brought him into the *casa*, prepared food for him, and coffee; she introduced him to the older children as their long-lost uncle. They were fascinated. The girls loved the little dog and played with it all the while, Esme all coos and smiles.

James was more taken with the man himself. Jaime, we call him now. He is fourteen years of age and among the Crows would already be a fledgling warrior, going off on raids with one soldier band or the other. He'd be stealing horses and lifting Blackfoot hair. Instead he had to attend the new English-language school in Santa Fe, founded only last year. He could only *read* about war and, what was worse, in Latin. Owen captivated him with the tale of our fight with the Gros Ventres, his capture and imprisonment at the copper mines, the Mimbres massacre of the Apaches and their later slaughter of the Santa Ritans, his escape from Mangas, and his subsequent adventures in the mountains of Mexico; of treasures waiting to be discovered in the wild, dangerous *malpais* of the Great West. What boy wouldn't be captivated?

Plover told my brother again and again that I was only with Dade and the Delaware to protect Owen from harm, when and if they caught up with him. Finally he rose from the table and laid a hand on Jaime's shoulder.

"That may well be," he said. "But best intentions are sometimes frustrated by subsequent events. *Con permiso*, I will take young James with me now, to ensure my brother's good will in the future. I hope to see him soon, unarmed and unaccompanied by my sworn enemies."

"You do *not* have my permission to take our son," Plover told him.

"It's all right with me!" Jaime piped up. Plover said she wanted to swat him, pull her knife on Owen, and have at him right then and there. But motherly caution prevailed. Owen was heavily armed—two revolvers in his belt, a bowie knife in the top of his knee-height moccasin—and the girls were in the room. While Jaime gathered his bedroll, foul weather gear, spare clothing, and the double gun I'd given him (an Allen & Wheelock over-and-under in .38 caliber for the rifle barrel, twelve-bore for the shotgun), Owen handed Plover a letter.

"This is for Dillon, but you can read it, too, after we're gone," he said. Then he whistled up his dog and they went out to saddle Jaime's horse, a sturdy little gray Morgan gelding with a pacing gait and a deeply arched neck. As they rode off, Plover said, Owen was asking Jaime how comfortable he was working with large quantities of gunpowder.

THEY BLEW UP the remaining two shafts of the Hidalgito mine that very night, a few hours before I got home. Fortunately, the foreman, Ings, had dismissed the night crew before the bombs went off. No one was killed this time, but the shafts were totally collapsed. I could not help but think that Jaime must have gotten a big bang out of it, though I said nothing like that to my wife. In her current humor she would not have appreciated it.

But of course I was outraged as well once I read Owen's note.

CHAPTER VI

"MY DEAR BUT traitorous brother," it read. "I pen this in haste, having just returned to Santa Fe from a pleasant northward excursion to the vicinity of the Sangre de Cristo Mountains. I recommend them to you for their salubrious waters. I must admit to considerable dismay, however, on seeing you following me north in company with Don Lafcadio Dade and his Delaware butcher boy. Are you working on the side of the Devil these days? I understand from local gossip that you are Dade's man these days, along with your partners Captain Beckwourth and the Shawnee Spybuck. So angered was I at finding you hot on my trail that I decided to return to Santa Fe before continuing my journey. My intention is to impress your wife with the gravity of your transgression. Blood is thicker than *dinero, Hermano mio,* and I am willing to shed some of hers to prove my point, along with that of your children, should you have proved so blessed as to have any. Make no mistake: *I will have total satisfaction* from Senor Dade and his ilk. If you are part of that ilk, you, too, shall feel the heat of my anger, even unto death. If, however, you choose to join me in my battle for justice, you will—if you can see the inevitability of my choice for a final stand—know where to find me. Sincerely, Owen Glendower."

He was mad—*loco* as a loon. A surge of rage flooded through me as I read that awful letter. He'd kill Plover? He would harm my lovely daughters? He would go against even the most sacred ties of blood to ensure my cooperation in his vengeful scheme against Dade. And now he had my unwitting son as his hostage, forcing me to go along with his will. Since early childhood Owen had always demanded compliance with his wishes. If I wanted to hunt rats, he made us fish trout. If I wanted to climb a mountain, he insisted we explore a cave. When I wanted to continue trapping beaver with the Crows, he had had his way, and we ended up digging for gold in White Hart Hollow. And that's what got us into this whole infernal mess to begin with.

"What does he mean by this 'choice for a final stand'?" Plover asked. She stared at me over her glasses, his letter in her hand. "Where is it?"

That stare brought me back to reality. "I guess he means White Hart Hollow," I said at last. "He was always reading romantic novels when we were growing up—Scott, Fielding, Captain Maryatt—and prating on about the beauty of structure. If a story began with some particular event, in some particular place, it must follow an almost circular course back to that place, and the denouement echo in some respect that event which set the whole sequence of events in motion."

"Whatever that means," she said. "But I take it you think he's heading back to where it all began. Well, we'd better pack up our stuff and get going."

"What do you mean?"

"I'm going back north with you, to find your brother and bring back our son."

"What about the girls?"

"We can't leave them here, even if we hired a responsible woman to care for them," she said. "I couldn't stand it. They'll come with us."

"But the baby? She's only just learning to walk."

"My mother packed me on her back for hundreds of miles when I was an infant," Plover said. "Or else I rode in a bundle on a travois, behind the dogs or horses. By the time I was five years old, I had my own pony. Gwen can ride, and I will pack Esme along, on my back if necessary." She rose from her chair and came over to me, took off her glasses, leaned down, and kissed me atop the head. "I will not remain here worrying about you and tending to my knitting like these gringo cows. I'm a Sparrowhawk, by God. I fly. And if necessary, I kill."

I SLEPT UNTIL nearly noon the following day. When I woke at last, it was to find that Plover had made all the arrangements for our departure. She'd ridden down into town and asked our wrangler, a reliable New Mexican named Pánfilo Ramirez, to occupy the *casa* with his entire family during our absence. His wife and children would love it. They would tend to the animals—there were chickens to be fed, half a dozen porkers to be swilled, a cow to be milked twice daily, and about two dozen long-horned beef cattle, wild as deer, to keep an eye on out in the pasture. Pánfilo's eldest daughter, Rosalinda, could read and write, so she would tend to the office affairs of the B, S&G stock detective agency during our absence. Plover had packed a kit with Esme's necessaries, while Gwen had stuffed her own bedroll with plenty of extra clothing and her favorite kachina doll. Plover was traveling light, Indian fashion, and had added only a few items to my always-ready traveling pack.

As I came into the *cocina*, I found Spy and Jim seated at the kitchen table drinking coffee. I showed them Owen's letter.

"He'll head for White Hart Hollow now; I'm sure of it," Jim said. "But Dade doesn't know that. He's organizing what he calls a *posse comitatus*— a lynch mob made up of his local caballero pals and whatever Missouri toughs he can find."

"He'll find plenty, the money he pays," Spy said.

"Dade says they'll ride Owen down now, once and for all. He's even sent a man up into the mountains near Taos to find that Delaware, the Big Nigger. I know the fellow. He's a damn good tracker, a far tougher case than the late Mister LeNapier. Dade's arranging a pardon for him from the governor."

Dade didn't want us along on this hunt. He'd made that quite clear to Jim and Spy while they were standing around the ruins of his mine.

"He says we purposely dawdled and misled him on the trail these past few days," Jim said. "And by refusing to join Lenny in that damn fool attack on Owen up in the Sangre de Cristos, we 'needlessly if not indeed maliciously brought about the death of my good friend and trusted *secretário* Monsieur Leonard LeNapier.' He's even considering pressing charges."

Well, we could count on no further help from Lafcadio Dade in our business affairs; that was for sure. As for my dream rancho in California, forget it. . . .

"Dade's still going to need a couple of days to pull his posse together," I said. "We can get the jump on him if we start today."

"If he doesn't know where Owen's headed," Spy said, "he'll probably go to his new mines in Colorado first off. He's already sent riders ahead with warnings to the supervisors to take all precautions against more bombs. That'll give us more time."

With luck we could get to White Hart Hollow a week in advance of Dade's gang, intercept Owen before he made his attack on the mine, rescue Jaime, and hustle them both out of that country—even if we had to overpower my brother and carry him off in chains to do so.

The sooner we left the better.

Plover was out at the stable, saddling horses.

"So, she's coming with us," Jim said.

"There's no gainsaying her. The girls are coming as well."

"You've allowed her to get too sassy," he said. "Give a woman an inch; she'll take a mile—no, two miles and half. Perhaps you should consider a brief course of the Plume treatment."

He reached for the tomahawk at his belt.

"Goddamnit, cut it out."

"Easy," he said. "Aw, hell, I was a just young hothead in those days. Maybe I shouldn't have clouted her. She was a good wife while it lasted. But you don't have to worry about Plover and the girls slowing us down. Crow women travel well. They're tough, these Indians. They've been wandering for longer than they can remember. I've known many a woman to give birth on the trail while the band's on the move. The whole business is over in twenty minutes, wherewith she rejoins the main body as if nothing had happened. The kids start riding horseback when they can sit up. I've known some who could ride before they could walk. Esme's not too young to learn. And I've watched Gwen ride. She'll do."

"Girls make better riders than men anyway," Spy said. "They're lighter, easier on the horse. As for fighting . . . well, look at Pine Leaf."

A point well taken, but perhaps the Quick Killer had carried that quality a bit too far. Still, Spy's mentioning her renewed a worry, and gave me an idea.

"I assume she's still out there, somewhere in the hills," I said. "She'll follow us up to White Hart Hollow."

"No doubt about it," Jim said.

"But on the way back to Santa Fe she allowed us to see her," I told him. "It's as if she'd like to approach us but doesn't quite dare. You know how a horse that's left the herd and run wild for a time is pulled by the sight of your horses but can't quite get up the nerve to come in? Spy thinks Bar-che-am-pe may want to rejoin our merry band. Perhaps you could get her to do it. After all, you're her old war chief and would-be husband. At least, if she'll talk with you, we might be able to figure out her intentions in all this. I must admit I haven't been sleeping well knowing she's out there, not after having seen what she did to Lenny. And now with Plover and the girls along, well . . . What do you say?"

"She never really liked me," Jim said. "But I guess I can try."

PLOVER AND I made a quick dash down to the *oficina* to show Rosalinda what to do while we were gone. It only amounted to collecting payment from the gringo rancher, Eli Boardman, whose horses Spy had retrieved from the Apaches last week, and taking the names of any prospective new customers, explaining to them that we would be back in a month or six weeks. As we went back out to the buckboard, Plover saw her friend Doña Ana across the road. Doña Ana was a blind old Pueblo woman, a *bruja* and *profeta* who told fortunes. Plove only half-believed her prophecies, which were all rosy at any rate, but paid her handsomely for them nonetheless. She felt sorry for the old dame, whose eyes had been put out by a brutal husband of hers whom she'd caught in flagrante delicto with another woman.

"I want to say good-bye to Doña Ana," Plove said. "Come on over with me; let's see what she says about this journey we're about to undertake."

"Ah, la Senora Griffit'," said the old dame, all gums and winks and wrinkles. Tobacco juice had dried in the runnels of her sagging jowls, and sprouts like those on potatoes that have been too long sequestered grew from her witchy chin. "I knew you would come to consult me today, though I had expected you earlier. The baby has recovered from her illness as I predicted, no?"

Plove explained that we were about to depart on a hazardous journey to the north to save our son from a *bandido* and asked her to foretell the outcome.

Doña Ana sat there a moment, summoning up the proper gravity. "I knew your son was in grave peril, though I knew not the source. Your *esposo* is with you now; that I can feel," she said at last. "I must place my hand on his brow to know what will transpire."

"Kneel down before her," Plover told me.

"Don't be silly. This is stupid. Let's just pay her something and get going."

"Please, for me?" Plover asked.

I knelt. Doña Ana spit in her grubby palm and slapped it to my forehead. Tobacco-flavored spittle ran down my face and stung my eyes. Doña Ana seemed to go into a trance, then inhaled sharply in surprise. In a suddenly deep, throaty voice she intoned; "You will lose something precious to you—your life, perhaps, or your love? I see bodies lacquered in blood. Skulls green with mold. I see fire, strangulation by smoke, a heart lost in smoke, drifting away on the smoky horses. Do not undertake this journey. It is fraught with peril—a *jornada del muerto*."

When I arose, Plover was ashen beneath her tan. Her eyes seemed glazed.

"Are you happy now?" I asked her. "Come on; this is a lot of rubbish. She doesn't want you to go because of the money. Every day for the past year you've given her a few pennies. She needs it to live. I suggest that you give her—here, five dollars. No, make it twenty." I fetched a gold eagle from my pocket and thrust it into Doña Ana's palm. Then I grabbed Plover's arm and hurried her to the buckboard.

CHAPTER VII

WE LEFT THE *casa* well before sundown and rode hard to the north, on into the dark. We were out of the mountains now, in open prairie on the high road to Taos. A three-quarter moon rose before the trail got too dim to follow, so we pressed on. Gwen seemed tireless astraddle her pinto, and Esme slept soundly in a pack on Plover's back. Toward midnight we halted and made a quick, rough camp. Supper was tortillas, chilis, and beans. No coffee. Plover was up before dawn, making breakfast. When the smell of ham, beans, and coffee woke me, the sun was just clearing the horizon. We hit the trail again. Barring disaster, it would take us at least three weeks to cover the distance from Santa Fe to White Hart Hollow—seven or eight hundred miles—and we all wanted to make time.

Once out on the prairie, Plover seemed a new woman. Or, even better, the girl I had known and loved of old. She was dressed in the height of Crow fashion: her old deerskin shift with all its beads and spangles, her hair flowing loose in the wind behind her. The reading spectacles were stowed in her possible sack, dangling from the tall pommel of her saddle, and her eyes seemed young again. As we rode onward, day after day, she told the girls Crow stories, of how the world came into being, of the tricksters and heroes of her tribe, tales of talking animals and foolish humans, and of the great wars with the Blackfeet and Cheyenne. She told them at first in English and Spanish, but slowly she shifted to the tongue of the Sparrowhawk People, which Gwennie had known as an infant but long since abandoned in favor of those other languages. Suddenly I realized that in their day-to-day conversations Gwen was talking Sparrowhawk again.

I recalled a time, trapping with Bill Sublette up in the Winds, when I mentioned that I was married to a Crow woman. "Good for you," he said. "They're a cuddly lot, very handy around the lodge, too. But I do not think I could last very long, were I married to one."

"Why not, Bill?"

"Well, in my experience they talk your ear off. Jabber jabber jabber all day long, and often well into the night."

Thank God for that loquacity, I thought now out on the trail.

Esme, who had tanned up under the kiss of the sun so that her eyes glowed like their namesake gems in an Indian-dark face, listened to these tales enraptured. She rarely cried and now spent most of each day riding just forward of Plover in the saddle. Soon I noticed that my wife's hand, which had been resting lightly on Esme's back or shoulder to help the child keep her balance, was now touching her only occasionally. Then not at all. A week up the trail and we allowed Esme to ride by herself, on one of the half-dozen spare horses we'd trailed along with us, a gentle elderly mare with a gait smooth as tallow. Spy took to riding beside the child, ready to catch her if she teetered, but Esme seemed born to the saddle. He was fond of both my daughters. In the mornings he and Gwen would saddle the horses, two by two, and buck the wildness out of them before we mounted up. In the process, he made a proper bronc peeler of her.

Gwen sometimes rode at the head of the column, alongside Jim. He was teaching her such things as how to distinguish a horse track from that of a mule, a deer from a prongbuck (the antelope has no dewclaws). He pointed out elk feeding on the horizon by the flash of their dirty yellow rump hairs and once a huge grizzly, white in that hot sunlight, lumbering toward the mountains like an ox wagon. He named the hawks that circled over the hills, named them both in the Crow tongue and in English or Spanish. He taught her how to select good wood for our cookfires, hardwoods like scrub oak or mesquite or madrone that wouldn't make too much smoke and yet would give off an intense heat, then die down after the meal to an enduring bed of coals that could be banked to last the night. He allowed her to help him at night, when he'd shot some meat for our larder, by cleaning and reloading his rifle. When she failed to get the barrel entirely clean the first time, he made her boil more water, pour it down the muzzle, and then work the brass brush through it once again, followed by patches on the cleaning rod, until the bore was spotless. It amazed me that she obeyed him without argument until Plover pointed out the obvious: "He's Tío Jim; you're only Papa."

Indeed, it was sharp-eyed Gwenivar who descried our first visitors on the trail, a hunting party of Indians following a buffalo herd north of the Arkansas River. I had been watching the dust from the herd, trying to determine the line of their movement, when Gwen, who was riding beside me, said, "Papa, those aren't buffalo behind the herd. Those are men on ponies." I hadn't even seen them up to that point. Now I pulled the spyglass from my saddlebag and focused on the riders. "I can't make out their tribe, but ride back and tell Jim that we may have company soon. Warn your mother to stay back with Esme, and you stay back there, too."

The Indians had spotted us by this time and altered their course in our direction. I checked the Hawken to ensure it was loaded and placed a fresh copper cap on the lock. Jim and Spy came galloping up.

"I think they're Cheyennes," Jim said after studying them through the glass. "There's an outlaw band of them in this country. I made their acquaintance ten years ago or so when I was trading up here for William Bent. A testy lot, if it's Old Smoke's outfit. Better check our locks and loads."

We spread out abreast of one another, about ten yards apart, so as to present them with three distinct targets rather than a knot of men who could be covered by a single blast of buckshot from a fusee. The Indians, a dozen of them, reined in their ponies just beyond rifle range. I was glad to see they were not painted for war, but nonetheless they presented a fearsome picture, wild black hair blowing in the prairie wind, hard faces dark with the sun, eagle plumes fluttering from their lances, and scalps flapping down the outer seams of their leggings. A few of them wore serapes taken from Mexicans they'd killed or captured, but the rest were bare-chested. An older man with much gray in his tangled hair rode out from the band at a gallop.

Suddenly I was aware that Gwen was sitting her horse just beside me and slightly to the rear. "Dammit, Gwennie, I told you to stay back with Mother."

"I wanted to see the wild Indians," she said.

"Jim, tell her . . ."

But now Beckwourth was riding out to meet the leader. They stopped about twenty yards from one another.

"Old Smoke!" Jim shouted in Cheyenne. Both Spy and I had enough of that tongue to follow the exchange that ensued. "It is I, the Medicine Calf of the Crows. Come in and drink black soup with us."

"Ah, yes, I can see it now!" he yelled back, squinting his eyes to slits in his wrinkled brown face. "You are indeed O-tun-nee, the Crow from Bent's Fort! You always gave us strong whiskey! You traveled with Left Hand in those days"—that was the Indian name of Andrew Sublette, Bill's younger brother and a partner of Beckwourth in the early forties—"but now you travel with women and children. Or is that Shawnee a man?" Old Smoke laughed. "Do you wish to trade? We have no robes, and that is why we chase the buffaloes. But we are dry, and a pot of *mo'kohtávi-hohpe* would taste good right about now."

He wheeled his pony and galloped full tilt back to his men.

Again I told Gwen to ride back to her mother. "Ask her to brew some coffee for our guests. And stir in plenty of sugar."

"Aren't we going to fight them?" Gwen asked.

"No, thank God. Now get a move on."

Her face fell, but she obeyed.

From Old Smoke we learned that the road ahead, crossing the ridge that separated the Arkansas River from the South Platte, was bone dry. It had been a near-rainless spring, and the waterholes along the way had gone alkaline through the heat of the summer, then dried up entirely. He advised us to stay close to the mountains as we proceeded north, for there we would still find an occasional spring creek that hadn't submerged into the sand yet.

"Near the Greasy River," the South Platte, "you will find the village of your friend Mo-he-nes-to, the Bugling Elk," he said. "There you will be welcome. I wish we had robes to trade with you, fat meat to offer you, but we are poor right now."

Mo-he-nes-to was another outlaw chieftain, he and his small band of warriors driven away from the mainstream Cheyennes for transgressions against the All-God, in most cases the killing of another Cheyenne but sometimes nothing more than a failure to observe certain taboos.

Gwen found the old chief fascinating. She slipped away from Plover's side and eased slowly over to him where he sat crosslegged before the campfire. She hunkered down at his knee and began stroking the scalp hair sewed to his leggings.

Old Smoke laughed. "She will make a good wife someday, always urging her husband on to greater coups."

"Perhaps she will be a soldier-woman herself," I said.

The old man frowned at that remark, then finished off his coffee and held out the tin cup for more. "A soldier-woman," he said. "Such a one is following you, do you know?"

"Yes," Jim said. "Have you seen her?"

"Ask Oh-kum here about her," Old Smoke said, indicating a young warrior seated beside him. "The Little Wolf nearly lost his hair to her yesterday."

"I cut her track where she forded the Flint-bottomed River," their name for the Arkansas, "and followed her over the prairie for a while," the young man said, unsmiling. "When I finally caught sight of this person, I could see it was a woman, though dressed like a man. An Apache, I thought. She rode a gray but trailed two ponies with her, a bay and a sorrel, as for a long journey. What could a lone woman be doing this far from the Apachería? I thought to catch her up and, if she was young and pretty, to make her a wife. She never looked back, but when I followed her into an ash brake near the river suddenly she was behind me. Running at me on the gray. An arrow nocked and full-drawn on her bow. I spurred my horse out of there fast, let me tell you. What a face! Like death itself: black with the sun, lined cruelly by war and hardship, with no spark of life behind the glitter of those wide, cruel eyes. I am no coward, but in that moment I felt my bowels turn to water."

"She is no Apache," Jim said.

"I thought not," Little Wolf said. "Of what tribe is she then?"

"She was born a Crow, but now she is a tribe unto herself. She is Tats-ah-das-ay-go, the Quick Killer."

"Such a tribe deserves extermination."

"No," Old Smoke said. "She needs a man strong enough to run her, to fuck some softness into her heart. Fatten her with babies and she will quit the war trail. I would take her myself, my old wife having died last winter, but I prefer younger females. That girl there"—he pointed to Gwen, who had been sitting beside him—"who just stole my knife, she would make me a good wife in a few years. Will you sell her to me?"

"No," I said. "Gwen, give him back his knife."

"She may keep it, with my wish that she use it with good fortune. I may forget her, but perhaps she'll remember me." He got up from the fire and mounted his pony. "Who knows? Perhaps someday I'll appear in your camp to reclaim it."

With that Old Smoke departed, his men at a gallop behind him. Soon they were dust on the horizon.

WE FOUND MO-HE-NES-TO'S village at the confluence of the South Platte and Crow Creek, near where the town of Greeley, Colorado, now stands. Jim was welcomed like a long-lost brother, until the Indians learned he had brought no whiskey, as in days of yore. We assuaged them with gifts of Navajo blankets, gunpowder, and bar lead, which Jim had had the foresight to pack along on one of our mules. "Yes, I used to trade liquor for robes," he admitted, "but truly it's the most infernal practice ever entered into by man. Nothing but trouble comes of it: war, thievery, murder, poverty, death. But think of the profits. A gallon of whiskey costs thirty cents in Saint Louis. You add four gallons of water and sell the resultant forty pints at a buffalo robe apiece. Each robe will bring five dollars back east. That's $200 on a thirty-cent investment. I'd show up at this camp with 200 diluted gallons—1,600 pints. That's $8,000 a visit. All the poor redskin got out of it was a headache, and a thirst for more firewater. Meanwhile the buffalo are slowly being exterminated, and with so little remorse that their very hides are now known among the tribes as 'a pint of whiskey.' "

"Then why did you do it?"

"It was the only way the Indians would trade their robes. I was ambitious. I don't do it anymore."

From Mo-he-nes-to we learned that the Oglalas were raiding along the Oregon Trail and had last been sighted between the headwaters of Lodgepole Creek, which lay not far to our north, and the Laramie River. "Go west from here, through the Medicine Bow Mountains," he said. "You have no wagons to slow your progress; your horses look strong. This way you will not encounter the Sioux. Traveling fast, you can make Green River in five days easily. Fort Bridger is not far beyond."

We wanted to stop at the fort to recruit both ourselves and our riding stock, as well as ask its lord and master, the Blanket Chief himself, about conditions to the north. Who knows? Owen may have stopped at Fort Bridger for the same reasons, en route to his destination.

THAT EVENING WE all took advantage of Crow Creek for much-needed baths. Plover and the girls went separately, for modesty's sake: my wife had picked up this fear of nakedness in the course of living with civilized people. When they returned, Plover was clearly shaken. "I saw her," she said.

"Who?"

"Bar-che-am-pe. She appeared suddenly out of the willows across from the pool where we were bathing. She stood there in the shadows, still as a deer, watching us. I could not make her out at first, and eased my way back to the bank where I'd left the pistol. But the setting sun broke clear of the willows across the way and struck her face, and then I knew her. It was awful."

"What do you mean?"

"Her face is ruined."

"How?"

"Her nose has been split, by Mangas probably. They must have caught her and tortured her. I hear that it's the custom of the Apaches to slice the noses of wives who've been unfaithful. There are other things as well. . . . No, I don't want to talk about it anymore."

"Tell me," I said. She was shivering now, huddled beside me at the fire. I put my arm around her and held her close. "I must know. Anything we can discover about her may tell us if we must fear her, or if we might recruit her for an ally. Tell me, Plove."

"I think Mangas cut off her breasts. She lifted her shirt. Just scars. . . ."

I sat there for a while, holding her until the shaking stopped.

"She was my hero when I was a girl," Plover said. "All of us loved her; we admired her courage and her scorn for death. She was better than a man at war. Stronger than the Medicine Calf, braver than Long Hair even, the deadliest soldier of our tribe. And she was beautiful. All the men wanted her, especially the Medicine Calf. But now, no more. No man could love her." She shuddered under my arm. "Those eyes . . . The eyes that stared at me there from the riverbank were those of an animal."

"Easy now," I said. "Did you try to talk to her?"

"I didn't have the wit to try. By the time I recovered my senses she'd faded into the shadows again. She was gone. Like a ghost. Like smoke on the wind."

Chapter VIII

F ORT BRIDGER IS located on Black's Fork of Green River, with
the snowy Uintah Mountains rising far to the south. A simple trading post with a blacksmith's shop and an ample supply of foofaraw
to serve the needs of the many wagons that pause on the way to
Oregon, it is not much to look at: just a square of peeled poles
daubed with mud, surrounding a few slant-roofed log cabins and
sheds, and surrounded by about twenty-five scruffy lodges full of
trappers, their Indian wives, their families, and their fleas. But to us,
after a rough crossing of the Medicine Bows and the arid mesas beyond them, it looked like Eden. Tall cottonwoods, willows, green
grass, watered by the braided crystal cold water of the Black, made
the area an oasis in the midst of a prickly pear desert. All the horses
needed new shoes, the girls needed rest, and I wanted to learn the
news of the country.

Jim Bridger is a tall hombre, lanky, with the stooped slouch of
mountain man or an Indian. He looks far older than his years, which
in this year numbered only forty-four, four fewer than the Medicine
Calf's. Usually full of horseplay and tall stories, Bridger was unwont-
edly somber during our stay. His daughter Mary Ann had been mur-
dered the previous November by Cayuse Indians at the Oregon

mission Waiilatpu, on the Walla Walla River, in what has come to be known as the Whitman Massacre.

The Whitmans, man and wife, were missionaries to the Cayuse. Marcus Whitman was a doctor as well as a preacher, and the Cayuse figured him for a *brujo*, a witchman, especially after their children and many of the grown-ups as well started dying from measles and dysentery, imported from the East by emigrants along the Oregon Trail. On November 29, 1847, after Whitman had conducted a burial service for three children of a Cayuse chief, the Indians followed him back to the mission. There, without warning, they tomahawked him. When his gentle wife, Narcissa, she of the golden-red hair, rushed to his aid, they shot her. Mary Ann Bridger and little Helen Mar, the daughter of Joe Meek, another mountain man, died along with nine others in the slaughter that ensued. It was a sorry day.

Bridger had known Whitman from the beginning. On his way west the first time in 1836, the doctor had removed a Blackfoot arrowhead from Gabe's back. It had been wandering around in there since the fight at Pierre's Hole in 1832, and a great knot of gristle had formed around it. When the good doctor expressed amazement at how Bridger could have survived this wound without a fatal gangrene setting in, Gabe told him, "Meat don't spoil in the mountains."

Would that it were true.

The two Jims, Beckwourth and Bridger, had been friends since the mid-1820s, trapped many a stream together, fought the Blackfeet side by side.

"Where you headed, Medicine Calf?"

"You know that gold mine Lafe Dade has up in White Hart Hollow?"

"Yep. Dadeville, they called it."

"We're headed up there for a look-see."

"Won't find much when you get there."

"How's that?"

"Grovan."

"Wiped it out?"

"Last spring. Lock, stock, and barrel. A bunch of my trappers was through there last month."

"Nobody left?"

"Ghosts," Bridger said. "The boys got another name for the place now."

"What's that?"

"Deadville."

BRIDGER HAD SEEN no one resembling Owen or Jaime passing through the country on their way north, nor in any direction, but said that a Ute named Walking Bear might have. Walking Bear was still at the fort. We found him in the trader's store, swapping buffalo robes for white man clothes, iron pots, and arrowheads.

Yes, he told us, a few days ago on his way into the fort from the west he had seen two whites, a man with long white hair and a beard and a boy. Three pack mules, heavy-laden.

"Was the boy riding a gray with a steeply arched neck?"

"Yes, a fine pony."

"Did they have a dog with them, a little one that barked a lot?"

"A very fierce little dog. Yes."

"Could you tell what they were packing on the mules?"

"Kegs," the Ute said. "Like the small barrels that contain gunpowder. Two to a mule."

At 50 pounds a keg, that made 300 pounds of powder, enough to blow the padres' mine to perdition.

"Where were they headed."

"North, toward the Buenaventura it looked like."

"Didn't you speak with them?"

"I wanted to. Perhaps I could have bought that gray pony from them, or at least the fierce little dog. It would have made good eating at a feast. Whoever ate of it, he, too, would have grown strong for war. I wanted to trade, I had plenty of robes right then. But the white beard had strange eyes. I feared he was a sorcerer, and rode on."

"When was this?"

"Two suns ago. In the morning."

I thanked him and bought him a new three-point blanket to express my gratitude.

"So they're ahead of us," Jim said.

"I'd wanted to rest the horses here a couple of days, but I guess we can't. The girls need some rest, too."

"Maybe you should leave Plover and the girls here," Spy said. "We could borrow fresh mounts from Gabe and ride on, top speed. The three of us should be able to overtake them before they get to White Hart Hollow."

"Plover won't agree to it."

" 'Agree' be damned!" Jim said. "Who wears the pants in your family? Order her to stay, and if she gives you sass, give her your fist."

"I couldn't do that. My father used to whup my mam when I was a little boy. It turned her into a mean, sour woman with no love in her soul, not even for her children."

"Well then, ask Gabe for the loan of fresh horses, anyway. And if it don't shine, Spy and I can chip in and we'll buy some. They're only asking twenty-five to fifty dollars a pony here. Times have changed in the mountains. That beats Saint Louis prices in the old days."

Bridger was reluctant to lend us the horses, but he had plenty for sale. "You fellows are heading into a fight," he said. "I can smell it on you. I don't know who you're gunnin' for and don't rightly want to know, but if you leave your hair up there in the hollow, I won't get my ponies back."

"What kind of a price can you give us if we buy?" I asked.

"Let's go out to the lot and tap some hooves, look at some teeth," he said. "You tell me what you want, and I'll give you a fair bargain."

We bought a dozen fresh horses from him, and indeed he gave us a good price: $325. But it about cleaned us out.

"Don't worry," Bridger said. "If you survive this journey, I'll buy them back from you at a decent price. If you don't, it will mean nothing anyway. That's how it is in the mountains, always has been. Always will be, too, I reckon. You pays your money and you takes your chance."

We packed our gear, saddled and loaded the horses, and prepared to move out. It was still two hours to sunset.

"By the way," Jim said to Bridger after he'd mounted his horse, "if

Old Smoke should show up asking about us, tell him we headed toward Salt Lake."

"Smoke?" Bridger said. "Hell, that old varmint and his boys was here just before y'all arrived. Bought some gunpowder, bar lead, and a keg of whiskey. Said he was off on a wife hunt."

"Which way did he go?" I asked.

Bridger scratched his long lopsided chin. "Hell, I don't know." His arm described a circuit of the west. "Out yonder, I guess."

JUST BEFORE LAST light we saw Pine Leaf shadowing us, standing her horse on a ridge to the east, allowing us again to see her. Jim spotted her first.

"She wants to talk," he said. "I know it in my bones."

"Let's go up there," I said. He nodded. I told Spy and Plover to proceed onward to a creek we had marked in the near distance and there pitch camp. Jim and I rode up to where we had seen Pine Leaf. She wasn't there anymore. Jim saw horse tracks, though.

"She's asking us to follow her," he said.

"Playing games?"

"I don't think she's that devious, not now. No. As I said the other day, she's become like a horse or a dog that's gone back to the wild. It can scarce remember its time with men, but if it was treated well, maybe it would want to go back. Still, its wild instinct tells it to flee at man's approach. Let me tell you a story. When I first went west with General Ashley, I had every reason to leave Saint Louis. I'd thrashed the blacksmith I was indentured to, who'd forbidden me to chase girls during my time off. I was very reluctant to return to the city. Perhaps there was a reward outstanding for my capture. But more than that, I took pride in my ability to survive in the wilderness. I didn't want to leave it."

"Well, whatever the case," I said, "we have to confront her. And damn quick, too. With Old Smoke out here on the prowl, I don't want to leave Plover and the girls hanging out there with only Spy to guard them."

"Let's do it," Jim said.

By now the light was almost gone from the sky. Darkness descended fast. Jim never tracked surer or better than on that evening, and we rode down Pine Leaf's trail at a hard gallop. We found her on another ridge, maybe a mile east of where we'd first seen her. In fact, we almost collided with her there in the dim dark blue of early night.

She was halted just under the lip of the ridge, looking downhill into the draw beyond. She raised her hand as we came up, not looking back. Then she pointed below.

I dropped off my horse and crawled to the top. There was a small fire burning down in the draw. Figures moved around in its faint, flickering glow. Indians. Cheyennes. Old Smoke and his boys, a dozen of them at least. I crawled back down and mounted my pony.

"They're following you," Pine Leaf said in the Sparrowhawk tongue. Her voice sounded cracked and rusty from disuse. I noticed streaks of white in her hair, which she had chopped back to the length of a white man's. Then she turned to look at us. The scar on her face glowed faintly even in the dark. Her eyes glinted.

"Let's kill them," she said.

"No, not yet," Jim said. I hadn't heard that harsh, authoritative tone in a long while, it was his war chief's voice. "Too dark to shoot straight. Better we steal their ponies."

Pine Leaf almost smiled. "Is-ko-chu-e-chu-re," she said. "The Enemy of Horses."

In my old days with the Crow I'd known Jim to crawl right up to a Blackfoot chieftain's tepee and cut his favorite war pony free of its tether, then sneak out of camp lying flat on its back, with no one the wiser. This wouldn't be quite that difficult, I hoped. Still, it would be much more dangerous than our California expeditions. There we merely rounded up unguarded horses grazing the empty grasslands near the ranchos and missions and drove them away. Here armed and murderous men were camped only a hundred yards from the herd.

We picketed our ponies so they wouldn't wander off, then stripped down to loincloths and moccasins. I saw the scars on Pine Leaf's chest which Plover had mentioned. They weren't all that ugly. She looked no worse than many an Indian brave I'd seen after a session or two of the Sun Dance torture, hanging with hooks through his chest from the top of a lodgepole, or dragging a buffalo skull attached in a similar manner until the muscles tore out. Combined with her short hair, though, it was odd: you would no longer take her for a woman.

The Cheyenne pony herd was grazing in the grassy bottom of the draw, beyond the campfire. A single guard watched the herd. He looked like a boy. Carrying only our knives and a six-shooter apiece, we dropped to our bellies and slithered like snakes into the sage. More easily said than done, what with the prickly pears that covered the ground. Snakes have armored plates on their bellies. Men don't. In the dark you only knew you'd encountered a prickly pear when it stuck you. The spines often broke off in your bare flesh, then dug in deeper as you crawled on. But you couldn't afford the sound of a gasp or the time it would take to remove them. The horse guard was alert. We saw him circling among the ponies, walking slow and quiet, pausing at odd moments to listen for sounds that might indicate approaching danger.

"We might have to kill him," Jim whispered to me. "Can you do it?"

I thought about that for a moment. The young Cheyenne looked to be about Jaime's age. I'd have to kill him with the knife so that a yell wouldn't alert the other outlaws. If I didn't agree to the job, Jim would have Pine Leaf do it. I had no doubt but that she'd do a quiet, efficient piece of work. The kid would be dead before he knew his throat had been cut. Again I thought of Jaime. . . .

"Yes," I answered.

I worked my way into the cluster of ponies nearest him. I hummed a low, quiet Horse Song I'd learned years ago among the Crow on similar raids. The horses stared down at me. The horse guard was also singing a Horse Song, to keep the herd calm. He couldn't hear me. One by one I cut the picket ropes holding the horses, without frightening them. Jim and Pine Leaf were doing the same. Then one of the horses nickered. The kid stopped singing. He walked over in my direction. I flattened myself to the ground, trying to make myself thin as a tortilla. I was lying square on top of a prickly pear, and the flatter I made myself, the deeper its spines sank into my chest.

Jim must have seen what was happening, because when the Cheyenne was only a step away from me I heard a clink come from the darkness. Like a knife tapping a pistol barrel. The Cheyenne turned toward it, raised his fusee. As he cocked the hammer, I rose behind him, knife in hand, and rapped him hard on the base of the skull with the haft. I caught him as he dropped. He'd be out for a while.

All the horses were free to run. I mounted a pony bareback and began to crowd the others away from camp. Jim and Pine Leaf followed suit. We kept the ponies to a slow, quiet walk. Jim went ahead to lead the herd. They were Indian ponies, unshod, and if a hoof hit a stone it would make only a dull *thwock*. The more distance we could put between the herd and the outlaws in the next few minutes, the better. Indians on foot are loath to move fast, even when pursuing their own horses. Particularly at night. There's too much chance of ambush.

Tonight it took a little longer than I remembered. We reached the break in the draw, where the ridge tailed off. Our horses looked up from where they'd been grazing. One of them nickered. The Cheyenne ponies moved toward them. Pine Leaf came up next to me out of the dark, riding a pinto and leading three other horses. I'd been herding the remaining six or seven ponies. Jim's teeth flashed in the dark, a happy grin. I slipped off the pony I was riding and mounted my own horse. We drove the herd slowly to the west, staying to bare, rocky ground where we could find it. For half an hour we continued at a walk; then Jim signed us to gallop.

"They won't come after us till morning, if then," he said. "Old Smoke will recognize this as my work, and he remembers me of old, back in the days when they called me the Bloody Arm. He might come after us later, but not on foot. It'll take 'em nearly all day to hike back to the fort for more horses."

We rode on to our rendezvous with Spy and Plover.

Chapter IX

PINE LEAF SLEPT with Beckwourth that night.

WE BROKE CAMP at first light, rode hard all day to the north, and by sundown were in sight of the Encantadas. Once again I was put in mind of sawteeth, ready to rip the heart of heaven itself.

Pine Leaf rode beside Jim, saying nothing to anyone but him.

The sun was still high when we made camp on a ridge in the pine-clad foothills of the range. Spy, Plover, and Gwen busied themselves preparing supper. To replenish our larder the Shawnee had killed a half-grown buffalo cow the previous day, and while we waited for the meat to dry into jerky he prepared his *menudo norteño* from its honeycomb tripe and one of its feet. He was busy now fussing over his ingredients. Pine Leaf was tending the horses, rubbing them down and checking hooves.

I took Jim aside. "How is she?"

"Wild."

"How do you mean?"

"I'd rather not talk about it. But I didn't, well, *impose* myself upon her, if that's what you're getting at."

"Does she know about Owen's being alive? Does she know we're going after him?"

"I didn't mention it. Neither did she. We talked old Sparrowhawk stories most of the night. Heroes of the past. How the People found fire. That kind of thing. She's . . . like a child. Just learning to talk. Sometimes I think she doesn't remember anything that happened to her after leaving Crow country. But then she glances down at her chest and turns away. Goes dead quiet."

I was silent for a moment, too, thinking about that.

Jim said, "I think we've got to go slow and easy with her right now. I've seen this before, too many times. Usually it's white children, girls especially, who've been taken captive by one tribe or another. In their minds they revert to childhood to forget the horror of their experiences. But they always seem to hold onto something they loved in their old lives. A scrap from an old calico dress. The sole of a boot. A song or nursery rhyme they sing over and over when they're really down. Maybe it's a way of escape. I want Pine Leaf's scrap to be me, for right now at least. I don't want to remind her of Owen until she's good and ready for it."

"She's your soldier. Do what you think best."

The spicy scent of toasting chilis—*anchos* and *poblanos*—reached my nostrils, along with that of the soup itself, with its onion, garlic, peppercorns, and tripe, simmering uncovered over the fire. The quartered calf's foot bubbled along with them, softening and blending its rich flavor with the other ingredients. Later Spy would strip the meat from the bones and knuckles, chop it into chunks, and toss it back into the mix. Spy always added some hot chilis to his *menudo*, what he called *cuaresmeños*. He'd brought the seeds north with him from the Mexican state of Jalapa during his scalp-hunting days and grew them with great devotion in our backyard garden in Santa Fe. "My *menudo* can raise the dead," was his boast. He'd discovered it during his drinking days and found it a sure cure for the anguish of his hangovers.

When we sat down to supper, Plover wouldn't eat.

"What's the matter?" I asked her. "You're not getting sick, are you?"

She shook her head. "What did Doña Ana say about smoke?" she asked. "The smoky horses?"

She'd caught an echo of that prophecy in our pony raid on Old Smoke's camp the previous night. She could feel everything coming together now. She didn't believe for a moment that the wily old outlaw would give up on Gwen and go home.

"He might sneak into our camp this very night," she said, "and make off with her. Esme, too. And me, and . . . I know he's coming."

"He's too old to sneak very fast or quietly," I said. I ripped off a chunk of sourdough bread and sopped up the rest of my *menudo*, then held out the bowl for more.

"Or send in one of his friends to do the job." She ladled me more soup.

"All right then, we'll stand guard together tonight, you and I, and let the girls sleep between us as we watch," I told her. "Now eat your soup. It'll fire you up if we have to fight. Here, have a slice of liver. It's damned good, fresh and juicy still, and I dipped it in gall just the way you like."

She shook her head no. "I'm just not hungry," she said.

Pine Leaf was also off her feed, picking at her supper in a half-dazed, half-demented sort of way. And now Gwennie wore a solemn look. Her bowl was only half-empty.

Women. . . .

Well, all the more *menudo* for tomorrow. It gets better with the passage of time.

WE PUSHED NORTHWEST into the sawtoothed mountains. This was rocky country, and there were times when even Jim lost Owen's trail. But we didn't really need it. I knew where the mine lay from a distinctive symmetrically shaped mountain that towered over the Buenaventura's valley. It was one of those conical mountains that the Spanish call *pilóncillos*, sugar loaves, and I recalled Owen saying that it had a distinctly volcanic look about it. I thought I could make out its peak even now, over the crags just ahead.

I kept Spy on our backtrail, with orders to skin his eyes for the signs of approaching dust. Old Smoke couldn't be on our trail just yet; it would take him a while to get back to Fort Bridger, buy new horses, and then, if he were still persistent enough, which I didn't think he would be, catch us up.

No, I was worried about Dade. We hadn't made the kind of time on this journey that men can make traveling alone. Plover insisted on frequent stops to change the baby's diapers or to let the girls rest. The interlude with Old Smoke and at Mo-he-nes-to's camp had cost us nearly a day by themselves. I worried, too, about what we'd find when we got to the mine. Owen must surely have gotten there by now.

If, as Bridger had said, the *minería* was wiped out by Indians, Owen might very well have blown up the shafts already with his gunpowder. Even if he hadn't killed Jaime, which I doubt he would have, he might have moved on after the explosion to some other locale. I had no idea where he'd head next. Back east? Back down to Baja California?

"No," Jim said when I told him my concerns. We had halted at the top of a steep climb to let the horses blow. "He'll stay at the mine, waiting for you or Dade or both of you to show up. He's getting along well with your son."

"How do you know?"

"By the sign at his camps. He hasn't tied the boy up when they've overnighted or even restricted his movements. Just this morning we passed a spot, near that trapped-out beaver pond I pointed out to you, where they camped two or three nights ago. He let Jaime go out and rub down the horses; then the boy fetched firewood while Owen hunted up some meat. Judging by the burnt bones in the fire, all he got was a couple of blue grouse."

"Well, maybe—"

"Maybe nothing. They sat around the fire after supper, probably just jawing until they went to bed. The dog sleeps with Jaime. You'll have to get him one when you get home, if I know kids. Your brother is smoking cigarillos nowadays. I think he may have allowed Jaime to try one. There were two stubs ground out near the fire circle." He looked over at me and smiled. "Don't worry. Your boy is fine. They'll be there when we get there, safe and sound. Then all we've got to do is convince Owen to clear out with us before Dade shows up. And maybe the presence of Bar-che-am-pe will turn the trick."

I looked ahead up the trail. It seemed to top out just a quarter-mile ahead, but mountains will always deceive you. You reach the top of a pitch, figuring it's the summit, only to find another one ahead of you— just a *little* ways more.

"Hand me over that canteen of *menudo*," I said to Jim. "It goes down good cold." The weather had gotten very hot and oppressive. A rainstorm was looming blue-black in the distance, the thunderheads rimmed dirty white. We didn't have time to stop for a midday meal, no matter what Plover said about the girls needing their nourishment. They could suck *menudo* with the rest of us and ride on at the same time.

WE GOT TO the divide an hour or so later. The storm was nearly on us now. From the crest I could see the *pilóncillo* clearly. It looked to be about five miles away. In places the Buenaventura flashed silver or green through the jumbled hills, snaking its way toward the Pacific, into the gloom of the approaching storm. A quarter of a mile down the trail I saw the spot where we'd given up the hunt for Owen and Pine Leaf back in '33. Then I turned to look down our backtrail for any sign of Spy. I saw the flash of a mirror from the trees far below. He was signaling to us.

"Can you read what he says?" I asked Jim.

He studied the flashes, then raised his rifle over his head three times, to acknowledge receipt of the message.

"He says he sees a dust cloud a couple miles down the trail. Coming our way. Says many riders. Asks what we want him to do."

"What do you think? Who is it?"

"Could be either of them, Old Smoke or Dade and his boys."

"Let's get Spy back up here," I said. "We can decide then if we want to make a stand."

"All right, but I think when he joins us we ought to press on, and fast. This isn't any place for a fight. They could slip men around us and cut us off up here without food or water once we ran out of what we've got with us. We ought to push on to the mine. And fast. Make a stand down there."

"Get him up here, then," I said. I told Plover to strap Esme on her back and get ready for a fast downhill ride. I told her to put on their slickers.

Pine Leaf looked over at me, into my eyes, for the first time since her return. Her whole manner had changed, and for the better.

"We fight soon?" she asked in English.

"Mebbe so."

"Bueno!"

SPY APPEARED HALF a mile down the trail, leading his horse. The heat and humidity were intense now, in the moments before the storm broke. You could see the sweat on both man and horse. While Spy labored up the steep pitch, I went around securing all the loose gear on the horses, tightening cinches, retying pack ropes, rigging a tarp over the food bundles. Spy came up the pitch with the reins in one hand, his rifle in the other. His pirate kerchief was askew. He was breathing hard. His face gleamed with sweat. His horse was blown. Finished.

Then the storm hit. A few fat drops of rain at first, some quick gusts of premonitory wind, then a dirty white wall of wind and water hit the ridgetop. In a few minutes it would make the trail down the mountain impassable. We'd be trapped up here. "Ride for it!" I yelled to Plover. "Ride like lightning!" She and Gwen kicked their horses to a gallop and began the descent. Jim and Pine Leaf followed.

Spy reached the top. He cut loose the bridle and saddle from his blown horse and swung aboard the pony Esme'd been riding. He slapped the exhausted horse on the rump, and it sloped off back downhill toward a grassy shelf.

"How many?" I asked him.

"Couple dozen . . . maybe thirty." He was still breathing hard.

"Who is it—Dade?"

He shook his head. "Both of them."

"Old Smoke, too?"

He nodded. Then raised his hand, bent at the waist, and took some deep breaths with his head down, elbows on his knees. "Way I figure . . . Smoke's on his way back to Bridger . . . runs into Dade . . . 'Who put you afoot?' . . . 'The Bloody Arm.' . . . 'Same man I'm chasing.' . . . They join forces. Now they're coming on fast."

"How far back are they?"

"I think we've got a mile on them, maybe less."

"Are you all right now?"

"Yes."

"You know this trail better than I do. You lead the way. We're going to make a stand down at the mine."

He looked out at the pilóncillo, barely visible through the blowing rain. He nodded. He started down the slope, overtook the others, then led the way with Plover and the rest following. I waited a few minutes, watching the backtrail.

A rider on a tall horse appeared through the rain.

It was Ed Chambers, the Delaware they call Big Nigger. He was huge. His dark face was topped by a battered plug hat. He was dressed in black buckskins. I dropped to my belly behind the rock. Brought the Hawken to my shoulder. The range was about five hundred yards. I lifted the sights a foot and a half over his head. Fired. The bullet kicked up dirt ten yards ahead of him. He did not flinch. He looked up at me. I raised my rifle over my head and shook it. I grinned down at him. He stared. Then Lafe Dade came up the trail, his red beard gleaming in the rain. Chambers pointed up at me and said something. Dade threw back his head and laughed. I headed downhill, fast.

IT WAS A wild ride through the rain. Water raced down the trail, carrying loose stones and gravel with it in dirty brown rivulets. Littering the mountainside were downed lodgepole pines, which the horses had to clear in a single downhill leap. Old avalanche scars bled mud and gushers of white foam. Hairpin bends with sheer cliffs falling far, far to the Buenaventura below. . . . Gwen rode it like a centaur. We all rode like centaurs. The horses held up. No one skidded and fell. No one foundered. The slick black rocks sped past in a blur, and then we were in the flat beside the river.

Already the first spate of brown water had hit the ford. Trees and brush and deadwood came tumbling down with the current. In a few minutes the horses would have to swim. We splashed across the ford in the nick of time. Then we rounded a bend . . . and there it was.

Los Padres Perdidos.

We stared at it through the rain.

But my God, what had Dade done to the place?

The slopes of Garnet Creek had been clearcut to provide balks for the mine shafts and fuel for the refinery. Stumps and slash rotted in disarray on the eroded hillsides. The alder brake was gone, the mud bridged by a rough road of slabs and riverbed gravel. A cluster of roofless burnt-out cabins straggled down the riverbank, with stone guard towers covering both ends of the line. The compound was surrounded by a man-high stone wall daubed with adobe. This must be where the prisoners were housed.

The ruins of a stamp mill loomed on the bank near the spot where Garnet Creek emptied into the Buenaventura. Its overshot waterwheel, fed by sluices from a dam upstream, hung awry, partly burned, as was the roof of the mill. A tall chimney stood at the downstream end of the building. Dade's engineers must have roasted the ore in there, after the drop hammer worked by the waterwheel had broken it up. Slag heaps as high as barns surrounded the mill, leaching their poisons into the river. The water looked yellowish green near the banks, and tendrils of it snaked their way down through the riffles. A stink of brimstone from the crushed, roasted ore still hung in the air.

As we neared the stamp mill we began to see skeletons. First of fish, and then of the birds which had fed on their poisoned bodies. Ospreys and bald eagles by their rotting feathers. A rotting white pelican. Then the skulls of men. Some of them split by axes, some crushed by war clubs, others intact or with the hungry black mouths of bulletholes gaping from them.

The Grovan had done a thorough job, all right.

The rain stopped as suddenly as it had started. Bright sunlight broke through. Steam rose as if from geysers all along the mountain face.

Spy led the way toward a low building made of stone. It looked like the mine supervisor's headquarters and perhaps his living quarters as well. A thin column of smoke scrawled from its chimney. The roof was still intact, and the building itself hadn't been burned like the slaves' quarters. Wet horses were tethered in a corral beside the building, among them the gray Morgan. The ponies looked up at us and nickered.

Owen stepped out of the door as we approached. The dark sombrero was tipped back on his head; his white hair and beard gleamed in the morning sun. A revolver hung holstered at his hip, slung low on his leg like a gunfighter's. He wore a red, black, and yellow serape, its folds thrown clear of the gunbutt. He was smoking a long black cigarillo. The little brown-and-white terrier stood beside him, growling low in her throat. Her ruff was up. The dog looked like the reincarnation of Thump.

"Brother," Owen said in a flat, noncommittal voice. "Do you come in peace or war?"

AND THERE I stood, dumbstruck, smote between the eyes with awe and reverie. For I had not believed, or perhaps believed only in hope, that he would, could, still be alive.

Even after all this travel. This travail.

There he stood.

Tall (though in fact I was taller than he, had been since my early teens), bold (his eyes still flashed as always, yet death now glared from within them), dark and scarred by the sun, seared and seamed by events, ineffably aged, the scars on him from bullets and arrows and time and contradiction etched deep in his face, in the poised, coiled slouch of his body, in the slight crook of his fingers over the grip of the gun.

My brother.

The brother who'd been my childhood's greatest fear, the bully of my youth. Yet the brother who'd taught me how to fight with my fists, gig frogs, catch trout, shoot guns, ride horses, love women, kill men.

The brother who had worked the mines back in the nightmare East, who had been spared when a stroke of fate felled our father, who had first suggested the trip west. The brother whose lust for gold had triggered the sequence of events that had torn us all apart and led us through the years to this awful place, yet who seemed to have learned the error of his ways.

Or had he?

The brother to whom I now said:

"Not merely peace, Brother. Love."

He smiled his hard, dark smile and stepped forward. We embraced.

I stepped back, cool again.

"Where's Jaime?" I asked him.

"Right here," my son said.

He was standing on a boulder to our right, the Allen & Wheelock resting butt-down on his hip.

At that angle, in that mountain light, he looked six feet tall. He was tanned by the journey, brown as an Apache, all of the baby fat burned off his face. His sombrero was tilted back on his brow just like Owen's; he, too, was puffing a cigarillo.

A hard face, like his uncle's.

My son the *bandido*.

Then Owen saw Pine Leaf. She stared at him. His eyes slipped out of focus for a moment, and he removed the cigarillo from his lips.

"Válgame Dios!" they both said at once. "I thought you were dead!"

Jaime jumped from his rock.

Plover ran to him and hugged him, already asking a thousand questions.

Gwen slid from her horse and hugged the little dog.

Esme began to squirm on Plover's back; she wanted to join the fun.

"Let's postpone this joyous family reunion," Jim said, still watching the river where it coursed down from the great, cruel peaks. "We've got about ten minutes to get ready."

"Ready for what?" Plover asked.

Jim looked at her, sad, I guess, but serious.

"The battle of our lives," he said.

CHAPTER X

THERE WERE THREE possible defensive positions at the mine. The
stamp mill was the strongest. Built of stone and about forty feet high,
it would provide covering fire to the crossings of both the Buenaventura
and Garnet Creek. The Grovans had fired it, burning out the interior
and collapsing the roof, but Owen had already removed some rocks
from the walls to create rifle slits. It was close to the water, so a pro-
longed siege couldn't drive the stamp mill's defenders out by means
of thirst.

The supervisor's house was also stone-built and had windows in
all four walls which riflemen could fire from. The roof was made of
slate, or anyway a thin stone slab that resembled it, so it could not be
set ablaze by fire arrows. It had no independent supply of water, but
Owen and Jaime had lugged kegs of creekwater down to the house
from the unpolluted springs up the mountain from the mine.

The stone wall that surrounded the burnt-out cabins of the prisoners was the most vulnerable position. There were no parapets atop
the six-foot-high wall, no rifle platform behind the wall, and any man
firing from the top could easily be picked off by a marksman a hundred
or two hundred yards away, even from cover on the rocky shore across
the Buenaventura.

"Still," Jim said, "we'd better put one gun in there just to deny the damned thing to Dade and Smoke. If they get some guns in there, they could have us in a crossfire, or use the place to stage sorties on either the stamp mill or the house."

We were all standing in the open near the stamp mill. Pine Leaf was watching upriver for the first sign of the attacking force. The river was roaring now, brown and full of fast-moving junk.

"I've got a surprise for them in the prison yard if they do," Owen said.

"What?"

"I mined the compound with gunpowder. If we can get a bunch of them inside, I'll light it off. I've rigged a long fuse from the house. And don't worry; it's waterproof."

"Then we'll have to lure them into the compound," Jim said. "Have a rifleman out there when they show up, let him fire a few times to draw their attention to the place; then when they move in on it the gunner can dash to the house. Once they're inside the compound, *Bang!*"

"I'll do it," Jaime said.

"No, you won't," said his mother.

"It's got to be someone who can keep cool under fire," I said. "I'll go."

"Nothing but heroes in this little Alamo," Owen said. "I'd volunteer myself, except that I'd be more valuable here, to set off the charges."

"Spy?" Jim said.

"I'll take the compound," the Shawnee said.

I looked upriver, past Pine Leaf. Whole trees were coming down on the spate. I saw a drowned elk rolling over and over through the rapids.

"All right," Jim said. "Let's have two guns in the stamp mill: Dillon and Jaime. Owen, Pine Leaf, and me in the house. Spy will fall back to the house when we've got them coming to the compound. Later he could go out and reinforce you two in the stamp mill if it's necessary."

"What about me?" Plover said. "I can shoot. I can shoot straight.

So can Gwen. With light charges, anyway. And she can reload if you'll show her how on those Colts of yours."

"You and the girls will stay with us in the house," Jim said. "Reloading mainly, but shooting if and when necessary. If things get too hot in the stamp mill, Dill and Jaime can fall back here. Let's arrange a signal so you can let us know when you'll be coming back. That way we can cover you."

Owen went over to his saddlebags and pulled out a red shirt. He handed it to me. "Tie this on a stick and wave it when you're planning to retreat," he said. "Then give us a couple of minutes to start laying down fire."

"All of this makes for a good defense," Spy said. "But can't we do something *to* them? Hit them some way? Otherwise it's just going to be one long, hard siege. Smoke's an Indian. He'll cut his losses and ride out of here if his people start getting chewed up, just like the Sioux did in that second big fight with the Rees years ago, back east in Dakota. But Dade won't quit."

"Let's get a look at them before we make any plans for sorties or counterattacks," Jim said. "See how many men they've got. Look for openings."

Owen laughed.

"What?" Jim said.

"I've got another surprise in store for Don Lafcadio Dade."

He stood there smiling, smug. Maybe just a little bit mad.

"Where's the rest of that gunpowder?" I asked him.

Before he could answer, Pine Leaf said, "Here they come."

A STRAGGLING GANG of riders had appeared around the upriver bend. The first of them were already picking their way across the ford. Twenty feet out the horses had to swim. They came angling downstream toward us. The rest of the band hit the water—a good three dozen men, mainly Missourians and Mexicans, but Old Smoke's outfit mixed in with them. I could see Dade's red hair and beard flashing in the sunlight.

"Let's get to our positions," Jim said. "They'll be here in five minutes."

"Is there any food in the stamp mill, in case we need it?" I asked.

"I'll get some jerky and beans to you before Dade arrives," Jim said.

Jaime and I ran for the mill while the others scattered to their posts. I had two powder horns and plenty of bullets in the pouch. "Do you have enough ammunition?" I asked my son.

"There's spare powder and ball cached in the stamp mill," he said. "Owen was thinking ahead even before you showed up."

We went in and barred the heavy oak door. It was dark and dank. The reek of stale wood ash and brimstone hung in the air. Sunlight speared through a charred hole in the roof and a few small windows. A wooden ladder led up to the scaffolding that circled the interior of the mill and gave access to our firing positions. Far overhead in the darkness I could see the heavy drop hammer poised at the top of its cycle, waiting for a quarter-turn of the camshaft to release it. A wooden bar held the cam in place. We scaled the ladder and looked out the upstream windows.

Dade's little army had forded the river. Riders were moving down toward us at a walk, still far out of rifle range. The carcass of the drowned elk had cleared the rapids and was drifting downstream in the slack water, abreast of the approaching riders. I scanned the horsemen, looking for Ed Chambers. I couldn't spot him. Where the hell was he? What was he up to?

I went around the scaffold to the opposite window. Spy was standing by the gate of the prison yard, a rifle at the ready. It was Beckwourth's ring-lever Colt. He must have lent it to Spy at the last minute to give the impression of a larger force entrenched in the prison compound. With the Colt, Spy could bang off eight shots without reloading.

No sign of Chambers.

"They're charging," Jaime said from across the way. I ran over.

It was Old Smoke's boys, coming fast across the gravel. They were painted for war, reds and blacks and yellows and whites, and screaming like eagles. I could see Dade standing on a boulder with a spyglass to his eye. His hair and beard blazed red in the sunlight.

Smoke led the charge. I held him in my sights, fired when he was 100 yards out, and missed. I heard the bang of Jaime's rifle beside me. A Cheyenne pony stumbled and fell. Then Beckwourth and Owen opened up from the house. Two more Indians fell. Jaime had already reloaded as I reseated my ramrod. He was fast. He fired again at the same time I did. We both hit Old Smoke's horse. It fell into the shallows of Garnet Creek, spilling the Cheyenne into the water. Bullets smacked into the stones of the stamp mill. Dade's men had moved forward with the assault. I saw Smoke running back up the beach. Jaime chased him with a futile shot.

The attack collapsed. The Indians retreated to the main body.

But now they were much closer, maybe 200 yards away, huddled behind drift logs and rocks, popping away at us.

During the lull that followed, Plover and Gwen raced over to the stamp mill carrying a bundle of food and extra ammunition for us.

"How's it going?" I asked her.

"Jim says fine. Kill a couple more Cheyennes and Old Smoke will call it quits."

"Let's hope so. But there'd still be twenty of Dade's gang to deal with."

"Keep a strong heart," she said. "Owen is making some small bombs, gunpowder, and buckshot in empty tin cans we found. They'll have short fuses. They won't do much damage, he says, but maybe they'll scare the Indians off anyway. Dade's men, too, if we're lucky. I'll send Gwen over with some for you when they're ready."

She kissed me and they ran back, dodging and bending low to present more difficult targets to the distant rifles. A stitchwork of bullets dusted their path.

"WHAT ARE THEY doing now?" Jaime said.

I looked upstream. Dade's men were sewing greased buffalo hides to oval frames of riverside willow.

"Making bull boats," I said. "They'll cross the river out of range and try to outflank us, send at least part of their strength downstream, land down below, and attack from both sides. Good. That'll split their force and put the landing party in range of Spy and the repeater."

"And Owen's gunpowder," Jaime said.

There were two hours of daylight left when the boats pushed off. Five of them, with three men in each. Dade was in the lead boat. The pilots poled the bull boats across the current. We shot and may have holed one or two of them, but they all reached the far side of the Buenaventura without sinking. They swept on downstream with the current, and we saw them angle in toward our shore just below the prison compound. The river was still running strong. I noticed that the carcass of the drowned elk had drifted down to a gravel bar just below the stamp mill. It was within easy reach of us if we ran short of food and needed fresh meat. I figured that when it got dark I'd go down there and butcher it, take a haunch and the loins at least.

Just then the door of the supervisor's house opened and I saw Gwen emerge, lugging a heavy, lumpy sack. Owen's bombs.

I trotted back down the ladder, unbarred the door, and swung it wide. She was grinning, happy to be of help, part of this glorious battle.

Then the world changed.

A huge, wet, dark Indian burst from the water immediately behind the beached elk, rifle in hand, and sprinted across the gravel, coming up fast toward Gwen.

Ed Chambers. . . .

"Gwennie, go back!" I yelled.

She looked back and saw him too late, dropped her bundle, and ran full speed toward me. Chambers was right behind her.

The big Delaware grabbed her up in midstride, spun around, and angled toward the cliff face, heading for the entrance to the mine.

"Spy!" I shouted. But he'd seen it already. He had the ring-lever Colt to his shoulder but must have realized that it couldn't throw straight enough for a safe shot. He ran out in pursuit of Chambers, leaving the prison compound unguarded. He looked over at me where I stood at the mill door, threw the Colt rifle toward the house, then drew his knife. Chambers was still ten yards ahead of him.

They disappeared only a few steps apart, into the black abyss of the mine shaft.

At that moment the Cheyennes charged again toward Garnet Creek and the landing force opened fire. Bullets whanged through the windows, richocheted from the walls. . . .

"I'm hit," Jaime said. He fell from the scaffold, his rifle clattering down with him.

Blood streamed from the top of his chest.

There was nothing for it. I pulled him to his feet and we made for the safety of the house.

Our neat little battle plan was fraying fast.

CHAPTER XI

———————◆•◆•◆———————

DARKNESS FELL, BLACK as the pit until a three-quarter moon crept over the Encantadas to the east. Its cold, pale light illumined a desperate scene. Old Smoke's men held the stamp mill, Dade's the prison compound. They were holding their fire, sniping only occasionally, waiting for us to make a move. They'd have us in a crossfire if we tried to make a break for it. One of the Cheyennes had sneaked in and stolen the horses and mules anyway. So how could we escape? In the supervisor's house we didn't know what to do. Jim and Plover had bandaged Jaime's wound. The bullet had shattered his collarbone but passed clean through the muscles of his left shoulder. It hadn't hit any major arteries, thank God. The boy was out of action, still groggy with the laudanum Jim had given him while Plover treated the entry and exit wounds. We'd built up a fire, heated a steel ramrod red-hot, and passed it through the bullethole to cauterize the wound. Then she went to work with her catgut and needle. He'd be hurting pretty bad when the drug wore off. There was no more laudanum. Perhaps he could still shoot, a revolver at least, with his uninjured right arm. But at what?

We'd heard nothing from the mine since Spy and Chambers entered it. No shots. Just silence. I was for going in there. Owen said no.

"There are too many tunnels," Owen said. "Go in and you'll only get lost. Spy is still stalking him. We've got to trust his stealth. I'm sure we'd have heard something from someone if a conclusion had been reached."

"Is Gwen all right, though?" That was my main concern. Chambers might have cut her throat already and Spy's, too, for all we knew.

"How the hell do I know?" Owen snapped. "You should never have brought her along. Plover should never have let her go over to the mill with those half-assed bombs of mine."

Plover got up and walked impatiently around the room.

"Why don't you blow up the compound?" I said. "Let's at least get rid of Dade and the men with him. See what this god-almighty explosion of yours can do for us."

"We tried just before you came in with Jaime," Beckwourth said. He was standing at the window, to one side, watching both the mill and the compound wall in case of an attack. "Owen's fuse fizzled. That rain must have got it wet despite his waterproofing."

"What's the other surprise you were talking about?" I asked Owen.

"I've planted charges in the mine and on the cliff above it," he said. "I can blow the whole infernal thing to hell and gone."

"If the fuse ain't wet."

"It'll be dry inside the mine if I can get there."

"But now Spy and Gwen are inside," Plover said. "I won't let you do it."

Owen turned away. Did he want to blow the place anyway?

"Enough of this bickering, children," Jim said. "I'm sure Chambers won't kill Gwen, not yet anyway. He's holding her hostage. I know the man. He had a wife and three kids in the Taos pueblo. He's mean, sure, but he's no child killer."

Unless he's gone crazy with sorrow, I thought. Vengeance is strange medicine.

"No," Jim continued, "what we have to do now is what Spy said just before Dade and Smoke showed up. Find a way to hit them so it hurts. Go on the attack."

"How?" I asked.

"There are only five or six Cheyennes in the stamp mill," he said.

"At most a dozen of Dade's boys in the compound. How many of those grenades do we have left?"

"Half a dozen," Owen said.

I said, "And there's that bundle of them Gwen dropped when Chambers jumped her. It's still lying near the mill. I saw it just before dark."

"All right then, here's the plan."

After moonset, Pine Leaf was to put the sneak on the mill, crawling over there under cover of darkness. She'd recover the grenades Gwen had dropped. Then at first light she would light the fuses one by one and throw the bombs into the mill through one of the windows.

Meanwhile Jim, Owen, and I would slip around to the far side of the compound. When Owen, and I were in position near the back gate, Jim would go over the wall into the midst of Dade's boys. "I've done it before," he said. "In early '33, the year you fellows came west, we had a war party of Blackfeet forted up in a similar situation. There were about thirty of them holding a rock-rimmed bastion down on the lower Bighorn. It was a huge mass of granite, forming a natural wall in front that ranged from six feet high to about twenty-five feet, nearly perpendicular all the way around. They were safe as bugs in there, sniping away at us. Every time we tried to storm the place they beat us back. Our losses were getting way too high. Long Hair, the old Crow chief, wanted to quit. 'Our marrow bones are broken,' he said. 'We cannot drive them from the fort without sacrificing too many men. Warriors, retreat!' "

"I told them that if they ran, the Blackfeet would shoot them in their backs and kill more than if we went over the wall and charged them. I led the way with nothing but my battle-ax and scalp knife. Soon they were fleeing the fort, where the rest of our people were waiting. We killed those Blackfeet to the last man."

"All well and good with Blackfeet," I said. "But these are white men. What if they don't run?"

"Then I'll be dead, and you shortly after me. But if they run, which I'm sure they will, you'll be there to pick them off on the back side of the compound, with Pine Leaf, Plover, and Jaime covering the front.

After we've whipped them, you can go into the mine and fetch out your daughter."

It was, I realized, our only hope, and a forlorn one at best.

DURING THE HOUR or so that remained before moonset, Jim familiarized Plover with the Colt eight-shot rifle. He had her shoot it, at both the windows of the stamp mill and the front gate of the compound, then reload it until she could do it in the dark. I went over to the fire. Esme was bundled up in a blanket, asleep, with Owen's dog curled up beside her. Jaime lay under a buffalo robe, his head propped against a saddle. His eyes were open. He was awake, and coming out of the haze imposed by the laudanum. I could see the pain in his eyes.

"How is it?"

"I can take it," he said.

"Do you think you're steady enough to shoot a revolver?"

"Damn right," he said. I handed him the Walker Colt. He'd shot it frequently back home in Santa Fe and could hit well from a rest at fifty yards. I told him our plans. He and his mother would have to shoot straight and fast when Dade's boys broke from the compound.

"Count on it," he said. "Now, could you give me some jerky and maybe a cup of coffee? I'm still kind of weak."

I fetched them from near the fire. We sat in the glow of it, drinking the brew Plover had boiled earlier. It was bitter black, strong, hot, and my son's face regained some of its color.

THE SPECTER OF death haunts every battleground, and the longer the participants have to wait for the action to be joined, the more insidiously it works its ways on their souls. We all knew we were in a tight corner here. We all knew someone would die. We hoped it would be Lafcadio Dade, and perhaps even Old Smoke, but we all knew that one or more of us, perhaps all, would probably be dead before sundown. Men in battle are not fools, though often they behave that way. The eve of battle is a time to set hearts in order. I had to get something clear with Jim Beckwourth, and took him aside so the others would not hear.

"Don't take this wrong," I said. "You've been like a father to me for many years now; you're my dearest friend; you've bled for me and risked your life for my family. We may both die today, Jim, and I have to know. You've always acted and spoken like a man who believes that race, color, religion, none of those superficial trappings of existence amount to a hill of beans when it comes to evaluating a man's true worth. But then why have you always so angrily denied being, well . . . black? Do you think it makes any difference to me?"

He looked at me, deep and hard, for a long minute. Then he said, "You cannot know the rage that comes with not owning your very own soul, miserable as it might be. Yes, I guess I am 'black' by the legal definition of the term in the Benighted States of America. My father was, as I've told you, a white man, a Virginian, and there it was I was born. But my mother, whom I scarcely knew, was a household slave on my father's plantation. She died when I was still an infant, and I was raised as my father's son. He was a good man despite the fact that he owned slaves. He educated me, saw to it that I learned a trade—blacksmithing—which would support me long after he was gone. But I always feared that, sooner or later, the law would descend upon me and return me to the condition of my birth. So I ran from it. I went west, and made myself the Enemy of Horses, the Bloody Arm, the Medicine Calf of the Sparrowhawks."

He sighed and stared out the window. The moon hovered on the brink of the western hills.

"Now civilization has come to the mountains, Dill. It's come even to New Mexico, the Land of Poco Tiempo. Sooner or later slavery will come trailing along after it, unless a great war is fought to eradicate it, a holy war like the one Spy talks about all the time. Men like Dade are working to make slavery the law of the territory. Look what he's done with his Mexican and *indio* prisoners! And if slavery does come to New Mexico, I will continue to deny I am black. I will make them prove it, and if they do so in their corrupt courts of law, which I'm certain they will, I will kill the first man—constable, sheriff, or marshal—who comes for me with chains. And I will kill all of them who come for me afterwards. I will make them kill me, before I submit to my mother's condition."

"I'll be there at your side," I said. For myself, I couldn't envision African slavery ever taking hold in New Mexico, yet less than ten years later, in 1857, the pro-Southern territorial legislature legitimized it and at the same time banned and annulled marriages between whites and blacks or even mulattoes, required all Negroes to carry passports when away from the homes of their masters, forbade the sale of firearms to African slaves, and at the same time made it illegal for free Negroes to remain within the boundaries of the territory for more than thirty days, any violation to be punished with fines and hard labor at the territorial penitentiary.

And it did take a holy war to eliminate that evil.

THE MOON WAS almost down. Pine Leaf stripped for action. For the first time, Owen saw what had happened to her breasts. She watched his eyes for a reaction. He stared at the scars for a moment, then went over and embraced her. "Do you have a strong heart for this bomb business?" he asked.

"Feel it," she said.

He placed his hand over the massive scar on her chest.

"Muy fuerte," he said. And kissed her.

"Ready?" Jim asked from across the room.

"Yes," she said. She carried only her lance and knife.

"Do you want one of the handguns?" Owen asked.

"No need to waste bullets on mere Cheyennes," she said. "But give me a *cigarro* to light the fuses." He lit one for her. She took it between her teeth, wrapped her gray blanket tight around her, and slipped out the back door.

Jim had peeled down to a loincloth and moccasins. He fetched pots of vermilion and ocher from his war bag and painted his face like the Bloody Arm of old: battle-ax in hand, the white-handled knife tucked in his belt. I kissed Plover good-bye. She sat by the front window, the eight-shot rifle at the ready. "Kill some for me," I said.

"And you the same," she answered.

Jim, Owen, and I followed the way Pine Leaf had gone.

IT WAS DEAD dark now. Just a fading afterglow of moonlight edged the mountains to the west. We crept unseen to the causeway, then through the mud of the late alder brake to the walls of the prison compound, moving from boulder to boulder as silent as snakes. The mud was cold. Near the gate we paused and listened. Dade's voice rasped through the dark.

"About ten or twenty minutes to first light," he was saying. "As soon as we can see our foresights, I'll give the word and we charge the house. Keep low and run a zigzag, fast. You men with fukes, load with buckshot. Stick your muzzles through the window and let fly. Old Uncle Richochet will take care of the rest. Ings, do you have that torch ready? When you get up to the house, light it and chuck it through the first window you come to. Let's get this damn business over once and for all. And try to capture that damn rapparee, the nigger Beck-wourth. I want to put him to work in the mines, the arrogant bastard. If you can't take him alive, bring me his head. Otherwise, take no prisoners, do you hear me—I'll have no survivors to tell this tale."

Jim grabbed my shoulder. "Do you see what I mean?" he whispered. He shoved me toward the back of the wall. Owen followed. Jim found a spot where a boulder would give him a leg up to the top of the six-foot wall. He gave us a wink. "Kill 'em dead."

A moment later we heard Pine Leaf's first bomb explode. Then the hollow crash of the drop hammer falling from its precarious lodgement near the roof of the mill. Screams of rage and fright followed . . . Cheyenne curses.

Owen and I ran to the rear of the wall. As I turned the corner, I glanced back in time to see Jim light his bomb, hurl it, then, with the roar of the blast still echoing off the mountains, leap like a great dark panther to the lip of the wall. He vaulted inside, ax in hand. A war yell rang through the dawn. The Bloody Arm at play.

All hell broke loose. . . .

Gunfire exploded from every direction. Screams and grunts of rage. I heard Plover's rifle bang, then bang again, and again. The sharper crack of Jaime's revolver followed.

Another bomb blast from the mill. . . .

Three men broke through the back gate of the compound, running fast for the bull boats. Owen dropped two of them in their tracks with a quick right and left from Manton. I caught the third through the small of the back and quickly reloaded the Hawken. Somebody poked his head out and stared in our direction. Owen popped him.

Inside the compound I could hear the clang of Jim's ax on the steel of a gun barrel. A fuke bellowed. Somebody screamed, once, twice, then silence.

Another bomb blew over in the mill, and through the echo I could hear horse hooves splashing across Garnet Creek, then rattling on the rocks as they faded to the south. The Cheyennes, those that were left of them, had decamped.

Then we caught a glimpse of a man running from the front gate of the compound toward the mine entrance.

"It's Dade," Owen said, snapping off a shot. The figure stumbled, then ran on. "I think I nicked him."

Suddenly I noticed the dog standing at Owen's side. She must have leaped from the window and tracked him after hearing the first burst of gunfire.

"Thump," Owen said, bending over to scratch her ears. "You'll find him for me, won't you, from the blood trail."

"To hell with Dade," I said. "We have to get Gwen out safely first."

Someone came toward us from the compound's ruined interior. I cocked the Hawken. It was Jim, limping from a bullet through his thigh. His right arm, his ax arm, was covered in blood to his elbow: the blood of his enemies. "I'm all right," he said. "They aren't. Dade went into the mine. Go get him, boys."

CHAPTER XII

INSIDE THE MINE shaft it was black as tarmacadam. Yet Owen had eyes that could see through the rocks themselves. Or so it seemed. The dog trailed Dade's blood spoor back through a maze of tunnels and side tunnels, deep, deep into the earth. It was hot down there, airless. I felt myself choking. But still I followed. Then we stopped.

Owen seemed to be pondering. A sideshaft led off to our right; the main tunnel continued straight. The dog ran a short way into the sideshaft, then returned and forged ahead, down the main tunnel.

"Chambers and Spy went down that way," Owen said. I saw his arm point to the right. Then he gestured ahead. "Dade's in there, where Thump went, not far ahead. He's bleeding bad."

"Let him bleed out," I said. "We've got to get Gwen."

"No," he said, and there was the edge of madness to his voice. "I must be sure of Dade. You go after her. I'll meet you back here later."

Later?

If there was one.

He and the dog disappeared into the blackness.

*   *   *

I WALKED SLOWLY down the side tunnel. Ahead I could hear what sounded like heavy breathing. A liquid, raspy cough. I felt my way along the wall. The breathing got louder. I raised the Hawken to my hip, muzzle aimed into the dark.

The breathing was right in front of me.

Then I remembered the lighter that the *cibolero* woman had given me, what seemed like months ago now. I struck a spark to the cotton cord and blew it into flame. I looked down.

It was Spy.

I knelt beside him. He was bleeding from a wound in his chest. He felt my hand on him, and his head came up. A knifepoint touched my throat.

"Easy," I said. "You'll be all right when I get you out of here. Where's Chambers and Gwen?"

"Straight ahead," he said. "Down there somewhere. Not far, I reckon. I put the knife into him an hour or so ago. Stuck him good. But he stuck me, too. . . . I think he's got her tied up back there. He gagged her so she couldn't attract our attention. Yeah . . . I think I stuck him pretty good. He may be dead, maybe not. Be careful. . . ."

He passed out again. I ripped a sleeve from his shirt and stuffed a wad of it in the slash I could feel below his collarbone. I felt around for more wounds but found none. He'd have to hold on now as best he could.

To hell with caution. I leaned the rifle against the wall next to Spybuck and drew my knife. With the lighter in one hand, the blade in the other, I trotted down the stone passageway calling Gwen's name. No answer. Panic grabbed my heart. I ran; the flame guttered, nearly died. I bounced off a wall, got up, and ran some more. . . .

Then I heard her, a muffled scream through the gag.

As I felt my way around a corner a rifle exploded; the bullet smacked stone chips from the rock beside my head. . . . The long tongue of flame illuminated the scene momentarily: Gwen huddled against a wall, a bandanna tied across her mouth; Chambers behind her with the rifle. The blast deafened me for an instant. Chambers was reloading, fast: powder first, then he spit a ball down the barrel, snapped on a cap. I rushed him. He fired again, from the hip, and next thing I knew I was flat on my back, stunned, numb from the waist down. The lighter lay burning weakly not far from my left hand. Chambers staggered to his feet, rising from a black pool of blood which had soaked his abdomen and his buckskin trousers. He threw Gwen aside and clubbed the rifle.

Swung . . .

I tossed the lighter into his face and he tripped, lost his balance, and tripped over my legs. I struck hard with the knife, felt it enter the side of his thick neck, just under his ear. He kicked once, spasmodically, and died. Then I must have passed out for a moment.

I AWOKE TO hear Gwen sobbing beside me in the dark. I reached for her, cut her bonds, and removed the gag from her mouth.

"Dad," she said.

"Listen, Gwen," I told her. "He shot me, down low I think. Gutshot. May have nicked my spine. I can't move my legs. I'm going to have to crawl out of here. Maybe you can help me some. And listen. . . . Spy's lying wounded, cut bad. He's back there the way I came, in the shaft about fifty yards from the entrance. You'll maybe have to help him, too. Can you do it?"

"Yes," she said, still weeping a little.

"Good girl. Let's get going."

Spy was conscious when we got back to him. He was strong enough still to crawl, even helped to drag me along. By the time we reached the main tunnel some of the feeling was coming back into my legs.

"Do you see that dim light off there to the left?" I asked Gwen.

"I can see it."

"Good. That's the main entrance. I want you and Spy to get out of here now, go back to your mother and Captain Beckwourth. Tell them I'm going in to help my brother."

"Christ, Dill," Spybuck said. "You can hardly move."

"No, no, it's going to be all right. I think the bullet just grazed my backbone, stunned it like, numbed my legs. But the feeling's coming back now."

"You're gutshot."

"It'll keep," I said. "What does Old Gabe say? 'Meat don't spile in the mountains'? Listen; give me one of your pistols. Owen's going to need all the firepower he can get."

They moved off toward the light. I checked the loads in Spy's Whitneyville. Then I staggered to my feet and edged my way down the main tunnel, leaning on the wall for support. Now the pain was working in there, sick and heavy, surging from sometimes to near-screeching intensity. I tried to put it out of my mind. It wouldn't go. Then it eased off some. . . .

Two shots came echoing up toward me, then a third.

"Owen!" I yelled. My voice bounced off rock down into the darkness.

"Get out of here, Dill!" came back his echoing answer. "This is my affair."

I heard Dade laugh, down there in the black. "Come on ahead, Dillon Griffith. Join the party."

I went toward the sound, feeling my way along the wall. . . .

Another shot, loud as a cannon this time, and Dade's pistol ball came up the passage, clipping from wall to wall. It whistled past my ear. He couldn't be more than twenty yards ahead of me now.

A hand grabbed my leg and Owen pulled me down beside him. He was lying behind what felt like a big, empty hogshead. The little terrier was crouched by his side. She growled low in her throat, then licked my hand.

"I told you to get out of here," Owen said.

"And I never much liked obeying your goddamned orders."

Silence for a moment.

Then he said, "Listen, Brother. I'm hit. Hard hit. Feel . . ." He pulled my hand over his chest. It came away hot and wet, sticky with blood. "He's killed me. Now I'm going to kill him."

Dade fired again, the bullet wailing away up the passage. I fired back, toward where I'd seen the flame of his pistol. He grunted at the crash. Then he fired again.

"I think I hit him," I said.

"I've hit him twice at least," Owney said. He laughed, then coughed—a wet, thick cough, with blood in it. "He doesn't die."

We could hear Dade reloading, a Navy Colt it was: the chink of a powder flask against the mouthed chambers of the pistol, the squeak of the hinged rod tamping the ball and powder charges home. The click of caps snapped onto the cylinders.

Owen was fumbling in his pocket for something. I caught the glint of a fire steel.

"But he will die when I set off the powder train." Now I saw the fuse cord, too, strung pale against the wall. "You've got to get out of here. I'm going to blow this infernal place."

"We'll never get out in time once you strike the spark."

"I'm not going. Look you, Dill, I'm finished anyway. The bullet went through my lungs. I'm bleeding out from the inside. Now get moving; get clear. Once I light this train it'll take only about thirty seconds to hit the powder charge, because it's right behind the spot where Dade is hiding."

Dade fired again, two shots this time. One of them nicked my shoulder.

Then we heard moccasined footsteps coming quick down the tunnel toward us, staggering some toward the end. It was Pine Leaf. She slid in beside Owen, silent. He put his arm around her. "Medio tonto," she whispered.

"Clear out, Dillon," Owen said again. And once more he coughed.

Pine Leaf lay beside him, breathing hard. She, too, was wounded, I realized; must have been hit by one of Dade's wild ricochets as she came down the tunnel to join the fight. I could hear blood dripping now onto the rock floor of the tunnel where she lay. She began chanting her Death Song.

"I can't leave you, Brother," I said. But I knew that I must.

"Get going," he said. He took my hand and squeezed it, hard. "As you love me, get out of here. And take Thump with you."

I picked the dog up under my arm and went.

WE EMERGED INTO full daylight a few minutes later. I put the dog down, and she ran to Gwen and Plover. Spy, Jim, and Jaime were sitting slumped in the sunlight, well away from the front of the mine entrance. Jim looked up, saw me, and rose stiff to his feet. I hobbled toward him, clutching my stomach. He came limping toward me.

"Where's Owen and Pine Leaf?" he asked. His wounds were bandaged, but dried blood still lay caked beneath his fingernails. He grabbed me just as my legs caved in.

"In there settling scores with Lafcadio Dade," I said.

He began dragging me back from the cliff. Just then a bellow roared from the cave, followed by a rumble from deep within the earth; then another, nearly synchronous roar shivered the clifftop overlooking the Buenaventura.

Smoke bloomed from the mouth of the mine, and the face of the mountain slumped in on itself. Jim hurried me away from the wall. Then a great, slow slab of rock toppled from the cliff and fell, blocking the entrance and shivering the earth with its impact. . . .

WE WERE A long time healing, and in some ways I'm sure my wounds still fester, especially those in my soul. Spy had lost a lot of blood, but Plover closed his knife wound with expert stitches and fed him slowly back to strength, there in the supervisor's cabin at Deadville, on herbal soups, deer and elk liver, and certain wild roots and barks which she said restored the vigor of the blood. She had learned herbal medicine from a captive Chippewa woman, a powerful *curandera* of the Midewiwin clan. Jaime's nicked lung seeped blood for a long while, but his mother dosed him regularly with what she called bear medicine—bitter draughts of pulverized dogbane root boiled in water—and slowly, slowly the bleeding stopped. His collarbone had been cracked by the same bullet, yet Plover's poultice of wild ginger and spikenard roots, along with the resiliency of youth, seemed to serve him well. A cast fashioned of steamed birch bark, which dries as hard as plaster, kept the boy's shoulder immobile while the fracture mended. The bullet Jim had taken through his left thigh had not involved bone or the femoral artery, and once the initial bleeding was stanched he quickly recovered. After a week he was scarcely limping.

I was certain that my own wound would end in a slow, painful death by septic peritonitis. An awful lot of guts and organs are packed into a man's lower body, and I had no idea which of them had been torn by Chambers' last shot. The bullet had ripped through my waist from the front left, just under the ribs, to exit above my right hip. It must have nicked a vertebra in its passage—the slow-working injury which more than half a century later would cripple me. For now, though, all I knew was the pain: sullen, intractable, sometimes intense, accompanied by severe nausea that kept me retching into a kettle day and night.

There were dark times as I lay there on my pallet of buffalo robes in that drafty, smoky cabin that I wanted to call for a pistol and put an end to it. I passed a lot of blood at first, which suggested a kidney or bladder wound, but Plover made me drink a decoction of mashed goldenrod root and water, bitter almost as death itself, and after a few days my urine cleared. The sharp, knifing pain in my left side which, with its sudden, unpredictable severity, caused the worst of the retching, she treated with a warm sludge compounded of young pine sapling chunks boiled together with the mashed inner bark of wild plum and wild cherry and applied as a poultice over the entry wound. The pains gradually abated.

Some months later, I asked an army surgeon, young Doc Hicks at Fort Marcy in Santa Fe, down near the Garita where they hang the Spanish *bandidos*, what organ might have been injured by the bullet to cause me that wracking pain.

"More than likely your spleen," he told me, after studying the healed wounds. "The organ serves as a blood filter and emergency reservoir, and is hence greatly vascularized. A gunshot wound involving the spleen is not, however, necessarily fatal, due in large measure to the contractile power of the membrane that envelops it, which narrows the wound and prevents further escape of blood. Or to put in plain English"—and here he scratched his head—"you're a damned lucky fellow."

I've often wondered if that trauma to my spleen accounts for my easy irritability these days. *Splentic* is the word for me lately, all right.

*　　*　　*

LATER, AFTER OUR wounds were sufficiently mended, Plover, Jaime, and I went into the hills in search of stray horses. We would need them for our return journey. Most of the horses had forgotten their panic at the gunfire and bomb explosions that had stampeded them during the fight. As we hunted across the scarred, barren mountain face above the *minería*, Plover stopped.

"Isn't this where we buried Yellow Calf?" she asked.

So it seemed. The peaks and river lined up correctly, but the trees were all gone: cut for timber and charcoal, for gold. We found the stump of the pine tree on which we'd built Yellow Calf's burial platform. Sifting through the dust, we came upon her remains, just a few of the long bones, leg and arm, and finally her skull. Plover gathered them into a bundle and placed them in an antelope skin. Later she would anoint them with ocher.

"We'll take her with us and bury her out with the buffalo," she said. "This is no place to spend eternity."

A few days later we rode for home.

When we got there a month later, it was to discover that our caretaker, Pánfilo Ramirez, had abandoned his family and absconded with our horses and cattle. It was months before we tracked him out and returned them where they belong. But that's the way of the West.

As for Deadville, may the mine and its tragic contents remain buried forever.

AFTERWORD

IT'S WINTER NOW, a bad one, perhaps my last on this earth. Things were touch and go there for a while. Back in December I was taken with a bone-rattling ague which old Doc Hicks misdiagnosed as calenture. Yes, the same Doc Hicks I talked to about my spleen more than half a century ago. After retiring from the army he settled in Santa Fe, having taken a Mexican wife. We get together now and then to play pinochle. He said that my fever this winter was perhaps a recurrence of an illness that's plagued me since a sojourn some years ago into the depths of Sonora, when I ran guns to the Juarista rebels fighting Emperor Maximilian. Instead, the illness proved to be a particulary wicked influenza, and it near did for me. Doc Hicks doubts I'll be able to ride again when spring rolls around, though I still have hopes for the horse and buggy.

But things could be worse, I guess. This writing has given me something to live for, and in the process carried me through a very bad spell. For hours on end, whole days, as my pen scratched out this account, it seemed I was young again, strong and fearless, as were my companions. They swarmed about me; I could hear their voices, laughing and cursing and blessing the glorious days; I saw them in action once more, smelled the smoke of old campfires blazing anew.

Otherwise our domestic situation is fine. The horses and the cattle seem to be managing the winter far better than I, despite more snow and frost than usual. And Speranza has found herself a fine young man, a spruce young cowhand named Nando Copál who used to ride for the Double K over near Bernalillo but now helps her with our herds since I am out of action. They ride my horses in the snowy hills and, unless I'm miss my guess, engage in a little spooning along the way. Or so I hope at least.

No motor cars putter up the road to the Casa Pequeña these days. None have done so since the summer afternoon that triggered all this reminiscence, and I have yet to lay eyes on my second horseless carriage. All the better, I might add. If I'm strong enough to sit up and raise a rifle come spring, I intend to take station on the veranda and shoot the next one that pokes its ugly bonnet over my horizon.

I never heard from Wentworth Champion again, and though I'm a faithful subscriber to the Santa Fe *Republican* have not found within its pages a "mountain man" story over Champion's name, or anyone else's for that matter. Perhaps he never made it home and the editor gave up hope.

If so, alas and amen.